BOOK 7 OF COURAGE ON THE OREGON TRAIL SERIES

# SEEKING HOME

# A.T. BUTLER

# SEEKING HOME

Women's Fiction Historical Saga

## COURAGE ON THE OREGON TRAIL
### BOOK 7

## A.T. BUTLER

James Mountain Media

# CHAPTER ONE

"And, so... all of this is to say, we're hoping that you all would consider moving to the Oregon Territory with us next year!"

Hope Waters let out the rest of her breath in a hurry. Supper was over and, as she said her say, she'd spoken so fast it felt as though she hadn't been breathing at all, wanting to make sure she said everything she had intended to say. As she finished her prepared speech from where she stood at the foot of the dining table, she looked brightly into the confused faces of all her five adult children, their two spouses, and her youngest daughter.

"Now, what questions do you want to ask your father and me?"

The entire Waters family—all ten of them—were crowded around the supper table, watching their matriarch plead with them to up-end their lives.

She was a short woman, pale with dark, graying hair;

even standing she had trouble commanding attention. But within her immediate family, Hope was often the driving force behind any choice or change. The fact that none of the Waterses had ever mentioned the word Oregon was beside the point. If Hope Waters decided she wanted her family to move there, she would do everything in her power to make it happen.

Hope caught her husband's eye; he smiled at her from the head of the table and nodded at her encouragingly. She just wanted someone else to say something. Even though she had known, deep down, that her idea would not be immediately seized upon, she had thought there would be more enthusiasm than this. She and Frank had invited the whole family over for Sunday supper with this very goal in mind; Hope had insisted they not offer any hint about what proposal they were there to hear. It would be far more exciting to surprise them. Now, as she saw confusion, questions and disappointment cross the expressions of all present, Hope wondered if maybe that had not been the best policy.

"You want us—all of us—to move?" Colin asked.

"Yes!" Hope nodded vigorously.

"To Oregon?" he added, deliberately.

Her third child, the most serious and most responsible, Colin had gotten married a mere month after his eighteenth birthday. His wife, Nancy, had been one of Colin's closest friends since they were twelve, and though Hope rarely detected the kind of passionate, exciting love she hoped for her children, there was no doubt that Colin and Nancy had a stable, content marriage.

And now she was asking them to pack up that stability and journey with her to the Oregon Territory, a far three thousand miles from the town they lived in in upstate New York. It was almost literally the farthest away they could get from home without leaving the continent.

"Mama, what are you talking about? Where did this idea come from?"

Angus, her oldest son, was always easy-going, always up to help if someone needed it. His expression now, however, was a mix of confusion that he seemed trying to hide with playful indulgence. Hope could see that this ask was too big for him to readily agree. His wife, Sadie, was watching her carefully, as though afraid Hope would show some sign she was kidding or even sick.

"I'm just surprised, is all," Angus continued. "You've never mentioned it before."

"I'm excited to go," Faith said loudly.

Hope beamed at her child, sitting at her father's elbow. Faith was the youngest and the only girl; though she was only fourteen, in many ways she was Hope's right hand. She sat at her father's side and played with the end of her braid, as she watched the reactions of her brothers all around her.

"I'm glad, young lady, because you don't have much of a choice."

"Do you think there will be other girls my age?"

"Wait a minute, let's all just calm down here," Colin said, raising his hands as though to quiet a noisy crowd. "Are you telling us that you and Pop already decided to sell everything you have and spend a year traveling to the complete other side of the continent? Without consulting any of us first? What if we don't want to move—you're prepared to leave your whole family behind?"

Hope looked at her husband again from across the table through the candlelight. The remnants of their big family dinner were spread across the table between them, and Hope had to remind herself that living out of a wagon for months would be a far cry from this abundance. But they would make it up again when they reached Oregon, rumored to be a land of green, verdant land, with rivers full of fish and forests full of game.

It would be the perfect place for her family to settle.

When Frank winked at her, she couldn't help but blush. She had been in love with Frank Waters since she was fifteen years old, and this would just be one more adventure in a lifetime of such she shared with him.

"Of course, your mother and me want you all to come with us," he said to his children. "And we asked you here specifically to consult with you and talk it all through. We'll answer any questions you have, and we hope that no matter what you decide, you can at least understand why we want to do this."

Though all six of her children seemed taken aback, this speech presenting her argument for moving to the Oregon Territory was nearly identical to the one she had prepared for her husband only a few days earlier. Frank, however, had interrupted her only four or five sentences into it to assure her he was already convinced.

"Hope," he had said, forestalling any more of her speech, "if this is what you want you don't have to convince me. I would rather walk all the way to Oregon with you than stay here knowing you would be happier elsewhere."

"I will be," she had said, fully convinced of the truth of it. "I will be so much happier, no longer doing the same thing here every day, the same faces, the same sights."

"I just want to make sure you know... Wherever we end up settling, if we are there any length of time you might find the same tedium, the same faces every day. Are you going to want to pick up and move every few years?"

"Maybe." She laughed. "But seeing as it's taken me nearly fifty years to decide on this move we will probably be all right."

That conversation had been easy and encouraging, and Hope realized now in talking to her children it had lured her into a false sense of victory. Convincing her children to let go of everything they knew would be far more difficult than convincing Frank had been.

"Why do you want to do this, Mama?" Beau asked softly, after taking in his father's words.

Looking at her second son, her gentle giant who sat at his father's right hand, Hope softened. Beau rarely spoke, which had the effect of ensuring that everyone listened when he did. If he was asking a question, Hope owed it to the whole family to answer.

She took a deep breath, and did not take her eyes from him. "We want to do this—I want to do this— because we have lived such a full life here, and I have loved so much raising you all in this community, but it just feels like the right time for a change."

"A big change," Colin mumbled.

"That's right." Hope turned to address him. "It is a big change. And it is a choice not to be taken lightly. So I hope that communicates a little to you how much we have thought about this and considered. I just feel as though if we stay here..." She softened, gazing at her husband again. The man who had been by her side through all of the adventures of the previous thirty years. "If we stay here I will always wonder what I had missed out on, what adventures or new friends I could be experiencing. I've had my fill of New York. It's time for something else."

"Hear, hear," Frank said.

Beau nodded, but didn't say anything further.

"Well, you don't have to decide this second," Hope said, as she took her seat again at the foot of the table. "Sadie, would you please fetch the cake?" Her daughter-in-law nodded, and went to the kitchen while Hope continued. "I made us a fat, delicious chocolate cake. I was hoping it would be celebratory, but I understand I can't ask you to make such a big choice so quickly. But we can't wait too long. We will need to make all our arrangements here before the end of October, which includes selling the animals, the house, paring down our belongings and all those difficult decisions."

"A lot of good-byes," her husband chimed in, as he accepted a plate with a slice of cake from Sadie.

"A lot of good-byes. As I say, you have time. Just not much. We need to be in Independence, Missouri, by the end of March, where we can hook up with one of the caravans going to the Willamette Valley. I've paged through the guidebook. We will want to look for a company with a trustworthy leader and enough families that we can have some security."

Angus was shaking his head in wonder at her, as he too accepted a slice of cake from his wife. "What do you two think about this?" he asked the two youngest boys.

Davis and Ernest, at eighteen and seventeen respectively, were both old enough to be out of school but not old enough to have homes of their own. The brothers looked at each other. They were only ten months apart in age and had been thick as thieves since Davis could toddle over to the kitchen and snatch a cookie from where it was cooling for them to share. Hope knew that whatever they decided, they would choose together.

"It's a lot," Ernest finally said. "What will we do if we don't go? Can we stay here?"

"We'll be selling the farm," Hope reminded them gently. "There will be plenty of time and no one is going to make you sleep in the snow, but if you decide to stay in New York then that will just be an opportunity for you to ... make a new home on your own."

She swallowed hard, tears stinging her eyes. Through all of this, all of her planning and cajoling and coming up with ideas, she had never really faced the fact that she might be leaving some of her children behind. Surely they would all see what an opportunity this was, and better if they stayed together. Looking around at the pensive faces that surrounded the table, Hope wondered how many more family suppers like this they would have.

She put that out of her mind. No need to borrow trouble. She would just have to try harder to convince them if necessary.

"Think about it," Frank added gently. "It's a big decision, but your mother and I would love nothing more than for our whole family to be settled out west next year."

Hope beamed gratefully at him as she settled back into her seat and listened to conversations bubble up all around her.

# CHAPTER TWO

The following morning, Hope had only just begun to open her eyes when she was jarred awake by a racking cough. She sat up quickly, blankets pooling around her waist as she hunched over, coughing and trying to catch her breath. Frank had already risen for the day, and Hope heard sounds of cooking in the kitchen below. Her family must have let her sleep later than she had intended. She clutched at the hem of the quilt, covering her mouth with it as she coughed.

The Waterses' married sons had stayed long after supper the night before, talking over the merits and drawbacks of emigrating to the Oregon Territory. Though Hope had felt her eyelids drooping as she listened to the murmur of conversation all around her, she didn't dare miss a second of it. She had only finally climbed the stairs to go to bed after midnight, losing her breath near the top and being attacked by another fit of coughing. When Frank followed her up, she had felt a bit dazed, a bit half-asleep already. Even first thing this morning, she could not remember what he had said to her as she climbed into bed the night before. Having her entire family under one roof was everything she had hoped for, and yet the whole experience had depleted her.

But today was going to be a full day. Now that she and Frank had broken the news to the rest of the family, there was no reason not to dive head-first into the rest of their plans. Now, at the end of summer, the Waters family had a mountain of chores and tasks around the farm to complete before winter and before handing the property over to a new owner. They would be selling most of their animals, most of their furniture. They would be stocking up on the essentials for traveling and sorting through what treasures were worth carting the three thousand miles.

So much to do; Hope could not simply rest.

Her cough had lessened, and Hope climbed out of bed to wash her face, brush and braid her hair and change into a fresh dress. The clock told her she had likely missed breakfast, but the voices from the kitchen hinted that there might still be someone down there cooking. Or, at the very least, perhaps there was coffee left.

The annoying cough found her again when she reached the bottom of the stairs. She tried to forestall it or hide it by clearing her throat, but it didn't work. Finally, she just stood at the foot of the stairs, both hands on the newel as she let her lungs settle.

"You're up."

Hope looked up to see her husband coming through the wide doorway to greet her.

"Coffee is waiting for you," he continued, and she grinned. "Faith is off to school, but there are biscuits still warm, with fresh butter, if you're hungry. Did you sleep well?"

Nodding, Hope allowed Frank to take her hand and lead her to the dining room table before he went to fetch her coffee. "Why did you let me sleep so late? There's so much to do."

"You've been sick and could use the sleep, I reckoned. An extra hour or two isn't going to make a difference in the list of things to do, but it could do a world of difference for that cough. Didn't you see Dr. Jansen about it? I don't like the sound of it."

Hope nodded. She was still struggling to catch her breath and didn't trust herself to be able to talk just yet. She took a sip of coffee.

"What did he say?"

"That I should take it easy. That it was probably just the plants and summertime air, pollen and such, that was getting to me, and I should stay inside as much as I can. That was a few weeks ago."

Frank chuckled darkly. "Well, that man doesn't know you at all, does he?"

"Very funny. To be honest, I might send Faith over there today and ask the doctor to come back. It's not getting better, even though I stayed home on Thursday before the quilting bee. Do you mind bringing me a biscuit as well?"

"I have a feeling the doctor meant to take it easy longer than just an afternoon," he said over his shoulder as he returned to the kitchen.

"Maybe he did, but if he meant that he should have said that," she retorted.

Frank chuckled again, setting her plate in front of her, with the small dish of butter next to it. "Well, I know better than most that I can't stop you, but you have to promise me that when that cough comes back you will at least sit down until the spell is over."

"I'll try."

"Hope Waters."

"I said I would try. I will."

Frank looked at her skeptically for a moment before changing the subject as he sat next to her. "I don't know if you overheard us last night, but I made the boys promise they would make their decision about Oregon as soon as possible. So we could make our plans."

"Thank you." She leaned in close to him and lowered her voice. "What do you think they'll decide?"

"Hard to say. I don't know Sadie well enough to be able to guess, and you know Angus won't do anything she doesn't want to do. I think Beau will come with us, and I think Davis and Ernest are waiting to see what the others do. This might all come down to the wives, truth be told."

"Nancy and Sadie." Hope nodded. "I suppose that's as it should be, men leaving their parents to cleave unto their wives and all that. Do you think we've done all we can do? Maybe I should go talk to Nancy this afternoon."

"Leave it alone," her husband said gently. "She needs time and space, and there's nothing new you can say that hasn't already been said."

"Yes, all right. Fine." Her relationship with her

daughter-in-law was already a little icy; she did not want to do anything to push her further away.

He looked at her intently.

"Fine, I said," Hope huffed, pretending to be offended by her husband's implication that she mind her own business. They both knew that if he had not specifically told her to leave it alone she could have very easily talked herself into meddling. But he was right. Most of her children were grown, building lives of their own, and she needed to trust that they knew the best choice for themselves.

"Don't worry," Frank said as he stood again. "Those boys know their mother. They won't make you wait any longer than possible." He kissed the top of her head. "Rest when you can, please."

Hope softened. "I will."

Once he was out the door, Hope looked around, taking stock of the mess that had been left in the kitchen. No one had wanted to leave the table to wash the dishes the night before, and now a stack of dozens of plates, bowls and utensils sat in the dry washtub, waiting for attention.

Her daughter would be home from school in a few hours; the men would be in from the field not long after that. Hope had the day ahead of her to get as much done as she could before she succumbed to her husband's insistence she see the doctor again. As she began heating up water for the dishes, Hope told herself there wasn't time for her to be sick. She simply wouldn't stand for it. This cough would just have to see itself out. She had been bedridden for long enough the previous winter when she had caught pneumonia and she wasn't going to do it again.

Even with that internal admonition, Hope found herself more tired than usual that day. Attributing it to her late night the evening before, she pushed through, getting all the dishes washed and put away, all the floors cleaned again after half a dozen big men had tread through her parlor, sitting room and kitchen. When her exhaustion grew to be too much, Hope set to work sorting through her rag bag. This was a task that did not strictly need to be done this moment, but as it allowed her to sit for a spell it seemed as good a time as any.

In the late afternoon, with the sun streaming through the full, green maples that lined the border between the western field and the house, Faith returned.

"I'm home, Mama!" the girl called as she stepped in through the kitchen door. She came through to the sitting room, and when she spotted her mother sitting on the window seat with scraps of fabric covering her lap like a blanket, she stopped suddenly. "Did you just get out of bed?"

"Very funny. I will have you know I was awake before you left the house. I heard you down in the kitchen. Thank you for making biscuits, by the way. I was just trying to catch my breath."

"Yeah, Pop told me you're sick."

"Do you think you could go fetch Dr. Jansen for me? I saw him a few weeks ago, but this doesn't seem to be getting better."

Faith nodded. "Any other errand you want while I'm gone?"

"Just the doctor, please. The sooner this gets taken care of the sooner we can get to all our Oregon tasks."

She left swiftly, darting out as quickly as she had entered. Hope didn't see her daughter out, but heard the kitchen door swing shut behind her. Not twenty minutes later, she again heard the door swing open. Faith had returned far sooner than Hope expected. She looked up at her daughter in the doorway.

"You're by yourself? What did the doctor say?"

"Mrs. Quinn is having her baby," Faith said excitedly as she flopped back onto the settee. "So the doctor can't come today. He was packing up and rushing out the door when I got there."

Hope frowned. "Oh, well. I'm sure that child needs him far more than I do."

"He said if all goes as planned he would be here tomorrow. And to tell you to rest until then."

Hope chuckled. "It must be nice to be a doctor and not have the same farm responsibilities the rest of us have."

"Mama, I think maybe you should—"

"Wait now," Hope said, interrupting. "Don't you go mothering me, Miss Faith. That is my job for just a few more years now. Don't take that from me."

Faith smiled. "All right. Well, then, I'll go feed the pigs unless you have some other mothering you need to do."

"No, dear. Thank you. Go on ahead. I'll call you when I need your help for supper."

In spite of her cough and her exhaustion, Hope had made a dent in the tall mountain of tasks that needed to be finished before they left for Oregon. Only another several months of the same before the family could be off on their adventure.

As Hope made supper that night—for a much smaller crowd than the night before—she almost managed to forget the annoying illness that persisted. Her mind was far too full of imagining what the journey west would be like. Who would they meet? What sights would they pass in their wagons? Frank had purchased them a guidebook for the overland trek, but she had not done more than glance at it. She would have to make herself sit down and read it cover to cover soon, so she could be fully prepared before they left New York.

# CHAPTER THREE

The following afternoon, Hope set Faith to hauling buckets of water as soon as she returned from school. The laundry had been a chore that she'd meant to get to all day, but any time she thought about the effort of bringing that much water up out of the well and then indoors Hope didn't feel up to it. Not in this summer heat. She must still be exhausted from her late night a couple days earlier, she reasoned.

So, after school while her daughter hauled another bucket of water into the kitchen, Hope poured the water she had already heated into her big wash tub. The steam curled up, into her face, and she took a deep, soothing breath.

"Mama," Faith called as she entered the kitchen, struggling under the weight of a full bucket. "Angus and Colin are back. They're taking care of the horses right now, but I told them you were in here."

Hope gasped and felt her entire face light up. "Oh, I

wonder if they have decided about Oregon. What about your father? Is he coming in too?"

Faith shrugged, and poured her bucket into the wide pot that sat atop the stove ready to heat up more.

"Faith Waters," her mother said in playful exasperation. "I was counting on you to bring me all the news so I don't have to get up from this stool."

Her daughter laughed and set the bucket down. "Sure, Mama. You're all set with water for now?"

"Yes, yes, go get your brothers. And Pop. Make them all come in here where I can hear every word they say."

Faith traipsed out the kitchen door, back to the yard where the men were. Though Hope couldn't make out any of the words from this distance, it sounded as though in addition to Angus and Colin, the three Waters boys who still lived at home had joined the conversation too. The din of male voices laughing and talking over each other grew louder and louder, until the whole crowd of them spilled into her parlor.

Hope realized she could not sit still. Her limbs felt tingly and her stomach churned at the unknown, the possibilities, the news she was about to hear that could change her whole life.

The previous week, when Hope had come to her husband with the idea to emigrate all the way to the other side of the continent, he had laughed at first. Frank had been utterly certain that she'd been kidding. Never before had they ever discussed even leaving their small town, let alone pulling up stakes to move that far.

Once she had finally convinced him that she was not making a joke, Frank had turned concerned.

"Why do you want to leave everything you know? Are you running away from something?"

For a brief instant, Hope considered deflecting from his pointed questions with more humor—that she was on the run from the law or hunting down a secret baby he never knew about. But the genuine concern on her husband's face had stayed her tongue. Though she had always been one to look for the next diversion, this was a far bigger step than she had ever before suggested.

"No. Honey... No, I'm not. I just feel as though... We are finished. We have succeeded. We have done everything we wanted to do here. Our kids are grown, or just about. Our home is paid for. Every day is the same, and I'm not sure what else there is for us here."

He shook his head with a frown. "But what about... What about all we've built? What about grandchildren that might come? Our friends that we've made over the years? We can't just walk away from all our years here."

"Oh, Frank." She laughed a little sadly. "The folks in this community are lovely, but not a one of them is a true friend. Who would we call on if we both came down with pneumonia at the same time? The doctor, yes. And our own offspring, but who else? I'm sure we'll miss the Quinn family or the Bentleys, but I guarantee that they won't try to write after the first or second letter."

Frank sat back in his chair, looking at the ceiling as though the answer would be written there. Instinctively, Hope knew to wait. Though she might be verbose, constantly checking in with her family, or explaining what she was doing whether they had asked her or not, in her long marriage she had learned that her husband was the opposite. Their son, Beau, took after him in this respect. Whatever thoughts or considerations Frank needed to go through would all happen in his head, quietly, without input, until he was ready to speak.

She wanted to bite her nails. She wanted to shake him. She wanted to repeat all her arguments using different words in case the new ones made more sense to him. But she forced herself to wait.

And she was rewarded. Though it felt like an eternity, in reality only a minute or two passed as Frank thought over her words. While he had initially agreed with whatever she wanted to do—anything to avoid her big speech—he still needed this additional time and information to be fully in agreement. Finally, he looked at his wife.

Hope took a deep breath and held his gaze.

"When I proposed to you all those years ago, I promised you I would always do whatever I could to make you happy, and I reckon this fits that promise."

"Really?" she asked, breathlessly. "Frank, are you sure? I don't want you to agree to this if you think you will hate it."

"You know, we're not all that young. This may be our last big adventure together. You sure you want to spend it in a wagon?"

Hope sobbed, which quickly turned to a laugh. Leave it to her practical husband to remind her that not all adventure would be fun.

"If we're doing it together, that's all I want."

"And the children?"

She nodded vigorously. "I'll convince them to come with us. I will. You'll see."

And now, after she had convinced her husband that this was the next big adventure for them, after she had put so much care into convincing her children, she was about to find out if it worked. If she was truly going to get everything she had wanted. When everyone entered, Hope stood, overwhelmed that the actual moment of decision was upon them. She opened her mouth to welcome her children, but closed it again when she saw their serious expressions. Instead, she watched as everyone filed in. Even Davis and Ernest had come in from the barn where they had been mucking out the stalls all day. They were dirty and sweaty and reeked of animals and Hope loved every single one of them.

She watched them all find seats in the sitting room, including Faith on the floor at her father's feet and the two youngest boys folding up their long legs as they sat on the stairs. Remaining standing in the doorway allowed her to see everyone, but it also gave her an outlet for her nervous energy. Shifting her weight from one foot to another, Hope silently willed her sons to speak.

"Well, now," Angus began, and all eyes turned to him. "I'm sure you're all wondering why I've gathered you here today."

A few chuckles were heard around the room, but Hope did not take her eyes off of him.

"An exciting opportunity has been laid before us. With the deep, thoughtful rumination of all the angles and considerations involved, we do have questions and concerns remaining, though I believe all will be answered in time."

He grinned, ever the troublemaker, drawing out

whatever suspense he could simply because he knew it would goad his mother.

"Oh!" Hope flapped her hands exasperated. "Just get to it, boy. Quit teasing me."

Angus grinned and looked at his wife. Sadie nodded. When he looked back at his mother, his expression had softened; it was less teasing and more soothing.

"We are going to come too, Mama. Sadie and me are going to join you in Oregon. This adventure of yours sounds like just the thing."

"We can't let you have all the fun," Sadie added.

Hope let out a sob. "Really?" She turned to Colin and Nancy. "And you too?"

Colin nodded. "Us too. It won't be easy. I tell you, I've spent the last day and a half really wrestling with if starting over completely was the right thing. I admit this is far from how we thought we'd be spending our next year, the idea of you all heading off so far away and leaving us behind is far worse."

"Thank you," Hope whispered. She glanced at Nancy's face, which remained passive, listening and letting her husband speak for her. Her husband put his arm around her shoulder and pulled her close. "Thank you, all of you. You've made me so happy."

"Wait, now, what about these three?" Angus waved a hand at the three Waters boys who had not yet said anything. "We leaving you behind?"

Beau shook his head. "I decided two nights ago. I'll go too."

Ernest and Davis exchanged a look, communicated something silently between the two of them, then turned and said in unison. "Us too."

"Not me," Faith declared loudly.

But the room erupted in laughter—the youngest Waters was always so indulged in her every whim that she occasionally had to perform any kind of rebellion.

Small conversations broke out among the family, in this corner and that, each person with their own idea of what was the most important thing they had to take care of first. There was much to decide, especially with so big of a family all traveling together with so little space. Hope remained in the doorway of the sitting room watching them all, and catching only snippets of what was said. But that didn't matter. She had gotten exactly what she had wanted and could not possibly ask for anything else.

Tears spilled down Hope's cheeks. This was all she had wanted, all she had thought about for several weeks. She would have danced in joy if she wasn't so tired.

"Mama? You all right?" Beau had appeared at her side and peered into her face with concern.

Hope turned to her tall son, and smiled wide, even as she wiped away her tears. "I'm so happy. I'm so grateful. This is going to be a wonderful adventure for all of us."

# CHAPTER FOUR

Humming a hymn to herself, Hope dried the breakfast dishes while she daydreamed about what their home in Oregon would look like. She may be wiping the bit of moisture on the inside of her large mixing bowl with her hands, but she was planting her new kitchen garden in her mind. There was so much to consider and plan for and learn. She felt as though she may not even be ready when they arrive a year hence. Surely they would have their pick of wild, open claims of land, maybe with a river running through it or a thick stand of trees that would serve as resources for the family for generations to come. The vagaries of the many months of hard traveling it would take to get to Oregon seemed distant and obscure in her mind. But the end point, the new home at the far end of the journey, felt crystal clear to her.

Hope was brought out of her imaginings by a quick rap on the kitchen door, and turned to see Dr. Jansen letting himself in and removing his hat.

"Mrs. Waters, I'm so sorry it's taken me so long to come see you again."

"Oh!" Hope had forgotten she'd asked him to come. Her cough seemed to have subsided—or at least she noticed it less—since the decisions about Oregon had been made. "Come in, yes. Thank you so much. I trust everything is all right with the Quinn family?" She set down the bowl and towel she had been holding and led the doctor into her sitting room.

"Twins," he responded with a heavy sigh. "Thankfully, Mrs. Quinn is a strong woman. She's going to need to be, with her hands full like that."

"I'll be sure to check in on her as soon as I can," Hope promised.

"But first let's see about your cough. We don't want to send you over to help with newborns while you're still sick."

She nodded obediently. "Is this all right?" She gestured to the room. "I've been feeling plenty well enough to cook and clean and all."

"Fine. Just fine." Dr. Jansen had set his medical bag on the settee next to him and begun to dig through it. "How long has it been since you've had a bad coughing attack?"

Hope answered his question, as well as several more about fevers, trouble breathing, and any other symptoms that she may have noticed. She took deep, slow breaths for him, while he listened; she allowed him to check her pulse and carefully consider her pallor. All in all, Hope felt rather silly. This cough was persistent, but not overwhelming, and after Dr. Jansen spending more than a full day with another patient, Hope was a bit embarrassed about wasting his time with this.

"I've been wondering if maybe this is related to my bout of pneumonia last winter?"

He nodded. "It could be. I imagine you haven't been resting as much as I've instructed you to, have you?" He smiled indulgently at her, well aware what the answer to his question was.

In spite of herself, Hope laughed. "I admit to being guilty of that." Her laugh turned to a cough, and the doctor watched her carefully. Once she had caught her breath again, she added, "And I'm afraid I won't be able to rest much for the next year or so. We've decided to head out west, you see. There's so much to do, and then we have the journey itself."

With eyebrows raised, the doctor prodded her. "West? To the territories?"

Hope gleefully explained, telling him about their plans, how the whole family would be traveling together. "All ten of us!"

"Well, perhaps the mountain air will be good for you. But, I will tell you again and again, Mrs. Waters, you need to rest far more than you do. Why have so many children if not to let them take care of you a bit when you need it?" He winked at her, and stood. "Rest as much as you can. And send Faith to come fetch me if you find the cough worsens before you leave. I imagine that will be sometime this fall?"

"October, if we can. We need to be in Missouri by the beginning of April."

"Then again, I'll say let your children help. If they know you're sick, I'm sure they will be happy to."

Hope stood as well to walk the doctor out. "Thank you so much. I am so sorry to have wasted your time this morning."

"Nonsense. Better to be cautious." He put on his hat, tipping it to her as he exited through the kitchen. "Please give your family my best."

Once Dr. Jansen had left, Hope had to sit again. She only got as far as the dining room table. She couldn't understand it. Hosting him for only twenty or thirty minutes had required very little of her, but she still felt exhausted. Sinking into the closest chair, Hope leaned forward and rested her head on her arms on the table. She hated that the doctor was probably right—she had not been resting as much as she should be. She had never truly recovered from the pneumonia in January. At the time, Hope had been in bed for nearly three weeks, leaving the running of her house and farm to the children. She had emerged from her sick room as soon as she felt able; Hope had never felt comfortable being taken care of.

When she had very first started feeling better after the pneumonia, she had come downstairs to find that Beau had brought home an upholstered armchair there was no room for and that Faith had set up a clothesline to dry garments across the dining room that they had not been using. The look of shock and guilt on the girl's face when she had seen her mother up and about still made Hope laugh.

As she chuckled at the memory, her lungs had other ideas. The spasm brought on another cough, and she could not get control of her breath. She began to think this wasn't as funny as it had been only moments earlier.

The muscles of her torso ached from all the coughing, and her expectation of productivity was continually being disappointed by the limits of her own body.

The cough continued, and Hope struggled to catch her breath as she pulled a handkerchief from the sleeve of her dress. After another long moment, the convulsions subsided. She put her hands in her lap, cleared her throat, and gasped. With a jolt of fear, Hope had glimpsed small dark spots on her handkerchief.

"No," she whispered to herself.

Inspecting the handkerchief more closely, Hope was assured that her first impression was, in fact, correct. Though the spots were quite small—barely flecks—it was unmistakable that she had just coughed up blood.

Blood.

She had coughed up blood.

It could be from inside her mouth, she told herself. Maybe there was some cut she hadn't noticed before (though even as that thought flitted through her brain, she knew there was no reason to uphold that theory).

No, she had coughed up blood from her lungs.

She had had a cough that had fatigued her for weeks, maybe longer without her noticing. And now she had begun to cough up specks of blood.

Every person of Hope's acquaintance knew what that meant. Goodness, every adult in 1849 knew what that portended.

Davis entered the kitchen at that moment, and Hope froze, praying that her turmoil from the previous few minutes was not written all over her face.

"Where is your father?"

The young man grabbed a muffin that sat cooling by

the oven. "Still with Mr. Barrow, as far as I know, negotiating about the stock. I guess it wasn't quite the easy sell he was hoping for. Did you need something?"

She needed to lie down, Hope thought. She needed to rest. She needed time to think that she would never get.

"No. No, dear, thank you. I'm fine. I was just wondering how the sale was going."

He nodded and headed back out again, snack in hand.

Hope had no idea what to do.

So she did what she usually did in other situations where she was at a loss: she found something else to occupy her mind. She wouldn't think about this problem; there wasn't anything she could think of to do in that moment, so she might as well spend what energy she had finishing drying the dishes, and then began sorting through their blankets and linens to decide what to take, as she had been intending to all day.

Even as she stood to return to the dishes, she remembered how strongly the doctor had advocated that she rest. And even Hope Waters was not so self-deluded to think that such recommendation would change if the doctor had seen her cough up blood.

But she couldn't rest. Not today. Not while the deadline of October was upon them to finish everything before leaving New York. Maybe she could rest in the wagon once they were on the trail. Yes, that's what she would do.

Because what else could she do at this moment?

Through a combination of pluck and sheer stubbornness, Hope filled the next eight hours of her day with plenty of chores and tasks and progress toward the family's imminent departure. When her husband finally returned ahead of supper that evening, she immediately peppered him with questions about his day, about the sale of the livestock and about his plans for the following day. Her interrogation did not distract Frank, however. As soon as there was a lull in her questions, he countered with one of his own.

"Did I see Dr. Jansen leaving earlier?"

"Oh?" Hope's mind raced. She was not ready to tell Frank any of what she suspected but neither could she outright lie to him.

He was watching her expectantly. "He came about your cough, didn't he? What did he say?"

Hope Waters blinked at her husband, opened her mouth to answer and made a split-second decision that she knew would affect the rest of her life.

"He said it's just a bad cold. I need to rest. Same as before, maybe a little remaining from my pneumonia last winter. Thinks it's good we're going out west, in fact."

Frank grinned at her. "Wonderful. I guess we better keep packing then, huh?"

"Yes, please. Let's be gone as soon as we can."

# CHAPTER FIVE



Once Hope had made the decision to not tell her husband about the depth of her illness, it was far easier to put the entire thing out of her mind and pretend it wasn't happening at all. The stained handkerchief was tossed into the stove, never to be used again. If she had to, she would come up with any excuse necessary to avoid another visit from Dr. Jansen.

Instead she threw herself head-first into all of the family's plans for the Oregon Territory. Even if her leg had been broken, Hope was not willing to give up on that dream. She would not be staying in New York, despite her cough—which was what she persisted in calling it to herself, unwilling to give the illness any extra weight or importance by naming it specifically.

The more days that passed when Hope did not share her fears with Frank, the easier keeping the secret became. After two weeks—in which she did, in fact, let herself rest more than before—Hope had almost entirely forgotten what she had seen hinted at on that handkerchief. She could convince herself even more easily when no one else knew.

Besides, she had more than enough to be occupying her mind. In addition to all the hundreds of small steps required to pack up their life in New York, in addition to all the research and preparation they needed to do to travel thousands of miles west, Hope found to her dismay that her normally easy-going, amiable family were in turmoil far more often than not. She told herself it was the stress and uncertainty of the journey ahead of them, but that didn't make mediating any of the arguments any easier.

Colin and Nancy—always prepared—had purchased their own guidebook to the Oregon Trail, and Nancy had read it cover-to-cover twice already. The pair had very clear, very set ideas about what all the family needed to do to be ready for the journey. It would be nearly a year on the road, from New York to Oregon, and neither Colin nor Nancy wanted to leave anything to chance.

Frank and Hope, after consulting the oldest three boys, decided that the entire family would travel west in two enormous, covered wagons. It would be a tight fit for all ten people along with all their supplies, but anything beyond that could become too much of an investment, too unwieldy, spreading the family's resources too thin. No, it would be better for the Waterses to remain united, together and focused, at least until they made it to the territory on the other side of the continent.

And so, for the next several months Hope spent her time divided between paring down their belongings to fit in the smallest imaginable space and overseeing the building of the wagons and the purchasing of the teams of oxen and all other necessary supplies. Hope lost count of the number of conversations she had with her sons' wives, making sure that everyone had everything they needed, but not an ounce more.

"I suppose I'm just worried that if we take so little with us, we will regret it by the time we get to Oregon," Sadie said, as she looked over the neat piles of pots, pans, dishes and utensils that had been slated to be packed. "We will have multiple households to set up there, won't we? This is barely enough for one."

"But the more weight we pack," Nancy responded, "the harder the work on the oxen, and the higher the possibility that we lose one, or more, and have to abandon a full wagon all together. Don't forget, we also need to pack literally hundreds and hundreds of pounds of food to feed all ten of us. Honestly I would feel better if we could do away with another fraction of all this."

"We should maybe not make too many permanent decisions too early," Hope said, trying to make both women happy. "We can always buy more food at the forts along the way."

"And always discard some of the furniture or other heavy things along the side of the trail, even after carrying them hundreds of miles," Nancy added darkly. "And then find ourselves without the very thing we need because we did not plan ahead."

"Right, well, we can make those choices when they come up," Hope said. "It will be fine. It will all be fine, girls. Really. Let's not borrow trouble just yet."

Nancy looked at her dubiously before turning back to assess her list. She had written out everything the family needed to take, broken up into three tiers of priority, organized and clear. "I think we also need to talk about the division of labor," she continued. "Both the cooking and cleaning between us and Faith, and the animals, hunting, wagon repairs, and all the other details for the men."

"Do we need to decide that now?" Sadie asked. She left the kitchen to sit at the dining room table, listening to her sister-in-law from a distance. "Would it not be beneficial to stay flexible? We don't know the full extent of what will need to be done. I've never lived out of a wagon, have you?"

"Well, no, but we still have a good idea of what is needed. And think of what a disaster it could be if we are all waiting around for someone else to take charge of something. Why, we could miss entire meals because none of us thought to be the cook."

"I am not sure that will be a problem," Hope said, lightness in her tone. "If nothing else, you know Davis and Ernest will remind us of every mealtime, likely multiple times."

Sadie laughed at that.

"Nancy, my dear," Hope continued. "I so much appreciate how thorough your research has been and how seriously you are taking this planning, but I hope you don't overdo it. We have a long way to go. You can't take on everything yourself."

"I don't intend to," she answered primly.

"Wonderful! Then just trust that Sadie and Faith and me will be there at every step. We will figure this out as we go."

"Very well."

All Hope wanted was for everything to work out, for her illness to go away and for her big, loving family to settle happily in Oregon. She had a very clear idea of how she would achieve those things, but it seemed as though Nancy did too, with far less optimism.

But Frank wasn't faring much better with the men. Colin had the same mindset as his wife, wanting to plan and control every detail as tightly as possible. No secrets. No surprises. Nothing that might alter his carefully thought-out culmination in their settling in the Oregon Territory. His brothers were used to that, though, and humored him as much as they could. Neither Beau, Ernest, Davis or Angus had any interest in being in charge as much as Colin did, so they simply trusted his decisions.

By the end of October, all the necessary decisions had been made, all the negotiations completed, all the packing and sorting and selling and disposing had been done. Frank and Hope turned over the ownership of their farm to a young couple, newly married, and the ten members of the Waters family said their good-byes.

The men would take turns driving the wagons, and caring for the oxen. They were also bringing two horses along, but had sold the rest of the livestock. One of the wagons would be for sleeping, as well as storing much of the clothing and blankets that would be used regularly. The second wagon would be for everything else—clothes, tools, furniture, odds and ends, but most importantly food. Enough sustenance to get them to Missouri.

When they reached the last town in the United States, they would have time to make whatever repairs the wagons required, and purchase whatever new food and supplies needed to be restocked.

But until then the Waters family still had nearly six months of travel. Through much of New York, Pennsylvania, Ohio and onward. Occasionally they would find a hotel or boarding house with room for all of them, and on those nights Hope relished the mattress underneath her and the roof over her head. Most nights, however, in order to save what cash they had, the Waterses camped in an open field or in a kind stranger's yard. The women had cots in the sleeping wagon, while the men slept in tents or under the stars on fine nights. They were able to use this time to fall into a rhythm, discover what they needed to do, and to learn what it meant to live out of a wagon day after day.

To Hope, this was merely part of the same monotony that had driven her from New York. She would not feel as though she were truly on her way to Oregon, had truly begun their adventure, until they were part of a community of emigrants, members of a wagon company on the Oregon Trail.

When they had left New York, she began knitting a sweater for herself, confident that it would be completed before the weather got too cold. A soft, ice blue sweater that calmed her when she looked at it. But as it happened, the travel the family did over that winter on their way to Missouri was far more exhausting than she had anticipated. Though Hope often went long enough between coughing fits to forget she was sick, her tiredness would never dissipate. She just kept looking forward, to their home, to the end of this trail when everything would be fine. The sweater would get finished eventually.

Until finally, at the very beginning of April, the two wagons rolled slowly toward the frontier town that had drawn them in for the previous couple days. The haphazard buildings, just south of the Missouri River, would be the final bastion of civilization for hundreds of miles. It would also be where the Waterses found the wagon company with which they would spend the next six months of travel.

It was both an oasis, and a way station Hope would be eager to leave behind.

"Welcome to Independence, Missouri," Frank said, taking off his hat and waving it in a wide arc. "The gateway to the west. Next stop, Oregon Territory."

# CHAPTER SIX

The Waters family's few weeks in Independence, Missouri, were not the quiet lull before the journey that Hope had intended. Not only were there far more wagon repairs to be done than she had anticipated, but with so many other families in the small town, each of them also repairing their wagons and purchasing their own supplies, the wait for everything that needed doing seemed unending. The long list of tasks was broken up between all the other members of her family, but even so the pressure to get everything completed in time mounted.

There was a sprawling campsite just outside the town limits where dozens of other families had made their temporary homes in advance of finding and joining a wagon company to lead them to the coast. Every day, it seemed, someone new was appearing, someone else was saying good-bye. The churn and chaos of so many men and women coming into Independence was enough to make Hope wish there was some other frontier town that they could try instead.

Every day she would page through the guidebook, reminding herself of what all the family needed to prepare for. Every day she would give her boys at least one task each—check on the wagon wheel repair or purchase the family oilskins to guard against the rain or replenish the medicine chest or any number of other small details. And every night, she, Faith, Nancy and Sadie would piece together a supper for the whole family using vegetables that needed to be eaten, potatoes that would be too heavy to carry west, and all the other odds and ends that they were trying to use up before they spoiled.

After leaving New York, Nancy had taken on more and more of the management of the family's food, and by the time they had reached Independence, Hope wondered if she should just give up and put the whole thing in her daughter-in-law's hands. It seemed clear that Nancy wanted to control what she could, so perhaps it would be easier to let her.

But her guilt at not contributing herself kept Hope as involved as possible, which unfortunately meant for some tense conversations with Nancy.

It was fine. It would all be fine, Hope told herself. Though this wasn't exactly the cheerful adventure she had hoped for, it was just a small hiccup as they sorted out their roles.

In this way, Hope and her family spent several weeks of April, until it finally seemed as though most of what they needed doing was done. One late afternoon, near the end of the month, her husband returned from town with a grin the size of the sun. He seemed utterly pleased with himself, and Hope didn't have to prompt him to tell her why.

"I've found us a wagon company." Frank sank into his seat with a long sigh. "They're leaving in just over a week. Do you think we'll be ready in time?"

"A week?" Hope thought quickly. "Yes. I think so. No, I'm sure of it. We can be ready. Even if I have to go without sleep—"

"You are not going without sleep, Mrs. Waters," her husband said tiredly. "How many times do I have to ask you to rest? That cough of yours isn't any better and it's been months."

"It's a little better," she fibbed. "I don't remember the last time I had a truly bad coughing fit."

"That's because you no longer notice it." He smiled up at her as she handed him a fresh cup of coffee. "Thank you. What I mean is, I fear that your coughing has become as natural to you as breathing, and that you forget that you're sick for long stretches of time."

Hope wanted to protest, but she knew he was right. She had far more reasons to ignore the fact that her body was failing than she had to pay attention to it. Instead, she changed the subject, counting on her husband to be easily distracted.

"Oh, I know you won't let me forget that. But tell me more about the wagon company, and the man leading it. We're putting our life in his hands, you know. I hope you vetted him properly."

Frank sat up taller in his chair. "Two men, actually. George Mills and William Sullivan. Both family men. Though neither have made the journey before, they both had been leaders in their hometowns, and Mills has a cousin living in California that has apparently sent him pages and pages of letters full of advice. Somehow, these men have convinced not only a doctor and a pastor to join their caravan, but we will even have a blacksmith. A good person to have, I should think."

As Frank prattled on about the wagon company, the fact that it included a doctor, and other details about their upcoming journey, Hope allowed the fact of her illness to float to the back of her mind. Her husband was correct that she often forgot that she was sick at all, let alone as sick as she feared. But, really, what else could she do other than what she was already doing? Getting her family to Oregon was the goal. No amount of resting would heal her in the small amount of time she had before they set off.

The weeks had passed far more quickly than Hope was prepared for, but, she reminded herself, perhaps that meant that the rest of the journey would feel as quick. She wanted nothing more than to be settled in her home, in Oregon, before...

Well, she would not think like that. There was nothing for her to be concerned about, no imminent threat that meant anything too terrible would happen to her. And with the question of their wagon company settled, she could relax even more.

Soon the final week of April had arrived, and the morning of their departure dawned. Hope was actually surprised by how prepared she felt for leaving Independence. She had to admit a big part of their preparedness was the tireless work of Colin and Nancy. Though there might be one or two small details that she had neglected or forgot about, all in all she was confident that the previous nine months of preparation had been used to the best of her ability. Especially as sick as she'd been.

Sadie and Nancy made the family breakfast, in their final campsite in the clearing outside of town, and as Hope washed the dishes afterward and Faith helped pack them away again, the Waters men hitched up the teams and made final checks of the wheels and joints of the wagon. Everything was coming together. Though there were a handful of forts and supplies between here and the Oregon coast, Independence, Missouri, would be their last access to anything resembling civilization for several weeks. Any split wood, missing nails, unsealed barrel or other minute detail needed to be addressed now.

Each member of the Waters family seemed to thrum with excitement—even Nancy—as they waited the final hours before they would be called to join the caravan.

About mid-morning, just as promised, the train leader George Mills passed by the campsite with his own two wagons and small herd of cattle that his family would be driving westward. Another half dozen wagons had fallen in behind him, and a small gap appeared that the Waters could take advantage of.

"Are we ready?" Hope asked excitedly, stifling a cough. "Today is the day."

She watched as Faith ran on ahead, along the trail, checking out the other families that were in the caravan ahead of them. Beau and Ernest had drawn first rotation driving the wagons, and they each guided their respective teams of oxen, bringing the two Waters family wagons into line with the rest of the company.

As the wheels turned slowly, gaining speed, Hope walked alongside the trail with her husband, out of the way of the dust that was being kicked up by the animals.

"Hope, why don't you ride up on the bench?" Frank said gently, leaning into her. "Me and the boys will handle the teams. You don't have to do anything but rest."

"Nonsense," she responded. "I can walk just as well as anyone else can. Besides, you know how uncomfortable that bench gets."

"But—"

"You will probably see me up there before this journey is over," she said, keeping her voice light. In fact, Hope was afraid that she would end up riding to Oregon from her bed inside the wagon, but that was not a conversation she was ready to have with Frank yet. Not on the first day. "Right now, however, I just want to breathe in the prairie air and see everything there is to see. Give me a day or two before I get tired of it all. This is the adventure that I have been dreaming of for months."

He smiled at her, nodded, and didn't make any other suggestions. He took her hand, and they walked with the rest of the family, with the rest of the caravan, with the rest of the emigrants all beginning the journey together.

And with that, the family was off, heading west into their future, toward their future home.

# CHAPTER SEVEN

The day the Sullivan-Mills wagon company left Independence was sunny and bright, with the light scent of prairie wildflowers filling the air. Purple, orange, red and yellow peppered the rolling landscape that stretched off in all directions. The sun climbed in the sky, and Hope felt the spring sunshine baking her shoulders and the top of her bonnet. Her son Beau wiped the sweat from his brow as he guided his team of oxen to follow the wagon in front of them. The dirt trail curved away from the town into the tall grass, where hundreds, if not thousands of wagons had passed before.

That thought brought Hope no end of comfort. Though their friends back in New York may have thought the Waters family were foolish, they were far from the first pioneer family to make this choice. All around her, Hope realized as she walked, were other women who had made the same decision. Other mothers who were taking this risk for the benefit of their family.

With a little lift in her step, Hope thought that maybe their big adventure to seek out a new home would also give them the opportunity to seek out new friendships, women who could be kindred spirits. Her family was dear to her, but the companionship of another woman who understood her struggles would be a gift.

"Mama!" Faith called from where she ran through the grass toward the wagons. A circle of yellow flowers rested precariously on her head.

"Where did you get off to?" Hope restrained herself from scolding her daughter about taking off her bonnet. This was their first day, and there would be plenty of opportunities for Faith to settle down into the drudgery of the journey. The sight of her elation, along with the chain of wildflowers that sat like a crown on her head— even if her nose got burned—was precisely how Hope had wanted the trip to go.

"Me and Sadie went out away from the trail to pick flowers." She gestured to the flowers sinking down over her forehead, and pushed them back up with a laugh. "I've seen a few other girls my age. Are all these folks going to be in our wagon company?"

"I think so." Hope looked on ahead, and then turned around to watch the line of wagons that followed. "There might be another company rolling out today, though. See all those wagons behind us? The first camp we're staying at tonight will be for some of the companies to organize or for stragglers to find a camp."

"Then maybe I should wait to talk to any of the other folks. Just in case we never see them again."

Hope smiled. "That's up to you. There is plenty of time for all of it. But I'm just tickled that you've already seen girls your own age."

"Sadie said she's hoping there are other young married women without children. Do you think there will be?"

"Oh, certainly. I think all manner of families are heading west to Oregon. Young people like her and Angus just starting out their lives, and older folks too. Someone's widowed mother-in-law they didn't want to leave behind, for example."

"Nothing like you, huh, Mama? Dragging everyone else with her?"

"Are you calling me old, young lady?" Hope tried to sound more stern than she felt, but her daughter saw right through her.

Faith laughed. "How much longer until we get there?"

"I'm not sure, child, but you know what the guide-books all say."

"Every minute of daylight used," Faith recited. She squinted up at the sun, as though to judge how much daylight was left in the day. "Well, then, if there's that much left to go, I'm going to back and pick more flow-ers. They probably won't last very long, but I thought I'd find the Bible to press one in."

Hope nodded. "All right, then. As long as you keep the wagon train in sight."

"I know, Mama."

"Have fun. Make friends!" she called after Faith as the girl loped away like a deer through the tall grass.

"Did you just tell her to make friends?" Beau asked.

Hope had been walking close enough to Beau and the wagons that he could overhear, though he stayed true to his character and did not interrupt or participate in the conversation in any way.

"I did," she retorted, as she moved to walk closer to him. "Even though we both know that of all my children, you are the one who needs the most prodding in that regard."

He just shook his head in response, and turned his gaze forward.

"Isn't that why you came?" she persisted. "Because of all the new people you are just so excited to talk to?"

He laughed at that, glancing at his mother out of the corner of his eye. "Precisely."

She smiled, pleased she had gotten a laugh out of her stoic son. "I'll be sure to tell your father that you don't want to be saddled taking care of the animals, as that will keep you from your blossoming social life."

Beau looked at her, smirked, and looked ahead again without answering.

"You'll see," his mother continued, stifling a cough. "By the time we get to Oregon you will be just as transformed as everyone else on the trail. A rugged pioneer, deeply tied to his community, constantly surrounded by loved ones. Perhaps even with a sweetheart. Or two."

After a moment, Beau said, "The only transformation I am concerned about is you getting rid of that cough. Do you want to ride on the wagon yet? I'll stop the team."

All the teasing and joy seeped out of Hope. She'd thought she had been able to hide her cough successfully, and to now hear that her own son wanted to take care of her made Hope feel like a child.

"No, thank you," she said primly. "I was just meaning to walk ahead to talk to your father anyway."

Beau nodded, not commenting on her protest as Hope sped up her steps to find Frank. There was absolutely no reason she needed to seek him out at that moment, but she could not think of another reasonable way to deflect Beau's offer. Walking some ten or twelve feet away from the trail, out in the grass, Hope tried to take a deep breath, but her lungs would not cooperate. Another wave of coughing hit her, and she was just grateful to not be anywhere near any other member of her family.

This would pass, she told herself. The air of the mountains out west would help clear whatever it was that was keeping her sick. She just needed to make it that far without someone or another insisting she hide away in the wagon. If they had any idea how sick she really could be, they would all be so worried. Hope did not want to do anything to gamble on their future, or even their enjoyment of the journey.

The rest of the afternoon, over the final miles to their campsite for the night, Hope kept to herself. The animals were in good hands, and there wasn't anything her family needed from her as long as they were traveling. Instead she spent the time paying attention to all the details around her, solidifying them in her memory. When they reached the first campsite, at the end of the long spring day, Hope felt both exhausted and energized by the start of their journey.

She walked wide of the caravan, trying to stay out of

the way of the thousand-pound animals and the vehicles they pulled. Everywhere she looked was the white, stretched canvas of the wagon tops. Most seemed new, eye-catching white, but here and there she realized some of the emigrants had painted words on the sides. "Oregon or Bust" or "Norfolk VA" to possibly indicate where they were coming from. Even in the midst of complete upheaval, of pulling up all of their roots, these families had clung tightly to their origins.

As she watched, Hope made her way between the wagons and camps that were already established, families that had arrived earlier in the day or in some cases possibly the day before. Though from her height she couldn't see the whole camp, it seemed clear that there were far more families, far more wagons than would make up a single caravan.

She found her family, the boys taking care of the animals, while Nancy was about to climb into the supply wagon.

"We're here!" Hope exclaimed. "I can hardly believe we've begun. I'll find the water and bring back a couple buckets for supper. We can settle into our evening and maybe meet our neighbors."

As she said that, somewhere in the distance the lilt of a fiddle floated on the air. Hope turned toward it, expression bright. Not only had one of these men brought an instrument all the way to Missouri and the wilderness of the plains, but at the end of the long day of walking had felt energized enough to bring it out, already.

That kind of energy and generosity was precisely

what Hope had sought in this new environment. Though it seemed too early to make any definitive judgments, at the end of this first day it sure seemed to Hope as though she had found exactly what she had been looking for.

# CHAPTER EIGHT

Supper at their new campsite that first night was a chaotic affair. Though the family had already spent plenty of nights traveling, with endless meals cooked over a campfire, the excitement, novelty and proximity of so many other emigrants lent more pressure to that evening's activities. Hope supposed that the fact that somewhere in the sea of wagons a fiddle was playing did not help her sons stay focused on their chores. There was so much to do, see, learn and meet. Their adventure was just getting started, and the simple necessity of checking the horses' shoes seemed mundane.

Though she maintained her focus, getting everyone taken care of, as soon as each member of the family was served their supper, Hope felt all the energy and excitement simply drain out of her. More than anything else at that moment, she wished she was curled up in bed, under a quilt, finally letting her body rest after the long, momentous day.

Her son, Davis, brought an empty bucket, and over-turned it close to the campfire, gesturing for his mother to take a seat. "My mama raised me to look after my elders," he told her with a smirk.

"Yes, yes, she sounds like a brilliant woman." Hope was too tired to banter back, and instead was simply grateful for the seat. She did not have the energy to find one for herself. As soon as she was settled, Angus's wife Sadie was at her elbow with the bowl of rice and beans with Hope's own supper.

"There's plenty more too," Sadie said. "You look just tuckered out. Nancy and me will take care of all of it."

"Thank you, dear."

Perhaps her insistence at not being taken care of would be tested on this journey, but she didn't see how the family could very well function properly without her looking over them all. Though Hope knew how blessed she had been, both with her own children and their temperaments, and also now with the women they were marrying and bringing into the family, it was still true that the broad variety of temperaments needed to be managed and soothed. It was still true that this entire journey had been her idea, and she wanted to make it as easy as she could for her children.

She focused on her supper, deliberately ignoring how difficult caring for her family might be with this sickness plaguing her.

Once supper had finished, Hope said her goodnights, and settled into her cot inside the wagon for what would be a full night's sleep, solid rest after the day of walking along the trail. Her children talked and laughed, late into the night, full of the vigorous energy that Hope herself had had at the same age.

The following day was one of rest and chores. The Sullivan-Mills wagon company would stay put for another full day, waiting for the final couple families who had not managed to leave Independence the day prior. Some of the women in camp took the opportunity to repack their wagons; some of the men went hunting. All were eager to get going to Oregon and so filled the extra day as best they could.

Though Sadie tried to press food onto Hope at breakfast, she wasn't all that hungry. Just a single strip of bacon would be enough for her for now. They would not be walking miles again that day, so her loss of appetite did not worry her overmuch. Once breakfast was finished and dishes packed away again, Hope realized she had nearly a whole day with nothing specific to do. This was the downside of being so efficient and on top of her planning up to this point. As the wagon company waited for stragglers, the Waters family was more than ready to start west.

"I think I might take a walk around the campsite," she said, standing. "Unless there's something to do here that I'm not remembering?"

Frank looked at her for a long moment, as though he was deciding whether or not to say something, until he finally nodded. "Don't get lost."

"I'll holler for you all if I do."

With a final glance back, noticing Nancy thumbing through her guidebook again, Hope set off on her own.

The campsite was both sprawling and crowded.

There were certainly more wagons here than belonged to a single caravan, and as Hope walked slowly between each settlement, she wondered which of these folks would be traveling with her, which of these women might be her friend in the days to come.

The day grew warm as the morning wore on, and though all Hope was doing was walking through the encampment, she soon found herself swaying on her feet. Her vision grew fuzzy at the edges. Hope blinked several times, shaking her head in attempt to settle herself. With weak knees, she took a couple more steps, trying to regain her balance. As her head swam, Hope realized with regret that she was far from anyone who knew her.

It was with that final thought that everything went dark and she collapsed.

"Goodness, are you all right?"

Hope blinked against the sunlight, and looked up to see an older woman reaching down to help her. She was tall and angular, with her graying hair pulled back in a tight bun, but in spite of certain severity of her appearance, the woman's expression was warm and sympathetic.

"Yes, I'm so sorry. I can't think what came over me. I must not have eaten enough this morning."

She struggled to a sitting position, her head still swimming a bit.

The woman grasped both of Hope's forearms firmly and pulled her to her feet, all while peering into her face with concern.

"You're a mite peaked. Looks to me as though you

could use a drink if nothing else. My husband would probably prescribe you white pepper tea or some other stimulant."

"Your husband? Is he a doctor— Oh! Dr. Martell, by chance? My husband told me we were lucky to have a doctor joining our wagon company."

"Yes, that's him. I'm afraid his elevated position might go straight to his head before this journey is over, so let's just keep it between us that his fame has preceded him." Mrs. Martell looped her arm through Hope's and guided her the few steps to her own campsite. "Come and have a seat, for a moment at least. I'll not let you wander off on your own just after fainting."

Hope only made half-hearted attempts to protest. Though she was reluctant to show that she needed anything at all, neither did she have the strength to make it back to her own campsite by herself. And then, of course, even if she did make it back she would not be able to hide her pallor from her family. So, instead, Hope allowed herself to be taken care of a little bit by the doctor's wife. It seemed like the best option available to her at the moment.

"Here you are. Let me just drain these leaves." The older woman wrapped a towel around the handle of the kettle that had been heating over the fire and poured the heated water over a strainer into two mugs. "I had just been brewing up some tea for myself, but I insist that you drink it first." She handed Hope the steaming mug. "That should fortify you a little bit at least. I won't let you go off by yourself again until you've had at least some of it."

"Thank you." Hope took a long sniff, the black tea strong and sharp. Mrs. Martell was right; this would be exactly what she needed.

"Where are you folks from?"

"New York. Upstate. My family is quite large." She chuckled. "I'm sure you'll get to know at least some of us Waterses. My husband and me, and six children, plus the spouses of two of them."

"Goodness, no wonder you fainted. You must be exhausted with your hands full like that."

"Actually, my boys are all grown, and my daughters-in-law are doing more than their share of the work. Mine might be the easiest crossing of the continent anyone has accomplished. Though, of course that makes me feel a bit guilty. I should be making my children's lives easier, not the other way around."

"I know just what you mean. When Randolph and I left Massachusetts, our daughter almost decided to move her entire family too, because she simply could not understand how we might make it without her."

"But she ended up staying?"

"She did. Her husband took over my husband's practice, in the end, so them staying was the best for all involved. I already miss her terribly, of course, but maybe a letter or two will make it to us out west."

Hope's curiosity was piqued. She wanted to know why this doctor had left his established practice and his daughter, especially at his presumed age, but she didn't want to pry.

"I had a whole speech prepared to convince my children to join us. It would have broken my heart to leave any of them behind. I don't mean that as any criticism toward you, of course."

"None taken whatsoever. I imagine if you were to poll all the families in this camp, you would come up with dozens of different reasons folks left their homes in the east."

"I'm sure you're right. All I want is to get settled in Oregon. New York wasn't terrible, but the territories will be so much better."

"We hope so. But in the meantime, there's laundry to do. I was on my way to collect water when I met you, and I'm afraid I have to get back to it. You're welcome to stay—"

"No, of course not. I don't want to take up any more of your hospitality. I'm sure we will have a chance to chat again. Thank you so much for the tea." Hope stood, steady on her feet again.

"Do you want me to have the doctor come look in on you before we leave in the morning?" Mrs. Martell said as she stood as well.

"Oh, no, no, thank you," Hope responded quickly. "No, but I'll be sure to send one of my children for him if a similar incident happens again. I'm sure I'm just worn out from the day of walking yesterday and I don't want to take any of his time. But thank you. Really, you have been absolutely what I needed."

Mrs. Martell smiled warmly at her while still seeming uncertain. "If you're sure. I won't press. I imagine there will be plenty of reasons for us to see each other over the next few months either way."

Hope laughed self-consciously. "Let us hope they are

purely social. But please do tell your husband that I look forward to meeting him."

Rather than continue her exploring through the camp, Hope elected to return to her own wagons, her own family, and not risk another fainting spell among strangers. She would have to be more careful from now on, if she wanted to be able to successfully disguise any weakness between here and Oregon.

# CHAPTER NINE

"When are we leaving?" Faith asked, slumped against the side of the Waters family's sleeping wagon. "What are we waiting for?"

"There's a lot to manage with this many families, love," Frank said soothingly. "We have plenty of time."

The family had two wagons to get them to Oregon, and they were divided between sleeping and supplies. The sleeping wagon held four cots, along with most of the family's clothing and bedding. The supply wagon held everything else—food for ten people, tools, what furniture they could fit, weapons and ammunition along with sundry other pieces. And both, at this moment, were hitched to teams of four oxen each, the animals pawing at the dirt, as ready to get going as Faith was.

With the exception of Davis and Ernest, who their father had to repeatedly nudge with his boot, the entire Waters family had been awake and up since not long after dawn. All of the members of the Sullivan-Mills wagon company had congregated, and today was the day they would be led west, along the Oregon Trail, toward their ultimate destination. Today was the day that they said good-bye to other emigrants still waiting for their own departures, that the caravan became fully self-sufficient, subject to the destructive whims of nature and the men and women's own abilities.

Though Hope was still cautious after her fainting spell the day before, she too was awake early, eager and ready to leave. She tried to at least oversee and direct what all needed to be done to get the family ready, but her daughter and daughters-in-law took care of most of the cooking, cleaning and repacking. Hope allowed herself the respite to be excited. Today would be just as exhilarating as the day they left Independence had been, and she could face what work would be required of her tomorrow.

Or so she had thought hours earlier when she awoke. Now it was mid-morning, long past the time they had been scheduled to leave, and yet George Mills had not guided his team out to lead the caravan. They all remained waiting, without campfires, without food, without any idea of what they were waiting for. Occasionally a young man would run by, in one direction or another, as though carrying a message, but none stopped to inform the Waters family what was happening.

"Any minute," Frank said, as he offered one of their oxen a drink from a bucket full of water.

"That's what you said half an hour ago," Faith said with a pout.

"And it's still true. This is what we need to get used to, honey. We are joining a caravan. There are dozens of other families, maybe a hundred or more people that we are traveling with now, and we have to be prepared to move at their speed. You wouldn't rather travel two thousand miles through Indian country alone, would you?"

Faith groaned. Her father chuckled. But Hope was sympathetic. She too wished to be moving; the extra day they had stayed at this first campsite had been a delay she had not foreseen.

Frank offered to help his wife up to ride on the wagon bench instead of walking, and again Hope waved him off.

"I will *tell* you when I need help," she insisted.

"Will you?" he raised his eyebrows in a question.

"Oh, now, you know me."

"I do know you. That's why I'm asking."

"Who is driving the wagons today?"

"Changing the subject?" He shook his head at her transparent deflection. "Angus and Davis are. So, of course, that means that you can ask either one of them for help if you find yourself too tired later. Beau is looking after the horses, and if you really want to, I'm sure you could ride all the way to Oregon. No one would judge you."

"We'll see," she said, even as she took several steps closer to him. Looking up at her husband of nearly thirty years, Hope batted her eyes, and rested her fingertips gently on his arm. "Does that mean you are free to walk with me? We could hold hands and stroll through the flowers like we used to?"

"Are you trying to flirt with me, Mrs. Waters?"

"Perhaps... Is it working?"

Before he could answer, they heard a whoop of

delight from one of their sons. Both turned to see what the commotion was, and noticed that the wagons had finally begun to move. One by one wagons fell into line behind the Mills family. The two boys urged their teams into motion, the heavy burden of the wagons making the animals strain in their harnesses briefly in the effort to get them moving. But soon the wheels began to turn, rolling over the dirt and flattened grass, slowly gaining momentum.

The Waters family were on the west side of the campsite, and fell into the row of travelers about ten families from the front. As the big, heavy wagons began their slow roll toward the packed dirt trail, the crowd of women and children who would be walking alongside the wagons moved too. As Hope watched, she saw girls about Faith's age, holding the hands of younger children, guiding them into the grass away from the enormous animals. She saw women walking together, gossiping and laughing. She saw young men without responsibility playing tag and ignoring the caravan completely.

Hope gave her attention back to her husband. "We're finally moving! Shall we walk?"

"I'm sorry, my dear. I had planned on spending a few hours, at least, talking to Mr. Thompson some more. When we met yesterday he said he had been corresponding with a friend in the Oregon Territory about the best crops for that region. I want to make sure that I get our farm started off on the right foot."

"Oh, then I won't keep you. I'll be fine. Walk with Faith, maybe, or by myself. Don't you worry about me."

"Ah, but I always do." He kissed the top of her head

and squeezed her around the shoulders. "I'll see you for supper tonight when we make camp, if not before."

He turned and made his way back down the caravan toward the Thompson family, even as Hope herself turned toward the front of the line of wagons.

"Mama!" Faith dashed up to her mother, her eyes wide with excitement. She seemed to be bouncing on her toes as she attempted to stay in place.

"Do you need to go run around?" Hope asked her daughter with a laugh. "All that energy you could easily beat us to Oregon."

"We're moving, can you believe it? Finally!"

"Finally," she repeated. "Come walk with your poor mother. I know soon enough you'll have a bevy of friends and I'll never see you."

"Mama, we are stuck in a wagon together for at least five months. You'll see plenty of me." In spite of her protests, however, the tall girl fell into step with Hope as the two began walking parallel to the trail, alongside the wagons.

With as late as the company had gotten started, the sun was already high overhead when they began, and each person knew there would be no stopping for a midday meal. Nancy had baked several extra batches of biscuits that morning, and all of the Waters snacked on what they could as they walked. Faith told her mother all about the women she had seen and met at the spring in their previous camp and in this way, several hours passed.

But even a girl of fourteen could only talk for so long. After Hope had traded her own story about meeting the doctor's wife, the two fell into a comfortable silence. There was not much else to do, other than keep up with the wagons, and in the lull of the warm afternoon, Hope let her thoughts wander. Her heart was full as she envisioned days and weeks of similar intimacy with her family, the satisfying feeling of accomplishment as they covered mile after mile. In spite of her weakness, this journey was turning out to be what she had so desired.

Those thoughts were interrupted when she heard a series of thuds and an anguished cry from up ahead, but from where she was walking out in the grass, Hope could not determine where the sounds had come from. Whatever it was would not be good, she knew. Even as she slowed her steps, wondering how bad it was, she noticed that the caravan of wagons ahead of her was also beginning to slow. Hope glanced over her shoulder, noticing as one after the other the wagons slowed to a stop, all the way back to the end of the train.

In a few rapid steps, she and Faith closed the distance to the caravan and their own wagons.

"What is it? Why are we stopped?" she asked her son.

Davis shrugged.

Hope tutted at him; that boy had no initiative, and even less so when Ernest was not around. He would simply stay where he was until the wagon ahead of him moved. Well, she wasn't about to wait around for someone else to bring her the news. Hope was a do-er, and whatever—or whoever—had made those sounds likely needed a helping hand.

She crossed over the trail, between her family's wagons, to see what had happened on the far side, with

Faith close behind her. As soon as she stepped out from between the wagons, Hope came within only a few yards of the disaster she had heard.

So soon after it had occurred, the scene was still chaotic, but one thing was certain: the woman's wail Hope had heard was that of what appeared to be a wife and mother whose man was now securely pinned under an overturned wagon. Hope swallowed hard, shocked at what she was seeing. Though she did not even know the family's names, the sight of two small children crying, and plucking at their mother's dress even as she vainly struggled to move the wagon broke Hope's heart.

"Oh heavens," Hope said under her breath. She reached for Faith's hand, squeezing it tightly when the girl slipped her palm into hers. "Don't look. You don't want that image in your memory."

"We should go help, Mama. Look at—"

"There are other people who can help, people who are not fourteen-year-old, impressionable girls." Even as they stood next to the trail, stunned, a dozen others were rushing forward to help the woman, to look after the children, to band together to lift the wagon off of the poor man.

Hope could not even imagine what that sight would be.

"I'm not delicate," Faith insisted.

"I know you're not, but that does not mean that this is anything you need to deal with."

"Mama..."

"Please, dear. Please. There will be plenty other opportunities for us to help, but not this one." Hope felt light-headed. She did not want to mention it to her daughter—or really anyone—but she worried about another fainting spell coming on just from the sight of all that blood.

Hope swallowed, noting her pulse racing, and stifled a cough.

"Come on. Let's go back to the other side of the trail. Staying out of their way is the best thing we can do."

The caravan continued moving a short time later, while the matter of the overturned wagon was taken care of.

When the company made camp later that night, word went around about the family who had already suffered a tragedy, only one day into the journey. Jeb Buchanan had died, leaving his wife Alma a widow, and his children Betty and Johnny without a father. In spite of this horrible tragedy, the widow had decided to continue the journey, hiring two of the older boys in the company to drive her wagon west. When Hope learned about this, from her son Angus who had sought them out, for the first time she felt as though maybe this adventure would not be the exciting dream come true that she had hoped for.

# CHAPTER TEN

The emigrants had left late the first morning, and then the following morning there was another delay. The Sullivan-Mills wagon company had to stay in camp longer than planned to hold the funeral for Jeb Buchanan. Though each man and woman in attendance held a sliver of hope that it would be the only funeral until they reached Oregon, not one person really believed that was possible. Hope Waters stood in the back of the crowd, with her hand tucked into her husband's, listening with head bowed.

She had not met the man; she had not even known his name until the previous night. But the loss of a member of their company so early into the journey put her to mind of all the other risks they were taking. All the other things her family could lose over the next few months.

Hope vowed to hold on tight to whatever she could, for as long as she could.

After the closing prayer, as the wagon company

dispersed, getting ready to leave camp for the day, Hope lost track of her family. Her husband and sons had eight enormous animals to attend to, while her daughters-in-law were taking charge of packing away the breakfast dishes. Hope took a deep breath, watching her beloved family scatter, all intent on their responsibilities and shouldering their part of the burden.

She made her way through the emigrants, who dashed here and there to find their own wagons, and reached her camp just as it was breaking up.

Though it was edging into summer, Hope felt a chill. She hiked up her skirt and climbed into the family's sleeping wagon to fetch her shawl. She had worn at least one shawl nearly every day since the previous summer; whatever hale and hearty constitution she'd had the year before was slow in returning.

Just climbing into the wagon had worn her out. She leaned against the bow near the back just to be sure she didn't fall over.

Hope coughed, cleared her throat, coughed again. And again. Soon the coughs were coming so fast she could barely get her breath. She could feel what seemed to be a coating in her lungs. Her coughs came fast and hard now. This was a coughing attack that she'd not had since they left New York. Sitting down on her cot, she pulled a handkerchief out of the sleeve of her dress and held it to her mouth, both trying to cover the sound of her coughing and... just in case.

Just in case of what, she would not admit even to herself.

Hope bent forward at the waist, over her knees, coughing toward the floor of the wagon. Somehow she instinctively thought to make her body as small as possible. As though it might offer some kind of suppression. But still her cough continued. With the handkerchief covering her mouth, Hope felt the spots of damp, against her lips.

She closed her eyes. Not wanting to see what she knew would be there.

After another long moment, the coughing finally subsided and she was able to draw breath. Not too deeply. Not too much. Nothing that might trigger another coughing fit. But her heart rate slowed and she soon felt herself again.

"Goodness," she said softly.

Knowing she could not avoid it, Hope looked at the handkerchief in her hand. Her heart dropped. She had seen tiny blood flecks come up in the past, but it was nothing like this. The bright red circle, the size of a penny, seemed like an angry eye, glaring at her.

Hope blinked back tears, wadded the handkerchief back into her fist where she could not see it and sat back up on her cot.

What was she going to do?

There was no doubt that she was still sick—her fainting and coughing proved that. But now she could not avoid the fact that the cough was bringing up blood. Everyone knew what that meant. Though consumption was not always a death sentence, there was a reason it had been called the 'white plague,' killing thousands of people.

Hope racked her brain, trying to remember if she had noticed any member of her family pale or coughing.

It could be that she was the only one who had contracted this mysterious illness.

Her next thoughts went immediately to how her family would respond if they knew. How much this sentence would crush them. How they might even insist on turning back, staying closer to the east and civilization so Hope could get whatever treatment possible.

Well, they could not find out. That was all there was to it. Hope would not be turning back, no matter what befell her. After all, Dr. Jansen in New York had plainly told her that the mountain air and heading west would be good for her. If Hope could keep this to herself until they reached Oregon, there was every reason to think she would recover.

Or, she *might* recover.

But she would be in the west, with her family around her, resting and enjoying her new home while she recovered. No one would need to know before then. She would be healthy enough until then, just one foot in front of the other for another couple thousand miles.

And she could always take up Frank on his insistence that she ride in the wagon some of the time.

Nodding to herself, certain about her plan, Hope stood again, and climbed out of the wagon. The company would be moving soon, and though there would likely be days ahead when she would need to stay in her cot, today was not that day. She gripped the back of the wagon with one hand, catching up her skirt with the other, and gingerly made her way back down to solid ground.

She paused a moment, letting her eyes adjust to the

bright morning light again, but before she could take a step, she heard a sharp voice.

"What is that?"

Hope turned, startled. Her husband had just come around the other side of the wagon and was looking pointedly at Hope's right hand. She looked down herself and realized too late that the bloody handkerchief that she had balled up in her fist had come loose when she had gripped the wagon's edge. She closed her eyes briefly, furious with herself that she had not tucked it back away in her sleeve.

"I— " Hope cleared her throat, flustered. "I didn't realize you were here. Who is hitching up the wagon?"

"One of our half a dozen sons," he answered impatiently. "Don't change the conversation. What *is* that, Hope?"

She heard the concern in his voice, braided side by side with fear and frustration. Though she had been able to keep her true fear—the extent of her illness—from him for eight months, it was clear he would not be put off any longer.

"It's nothing," she said in a small voice, while she looked at the ground.

He took two steps toward her, closing the distance to nothing, and held out his hand for what she had.

She held out her own hand, the handkerchief held tight in her closed fist. Without meeting Frank's eyes, she slowly, reluctantly unclenched her fingers, letting him see what she held. As she was now seeing it through Frank's eyes, the bright red droplets of blood seemed to stand out even more starkly than they had a moment ago. The spots that she had convinced herself were nothing now clearly announced the fact of her consumption.

Hope stifled another cough.

"Hope Waters," he said softly. "What have you been keeping from me?"

The crack in his voice, the anguish she so clearly heard, was what finally made her look up into his face and meet his gaze. She had never before kept such a secret from him, and now she felt a burning shame that she had done so.

"I'm sorry."

"I know you are. But you still have been keeping this from me. How long have you known? What did Dr. Jansen really say?"

She looked up at her husband, and was stricken to see the tears forming in his eyes. "I told you the truth," she insisted. "Dr. Jansen didn't say anything more than I needed rest, and the western air could help me."

"Hope."

"He did!"

"Hope..."

Young Norman Kirk, whose family had the campsite right next to the Waterses, walked by at that moment, glanced at Frank and Hope and continued on his way.

Hope lowered her voice, suddenly reminded of all the listening ears around them.

"He, um..." She shrugged, embarrassed. "He didn't see the blood," she finished quietly. "I didn't cough up any blood until after he had been there. And then we were getting ready to leave New York, and everything was happening, and I didn't see the point in delaying or redirecting anything. It's not like we could have done anything about it. And maybe he's right that going west will be good for me."

"Of course we could have done something! You could have rested much more, for starters. We wouldn't have left at all if we had known."

"I *know*, Frank! That is my point. I could not risk all of our plans changing, and missing out on this whole adventure. Not for a little cough. I couldn't do that, Frank. I am not letting go of this dream. Especially if…" Her voice cracked. She could not bring herself to finish that sentence, and looked down at the ground.

Frank was silent for a long moment; she did not meet his eyes. Finally, he sighed and leaned against the back of the wagon. "Give me your hands."

She stepped closer to him, shyly offering both of her hands into his.

"Hope. I know that over the course of our long marriage I have never once been able to convince you to do something you don't want to do. It's one of the things I love best about you. Some call it stubbornness, but I see it as steadfastness. I also know that you have far more energy than I often realize, and that you have never, ever rested as much as I would have liked."

Hope could not help but chuckle at that. The number of times her husband had marveled that she was still awake, still completing some chore, was uncountable.

"But I need you to take better care of yourself," he continued. "Our children need you to take better care of yourself."

"Are you going to tell them?"

He held her gaze for a long moment. "You need to tell them."

"I will. Just... not yet."

"Hope..."

"Please, Frank," she pleaded. "Let me just have a little while longer when I can believe that there's nothing wrong, that everything will work out. I'll tell them eventually. Not now though."

He shook his head. "I don't like this."

"I know. But you love me."

"I do love you. Which is why I need you to take care of yourself."

He pulled her into an embrace, her face crushed into the earthy scent of his shirt. He wouldn't push her any further. Not yet at least. There was a small part of Hope that was relieved her husband knew the truth, that she would not have to carry this burden by herself. But that did not extend to worrying their children. She could pretend everything was normal just a little bit longer.

# CHAPTER ELEVEN

Though the next several days traveling west on the Oregon Trail were blessedly uneventful, Hope felt anxious. Seeing the blood staining her handkerchief, having that conversation with Frank, trying to keep her strength and energy up without her children noticing a problem. She found herself no longer able to ignore this illness that had been affecting her for months.

But neither did she have the time or space to rest the way he wanted her to. As a compromise, Hope elected to spend the latter half of many of her days riding on the wagon seat. Not every day and not all day. Not more than a few hours. But a little bit, when she needed to. The afternoon sun beat down on the top of her bonnet, but being out in the open air was better than riding in the wagon. She was finally beginning to admit this might just be the kind of thing she had to get used to.

On the third day, however, the wagon company crossed into Indian territory, with all the danger and hostilities that brought. Hope felt the tension running through the community, and any idea of resting flew away. The company leaders, George Mills and William Sullivan, called a meeting with all the men, all the heads of household for each family that traveled in the caravan. Frank, as well as his two married sons, attended the meeting. The captains had a plan to make sure the families under their care would stay safe, but it would involve everyone's help.

While they were gone, Hope settled in with Faith to go over some of the schoolwork she still wanted to finish. Even though Faith had been committed to the move from the beginning, there were still bits of their home back east that she missed. Hope was proud of her daughter for continuing to pursue her education, even when it wasn't strictly necessary.

"Mama, did you know there's a teacher in the company?" Faith said, as she wiped her slate clean after her previous lesson. "We're doing math today, right?"

"Have you met this teacher?"

"Not yet. She's a spinster lady, traveling with the Robinson family, but Abby says the teacher wants to hold classes this summer, on days that we stay in camp longer."

"And Abby is...?" With all she had been consumed with her illness and secrecy, Hope had not yet had the chance to be as social and friendly as the rest of her family had been. As such, they were constantly mentioning names that Hope did not recognize.

"Abby Mills. The captain's daughter. She's my age, maybe. Maybe older. I don't know."

The math workbook fell open to a page in the middle.

"And did you want to go to these classes?" She peered at Faith's beaten-up workbook that had been used by all her brothers ahead of her. "This is the lesson we left off on, I think."

"I am probably too old, I think. I don't know. There are so many little boys and girls that she might be too busy."

Hope watched as her daughter tucked a piece of loose, dark hair behind her ear and bent over the workbook. They had been doing long division, but the last time they had been in one place long enough for Faith to pull out her work had been nearly a week earlier. At fourteen years old, she would have still been in school at least through the end of this year, but as the family had been traveling for months, the girl had missed out on the more advanced learning that the girls back in New York would be getting.

The knowledge that there was a teacher in the wagon company made Hope grateful. Even though her own children were too old for that tutelage, there were dozens of children in the company that could benefit. And if this teacher stayed near the same settlement as the Waters family in Oregon, maybe Hope's one-day grandchildren would also benefit. Her mind wandered for a moment, imagining their future settlement, complete with a school, a church, a general store. It could be absolutely perfect.

Someday.

Even as she daydreamed, she knew that starting over

completely in another territory was bound to be a much bigger project than Hope was ready for, though she was excited to try. Every foundation, every industry that they had taken for granted in New York now had to be built completely from scratch or brought along the same long, arduous journey that they were now on. The very luxury of having a teacher in their midst was intoxicating.

It was while she was considering this that the men returned from their meeting. She looked up expectantly, immediately recognizing the expression of worry on Frank's face.

"How did it go? Do you feel confident in the plans?" Hope asked her husband. The other boys dispersed, presumably to tell the same details to their own wives, and Hope poured Frank a cup of coffee as she settled in to listen. "Does it seem like the captains know what they are doing?"

He nodded, taking a sip. "Every man and boy above the age of sixteen is going to have to be on guard duty at some point, starting tonight. Four-hour shifts each. But there are enough men that any one person's burden should not be that difficult. And it's reassuring to see how many of these men are really excellent shots. Not many city folk in our company, I don't think."

"Oh, that is good," Hope said. "I was a little worried when we learned that one of the families doesn't have a man at all in their wagon, but maybe the rest of the men will make up for it."

"The Hudson sisters? They do have a young man, who might also be taking on guard duty. I'm not sure how old he is. And we are to pull our wagons into a tight circle every night for camp, letting the animals roam around in the center. Then chaining the wheels of the wagons together to keep it secure. But that wall, of sorts, should help protect us against any attack. I think. That's the hope, and what has gotten previous wagon trains across the plains safely. But some of the stories Captain Sullivan told us about caravans that have come through here before now... I know he was just trying to get us to take the danger seriously, but I still think it's a wonder anyone has managed to cross the plains at all."

Hope shook her head. "I knew we would be traveling through Indian country, and I know they were here first. I just wish there was more of a guarantee of safety. It's so scary to think about what could be out there in the darkness, watching us."

"I know, but we can get through this. Not every Indian is dangerous, just like not every white man is safe. We always knew there would be risk, and we can at least be grateful that our company is being led by such prepared and fore-thinking men."

He glanced over to his daughter who was still bent over her slate and workbook, only partway listening to him talk.

"What's this?" He kissed the top of Faith's hair as he looked over her shoulder. "Mathematics? You're a braver person than I am. Failing at math is why I always knew I would be a farmer."

"You need math for that too, Pop. Pounds of oats or the price of eggs is all still math. How are you going to know if someone is cheating you or not if you can't add?"

"Well, sure, but I can also pass it off to one of my many children, can't I?" He grinned at her. "You'll take over the books when we settle in Oregon, won't you, love?"

"Pop…" She shook her head, flashed her own grin back at him, and turned back to her work.

"She will," Frank said to Hope with a grin. "My brilliant girl."

Hope chuckled. The teasing look forward helped take her mind off of whatever native tribes might be in the prairie grass just over the horizon.

Though the additional danger and additional security made schedules even tighter and more frantic, after that the wagon company settled into a steady progress, a regular rhythm, that bordered on monotony. Every morning, Hope woke with the sun, and between her daughters and herself made breakfast and coffee for all of the Waters family. It had to be done in shifts; the pans they had brought were insufficient for cooking enough food all at once. The two men who would be driving the wagons were fed before all else, and the ladies were fed last, finishing the final bits of whatever food had been prepared while at the same time they washed dishes and packed them away.

At the time, Hope had been so proud of her efficiency and her lack of sentiment when they had packed up their belongings in New York. But now, with the reality of the day-to-day living on the trail, she worried that she had been too frugal. Even though the entire family shared one household now, that would not be the case when they reached the territory. Her married sons would want to set off on their own, and their wives would be severely limited by not having the same tools and household items that Hope had packed for the family to share on the journey.

But, it was too late now for regrets. And she had a feeling that despite their best effort there may still be more missteps that came to light in the future.

All she could do now was her best, feeding her family, resting when she could, step after step westward to their ultimate destination.

# CHAPTER TWELVE

Across the wide-open plains of North America, the Sullivan-Mills wagon company crept along. Hope continued to walk out in the grass, parallel to the trail and the wagons as much as she could. Fortunately, with as large as the company was they tended to move slowly. She could easily keep up without wearing herself out, though some afternoons she found it easier to ride on the wagon bench rather than fight with her husband about it.

Her sons took turns driving the two wagons, while those not so assigned scattered throughout the company. Hope had an idea that Angus and Sadie were making fast friends, while Ernest and Davis might be getting themselves in trouble. There were an awful lot of young men in the company, perhaps more than could be kept busy. Beau, as usual, tended to keep to himself, while Faith made tentative inroads with the other young girls of the company.

In spite of all the strain, Hope was content. She just

wanted the best for her children. This entire plan for the Waters family to make this journey was to give all of them a better life, more opportunity, new people and places. After the heartbreak of Jeb Buchanan's death, things had calmed down somewhat, and Hope could again imagine how perfectly her family's choice would work out. They were making progress; they were becoming part of the community. They were all settling into this new life in their own ways and Hope could not be more proud of them.

Just when it felt as though the Waters family and the wagon company had fallen into a rhythm, they reached the wide Kansas River and all that entailed. This would be their first major obstacle of the journey: getting all fifty wagons across to the opposite shore. This was to be the first of many river crossings that peppered their journey west, and the only one that offered the convenience of an established ferry. The two Papin brothers had launched their small empire on the frontier only a few years earlier, but it was already an essential service for most emigrants.

As the Sullivan-Mills wagon company approached the river, it seemed that all Hope could see was the long line of white-topped wagons, all funneling toward the river, each family waiting their turn. Because the wagon company was so large, and because the ferry could only take two wagons at a time, the caravan would need to camp on either side of the Kansas River for two days to allow time for everyone's passage. As they were near the front of the caravan, the Waters family anticipated getting their chance early on, and then spending the next day and a half waiting.

That did not mean they could avoid waiting some the first day, however. The line of wagons inched forward little by little. Frank and Colin debated whether or not to turn the oxen loose to roam while they waited, but eventually decided that they could not spare the time it would take to round them up again as the line moved forward.

And so, Hope waited too. She watched with a little bit of envy as one of the Valentine girls came to collect Faith for a morning of giggling and gossip. Hope had caught snatches of their conversation, and it seemed there was some kind of admiration-from-afar of one of the young men in the company. As they walked off, arms linked, Hope smiled to herself at her little girl growing up, but felt a twinge of loneliness. Though the friends she'd had in New York had been reliable, she had never really had a close female friend. Her husband was consistently wonderful, and all of the women in their church back home had been perfectly kind, but none had sparked the deep connection that Hope craved.

Well, she thought, if she was waiting around anyway, she might as well make an effort to do something. If Faith could make friends, then so could she.

Hope looked behind them, to the other wagons waiting to cross later that day. She had not yet met the family that followed directly behind the Waterses, even though they were living practically side-by-side every day.

It seemed as good of a place to start as any, and Hope made her way to where she saw the matriarch of that family leaning against the back of her wagon, on the shadiest side, and fanning herself.

"It's amazing how the breeze drops away when we're staying put, isn't it?" Hope said as she approached. "I'm so sorry to bother you. I'm your neighbor." She pointed up to her family's wagon not twenty feet away. "And I can't believe we haven't met yet. Hope Waters."

"Maggie Kirk," the woman said. "So glad to finally meet you. My husband is Paul, and he's off..." She waved her hand toward the river. "Worrying, I imagine. He likes to make sure everything is safe and taken care of, so I'm sure watching the ferry crossing gives him some feeling of control. I have just about had my hands full morning, noon and night since we left Independence. I'm sure you understand—I think we both have half a dozen boys or so, don't we? I've seen yours running around. Though it always feels like more." She laughed, a sweet lilting giggle that had a thread of exhaustion laced through.

"I do, yes, but most of mine are well grown, and I've got daughters-in-law to help. In fact, just saying that makes me feel a mite guilty; I should have offered your family help long before this."

"Oh, heavens, do not even think about that. We all are doing our best. And I trust if I ever have a real need of you I can ask."

"Of course."

Their conversation was interrupted by the sound of a rich baritone voice, belting out a swinging, catchy song. "Wild roved an Indian girl..."

The two women paused to listen.

"Is that..." Hope smiled, confused. "'The Blue Juniata'? Who is that? His voice is lovely."

"It's Jack Benedict. They're in the wagon just behind

us." Mrs. Kirk gestured over her shoulder with a twinkle in her eye. "I'm surprised you haven't heard him before this; it's not the first time and it certainly won't be the last."

Hope laughed. "You're not tired of it yet, are you?"

"Oh, no. I appreciate the change from listening to my boys bickering. And, besides, I'd like to think that if Mr. Benedict can keep up his energy and enthusiasm to sing like that throughout the whole journey, things won't be that bad."

"I'll be certain to keep an ear open for him in the future," Hope promised.

Behind her, the wagon inched forward a bit, as far up ahead another wagon was loaded on to the ferry to be taken across the wide Kansas.

"How old are your boys?" Hope asked, once the caravan had settled into place again.

"Let's see... the oldest is Judah. He's eighteen, all the way down to Norman who is twelve. Five boys total."

"Five boys in six years? Heavens, I wouldn't know how to manage that," Hope teased. "My husband is always telling me that we have more boys than we could handle, but even so. I think yours might be more."

"Oh, believe me, I know. I certainly would not give up any of my boys, but maybe if Paul and I had been more deliberate in our past choices, we wouldn't be where we are now."

Hope frowned in confusion. "Wouldn't be on the shores of the Kansas River?"

"No..." Maggie laughed a little awkwardly. "We are... Well." She blushed, shook her head, and then stood up straighter, with shoulders back, as though preparing herself to face the worst. "It's a bit embarrassing, but the truth is Paul and I... We lost our farm. We weren't careful enough with our money, or we were spread too thin. Truth be told, I still am not quite sure how things got so badly so quickly. But we found ourselves homeless and decided that Oregon could not be any worse than winter in Connecticut would be without a roof over our heads. So, we rounded up our boys, told them what we had to do and..." She shrugged. "Now we're here."

Hope was stunned—not by the fact that the Kirks had been unable to hang on to their home. That was unfortunately a common enough story when freak storms or blights could destroy a year of a farmer's work. What surprised her more was that the Kirks had been so candid with their children about what that meant for them.

"You— How did the boys take it? It cannot have been easy to tell them."

"Oh, there was some anger. Tears, even, but I won't tell you which one. Paul and me got a good earful of frustration from all of the boys. Imagine getting a lecture from a twelve-year-old. But, I couldn't bear to keep the truth from them. I wouldn't want them to be heading into this new life with the wrong idea about what we have and what we are hoping for. No, the conversation was difficult, but it's better that in happened than not."

"Mama," Colin called back to her from where he had a tight grip on the oxen's reins. "You coming?"

"Excuse me," she said, standing. "I suppose that's our turn. I'm so glad we finally got a chance to talk. I don't know where my head has been these last few days, being a terrible neighbor and all."

"Don't think anything of it. We are friends now, and have plenty of time ahead of us."

Hope wanted to hug the woman, so grateful was she for the promised intimacy and friendship. Maggie Kirk was like her in so many ways, even down to the number of boys they had each borne. She contented herself with a broad smile and a wave, as she hurried up ahead to join the rest of her family at the ferry.

# CHAPTER THIRTEEN

After waiting a couple hours, it was finally the Waters family's turn to cross the Kansas River with the ferry. All of their animals, wagons and belongings would be crowded onto a small floating platform and eased across the coursing current, all while Hope held her breath in agony wondering if they would make it to the other side without incident.

The ferry company had been providing this service to emigrants on the Oregon Trail for several years now. There was an entire practiced procedure with careful steps and no room for improvisation. In order to maintain the most vigilant safety, each man, woman and child was required to follow every instruction they were given to the letter. Hope listened in silence, worried but leaving it to the experts. There was nothing she could do that they could not do better.

The river here was several hundred feet wide, and with the late spring run-off, the water seemed deep and turbulent. Several of the men, like the captain's son

Daniel Mills, swam their horses across, alongside the ferry, shouting instructions, watching out for things falling overboard and helping keep everything safe as much as they could. Ernest would swim the family's two horses across himself, rather than try to fit them on the ferry with everything else. Hope watched as the horses struggled to keep their heads above the cold water; she shook her head. How had they managed to make this crossing successfully time after time?

As the ferry carried two wagons at a time, both of the Waterses' wagons were guided onto the platform together. Hope held her breath as each turn of the wheel, each step by one of her many tall sons seemed fraught with danger. Anything could overturn this ferry —it was merely a wide, flat wooden platform, lashed to canoes to keep it afloat. The animals—still hitched to their wagons—showed signs of distress. Hope wanted to go to them, but felt stuck, frightened and overwhelmed. This was beyond what she had prepared for. Frank and the other boys helped calm the teams somewhat, but it was apparent the animals craved earth underneath their hooves. Hope felt like her heart was in her throat as she watched.

Soon it was her turn, along with the remaining family. Hope felt certain that the ferrymen were going to say they were too heavy, that there were too many people, too big of animals, but instead the men watched with grim, set mouths, until all of the Waterses and all of their belongings were on the ferry.

Hope closed her eyes tight. She stood with her back against the railing, squeezed in between Faith and Angus, and only feet from the family's supply wagon.

With her eyes closed, she tried to focus her attention on the chatter of her family around her, and less on the fact that every single thing the family owned was crowded onto this uncertain vessel. If the ferry overturned, she did not know what they would do.

Though the crossing seemed to take forever, she eventually felt the ferry bump into something solid and she opened her eyes. They had made it to the other side, and now began the slow process of unloading all of the weight, animals and people without upsetting the balance.

Hope let herself be guided, instructed, waiting until Beau offered her his hand to help her step off of the ferry onto the small dock and then the shore beyond. With her feet on solid ground again, Hope felt far more ready to make camp and settle in for the day. She let out a long slow breath to steady herself, before following the rest of her family to the campsite.

It was early afternoon, and by the end of that first day, half of the fifty wagons in the Sullivan-Mills company would be brought over. All they had to do now was wait. They would be staying the night in place for the second half to cross the following day. Two of Hope's sons led their wagons to where the rest of the company was making camp, while their mother followed behind.

The crossing had been stressful, but it was done, and now she had nearly a day and a half to rest. Though she had not had a coughing fit in the last few days, at least, Hope felt tired to her very bones. She trudged after her wagons, step after step, looking forward to sitting by a campfire that one of her children made, drinking tea that another one brewed. Her need to oversee everything that went on in her camp was waning the farther west they got.

"Mother Waters?"

Nancy, Colin's wife, appeared at her elbow. The younger woman was taller than Hope, and regularly gave her the impression that she wanted to shield her mother-in-law from something, catering to whatever she needed. In private moments, Frank and Hope had called Nancy their headmistress, always a little disapproving but keeping them in line. She had an old soul, and in the chaos and struggle of life on the Oregon Trail, she had practically taken over the managing of the family's life. This was something, at least, that Hope and Nancy had in common: the desire to make sure everything was under her control. There were times that Nancy perhaps managed too closely, and Hope felt utterly useless. There were other times that she was grateful for the break, after nearly thirty years of being the matriarch.

"Yes, Nan?"

"I noticed you seemed a bit distressed on the ferry over. Can I make you tea? I've already sent the boys to collect water for supper, and I'm happy to brew a pot for us."

"Oh, you know?" She smiled up at Nancy. "I would love tea, dear. I was just thinking about how relaxing that might be."

Nancy nodded. "I'll start right away."

"And after that, do you think you and Sadie will have everything in hand for supper? I might go talk to Mrs. Kirk some once they're settled in camp. I'm feeling a bit neighborly. Unless I am needed here, of course. I am happy to do whatever you think best."

"Of course I have everything handled." She looked almost offended at the implication. "And if you want to be social, of course you should, though I think your son might prefer that you rest more."

Hope heard the pointed disapproval in her daughter-in-law's tone, but chose to ignore it. "Well, that's why I'm looking forward to your tea. Just the fortifying break I need."

Nancy nodded. They had reached the spot in the circle of wagons where the Waters family would make camp for the next two nights.

"You have a seat," Nancy said. "I'll bring you tea as soon as I can."

"You are an absolute blessing to me," Hope assured her.

She watched as Nancy hurried on ahead to direct her husband and brother-in-law with the wagons. She adored Colin's wife, and was being truthful when she called her a blessing, but just like Colin, Nancy was over-serious and did not have the sense of humor that Hope did. Sadie, Angus's wife, was another story. Often had the two women fallen into fits of laughter about the way the brothers all interacted. If Hope had a close female friend at all, it was Sadie.

But, Hope supposed, all families needed the person to which all else could look to for sobriety and responsibility. They were all quite lucky to have Nancy.

Especially as that meant that Hope could duck out and chat with a friend for the afternoon, rather than bake biscuits or do her sons' laundry.

Although, as soon as she was seated, Hope felt like staying put the rest of the night. The emotions of the crossing must have taken more out of her than she realized. She sat watching her boys make camp, and within a few minutes, Nancy had brought her a steaming cup of tea, brewed precisely as strong as Hope liked. She missed having a drop or two of milk in her drink, and wondered if maybe they could buy or trade something to the Sheldon family, who were driving their couple of dairy cows across the continent. She tucked that idea away to ask Frank about later.

By the time she finished her tea, the Kirk family, with the Benedicts behind them, had crossed the river and joined them in the circle of camp for the night. There were still hours to go before half the company would be over the river, safe and sound.

But, also, by the time she had finished her tea, Hope was already feeling sleepy. She would need to put off her visit for the following day. Nancy looked at her curiously when she said that she would be staying, but didn't press. Hope realized she would need to be even more careful if she meant to hide her weakening constitution from the children, especially with Nancy watching so carefully.

# CHAPTER FOURTEEN

Hope was woken the following morning by the sound of Angus's loud laughter. She rubbed her eyes, letting her vision adjust to the dim morning light within the wagon, and realized that everyone else had already risen for the day. She sat up abruptly, feeling slightly guilty that—yet again—Nancy had likely taken care of breakfast without needing Hope at all.

If Hope did not start taking more responsibility for the chores that needed doing, one of her children might notice. She needed to disguise her sickness as long as possible.

After finding a fresh apron and pinning up her hair, Hope climbed out of the sleeping wagon to find that half of the family had already scattered. Sadie was washing dishes, while Angus and Ernest regaled her with some kind of story. Hope caught the words "horse" and "Sunday," but she had only taken two steps toward them when Nancy appeared in front of her.

"Good morning. This is the last of the coffee but I can make a fresh brew if you would like it."

Hope accepted the warm cup gratefully. "No, don't go to any trouble. This is just fine. I'm so sorry I slept so late." She peered up at the sky, guessing it was at least an hour after sunrise.

"No trouble. You have a seat and I'll bring you breakfast."

Hope hesitated. She was the mother. She should be the one making sure everyone else was taken care of. But at that moment, Angus noticed her and waved her over.

"Mama, come tell Sadie about the time we left Ernest at church and he had to run behind the wagon for half a mile."

"Oh, goodness, is that what you all are laughing about? I could have slept a little later if it hadn't been for that guffaw of yours," she teased.

As if on cue, Angus let out another loud laugh. "It's not my fault! Little five-year-old short legs trying to run after a team of horses is funny!"

"No one ever thinks about me," Ernest said wryly.

"Oh, my sweet boy." Hope leaned down and kissed her youngest son on the top of his head. "No one thinks about any of you all once we were up to three children."

Sadie and Angus both laughed at that, while Ernest rose to offer his mother his seat.

"Well, then, I'm off. Davis and me are going to try fishing upstream a bit. But I'll be back for supper," Ernist added, before his mother could ask. "I'll see you all."

As he strode off, and Hope took a seat by her oldest son, she realized that not only did she have an entire day ahead of her in which to do whatever she pleased—maybe even rest as Frank had continually pressed her to do—but she had also made a new friend with which perhaps to spend it. Though her conversation with Maggie Kirk the day before had been cursory, she sensed a seed of something deeper.

"A whole day in camp," she said. "I'm not sure I know what to do with this wealth of time. Do we need to do laundry, or bake bread or ...?"

Sadie shook her head. "Nancy said that she would take care of the laundry that needs to be done today. I think it's a good idea to do that any time we're camping near this much water, since goodness knows there will be days that we have to do without. But, I think you can probably spend your day however you want, Mama."

"Mother Waters, here's your breakfast." Nancy had brought Hope a tin plate, piled high with bacon, beans and a biscuit.

"Oh, this is so much food!"

"But you've got to keep your strength up, don't you?" she said as she walked back to the campfire.

Hope kept her eyes on her food, feeling guilty about her secret, but did her best to eat all of the food Nancy had brought her. There would likely be a day in the future when she longed for this abundance; she would make herself enjoy it now.

But then, after she ate, Hope found herself with hours ahead of her in which to do whatever she wanted. Nancy insisted she was not needed at their camp. The rest of her family had scattered—Colin staying with his wife as she heated water for laundry. So Hope pursued her burgeoning friendship with their neighbor in the next wagon over.

Though she approached the Kirks' campsite cautiously, Maggie's exuberant welcome was plenty to assure Hope she had made the right choice. Once settled in with her new friend, the day seemed to fly by. Maggie, as the only woman in her family, had more than enough work on her plate, and while Hope knew she should be resting, neither could she just sit by idly and watch her new friend carry water, baking extra bread, or hanging laundry to dry. If Nancy didn't want her help, someone else did.

"I really hate to be taking you from your own work," Maggie said for what seemed like the fourth or fifth time, when Hope was flipping the flapjacks in the frying pan.

"Oh, I promise you, my daughter-in-law Nancy wouldn't let me do any of this even if I was over in our camp."

From where Hope sat near the Kirks' campfire, she could easily see her own family's wagons. Nancy had more than taken charge; from this distance it seemed as though she had roped Faith and Colin into collecting dry grass to refresh the family's mattresses. That was a messy, time-consuming chore that Hope would have put off as long as possible, but here was Nancy making sure it got done. That evening Hope would sleep on a newly fresh-smelling bed, instead of the moldering, musty one she had been making do with.

"They treat you like an invalid?" Maggie teased. "Or maybe a queen."

And though Hope could hear the joke in her tone,

she felt immediately defensive. "I would not allow that. I hope they know better. I keep offering but I'm beginning to think I might just be getting in Nancy's way."

Maggie did not seem to sense the coldness in Hope's tone; she was too consumed with the tiny stitches on the trouser patch she was making. "Well, regardless of why, I'm happy to have you here any time you can manage it. And not just to put you to work. I can't tell you how much I miss my women friends from back home. You have made my day in more ways than one. Please— please—feel welcome to come back any time."

Hope glowed under the praise, as she started another batch of flapjacks. The Kirk boys ate constantly, according to their mother. This food Hope was preparing would be gone by the following day, but even that small contribution made her feel better about not resting the way Frank wanted her to. At the very least, continuing to cook and clean, even if not for her own family, could help deflect suspicion from any of her children about how pale she was getting.

# CHAPTER FIFTEEN

After spending hours helping Maggie Kirk, Hope was back at her own camp before supper. It had been a full, satisfying day, but she needed to get out of Maggie's way as her own boys trickled back home for the evening. Nancy had already begun cooking supper by the time Hope returned home, and waved off her offer of help. One by one the rest of her family came back, gathering around the campfire. The boys were full of stories about their days—fishing, befriending other young men, teasing Ernest about a potential young lady. All of the Waters family was in one place for supper that final night by the Kansas River, and Hope felt a warm gratitude at getting this chance with them.

"When have we all sat down together before this?" she said, when Faith cuddled up to her side. "It feels like it's been weeks."

"Mama," Colin said seriously, "we have meals together every day. There's no need to be so hyperbolic." He sat on the opposite side of the fire, closest to his wife and seemed ready to jump up the moment Nancy needed something.

"I'm not!" Hope insisted, even as she heard Davis and Ernest sniggering behind her. "It's just that breakfast is always so fast, and this morning you all scattered to the four winds before I woke up. I didn't even get to see Beau until this moment." He nodded, silently acknowledging her. "And supper we often have to cook in waves, and once a few of you finish eating you're off to do whatever it is you do before the rest of us have started eating. I'm just saying ... this is nice. We should try to do it more."

Frank wrapped his arm around her shoulders and kissed her temple. "I understand, my love. We'll all do better about that, won't we, folks?"

"If you want, Mama," Angus began, "we can have breakfast together tomorrow too."

"Oh, you." She huffed, pretending to be more affronted than she was. Each member of her family knew that Hope secretly treasured being teased by her grown sons. The easy love and friendship between them was one of the best parts of her life. "I don't know why I bother being nice to you."

"I don't either," Angus said with a twinkle in his eye.

"Alexander!"

Their teasing was interrupted by a shout from nearby. Hope turned to see a woman with dark hair, wringing her hands and looking from side to side. She peered through the fading light, looking for something. Her son, Hope guessed. Alexander. As the company had been in camp for two days now, there had been veritable packs of children running around, playing, getting into trouble. Hopefully wherever this Alexander boy was, his mother would not be too angry with him when she found him.

"We're leaving tomorrow, right?" Hope asked her husband. "These two days of waiting have been lovely, but I can't see that we have much more time to spare. Not if we're going to reach Oregon before winter."

"We're leaving tomorrow. I believe there are some obstacles over the next few days of travel, so expect more slow progress."

Hope sighed. "Well, you know if I was in charge—"

"Stop," Frank said with a laugh. "If you were in charge you surely would have discovered or invented some way for us to be in Oregon already. Let's just let the captains do what we have elected them to do."

"All right," she said, acquiescing. "But I still think that we should not spend any more time here than necessary. I have half a mind to tell Captain Mills so."

"Maybe he'll let you drive the lead wagon, Mama," Angus said, as he lounged back in the grass. "We should ask him."

"Mama," Beau said, seriously. "You're supposed to be resting. You should not be getting yourself upset."

"Told you," Frank said to her, before he walked off to check on their horses. They too had been given a day off and spent much of the day grazing in the wide-open space in the center of the circle of wagons.

"I don't need you scolding me, Beau Waters. Did your father put you up to this?"

He shook his head. "I notice things. I listen. I know what the doctor said before we left New York, and I don't like what I see."

"I'm perfectly fine," she said, dismissively. "And I'm getting a little tired of no one believing me. I won't be driving a wagon"—she looked pointedly at Angus—"but I am perfectly capable of having an opinion without upsetting myself."

She was saved having to defend herself any more adamantly when a piercing cry cut through the air. Both Hope and Beau turned abruptly toward it.

"Who was that?" she asked in a whisper. "What happened?"

"I'll go," he said simply, before striding off toward the river.

The sound had shaken Hope. It was a cry of such despair, such pain. Whoever had made it was wounded badly, though whether physically or emotionally she couldn't say. Faith leaned into to her and linked her arm through her mother's, even as they both kept their attention focused on Beau's back, waiting breathlessly to hear what had happened.

"It will be fine," Angus said, with little conviction. "We're all here. We're safe. It will be fine."

Hope whispered, mostly to herself, "Thank goodness we're all safe."

Beau returned shortly, with the somber news that Alexander McKinnon—a boy of only six years—had drowned in the shallows at the edge of the river. He must have wandered out of sight, away from friends, was the thought. Maybe he hadn't realized how deep and fast the river was. Maybe he had thought he was stronger than he was.

Supper was a quiet affair, a far cry from the peaceful delight of the family gathering before that news. Hope could not stop thinking about that distraught mother. Any comment made to her had to be repeated, as her mind was elsewhere.

Whatever had happened to that little boy, Hope went to bed that night in agony, thinking about the poor mother's suffering. While her own children were safe, this woman was now ending her day with the knowledge that hers were not. She would have to live each day now not only without her precious little boy, but also far from his final resting place. The wagon company would keep heading west the following day, and the tiny grave would have to be left behind.

Hope stifled a sob, and rolled over in her cot, pulling her quilt up over her head so no one else in the wagon was woken up by her crying.

The McKinnons had had no chance to prepare. There was no warning such a disaster was coming. The little boy's mother must have woken up that morning with no thought about losing one of her children, and now their lives were changed forever.

It was no wonder Hope had a difficult time falling asleep that night. Thinking about Mrs. McKinnon's loss inevitably led her to thoughts of her own health, and what a similar loss might mean to her children. She rolled over again on her fresh mattress, trying not to wake the others, as her anxious thoughts spiraled into the night.

# CHAPTER SIXTEEN

The following morning, Hope stayed away from Alexander McKinnon's funeral. She could not bear the thought of his mother's grieving face.

After a quick breakfast—her appetite was negligible, especially after so little sleep—she returned to her cot in the family's sleeping wagon to wait until it was time to leave while the rest of the Waterses went to pay their respects. Given how much her family had been encouraging her to rest since they had been in New York, no one batted an eye at ger choice. She leaned into that explanation for her staying in bed an extra hour; in reality she was still shaken by the empathy she felt for the McKinnons' loss and could not stop picturing her own family in such a situation.

It was not until Hope was forced to look at the possibility of her own death that she recognized that perhaps keeping her illness from her family was doing them an unkindness. How would they all feel if she was gone suddenly one day, like Alexander?

But she didn't want to think about that. As she lay on her narrow bed, looking up at the canvas stretched over the wagon, Hope mentally pushed away such a possibility. She did not want to believe such a thing could happen. Yes, she knew she was sick, and, yes, she dreaded an actual doctor diagnosing her, but neither of those things necessarily meant that she was in any real danger. She could still walk alongside the trail for hours every day, and it had been days since she had coughed up any blood.

No, Hope decided. She simply could not bring herself to admit to her children how sick she really could be. Looking at the conversation from every angle did nothing to help. There was still every chance they would rebel against the journey all together and insist they return to the States. She could almost hear Colin suggesting that very thing. For everyone's own good, Hope needed to pretend she was perfectly healthy. For just a little while longer at least.

After the brief funeral, Hope's family trickled back to camp. The animals were hitched up. Preparations were made in silence, each person distracted by the sad reality that the wagon company had lost yet another member.

When the Sullivan-Mills wagon company left the shores of the Kansas River later that morning, Hope was still in her cot. Her daughter-in-law Sadie had ducked her head into the wagon to bring her tea, but otherwise the rest of the family left her alone. She overheard snatches of conversation through the canvas, and none seemed to be overly worried about her. Davis, even, made a joke about what big new project she might be working on inside the wagon instead of resting as she was claiming to.

She had not had a bad coughing fit since the day that Frank had caught her, but Hope knew better than to assume she was completely healed. With all the dust that was kicked up by wheels and animals as the caravan progressed westward, Hope did not really believe any healing would start until they reached Oregon.

She just had to hang on long enough to get there.

As the wagon pulled out of camp, taking its place in the long caravan just behind the Pierce family, the vehicle swayed and bucked. The ground was uneven—small rocks, deep ruts, packed earth where hundreds of wagons had gone before. While the wagon was sturdy enough, the jolting and movement caused by traveling over worn dirt trails made riding inside feel like what Hope imagined a boat must be like. She lasted only an hour or so, resting inside, before the nausea and sickness caused by the side-to-side movement drove her out.

Hope stuck her head out through the canvas flaps at the back of the wagon, trying to judge the right moment for her to climb down to the ground. She needed to wait for her own wagon to be going slowly enough, but also ensure there was enough space between this and the family's supply wagon behind that she would not be in the way.

"Mama? Do you need help?"

Angus drove the supply wagon that day and had spotted her face, peeking out from between the canvas.

"I can't ride in here anymore. I need to walk."

"Davis!" Angus called, and his younger brother

dashed back to the trail in moments. "Help Mama down."

"I can do it." She held up a hand to stop him.

"Absolutely not. If your dress gets caught in the wheel, or you lose your balance and break your wrist, it will just make everything more difficult for everyone else."

Hope scoffed at her son's exaggeration, but allowed the help.

"Come on, Mama," Davis said, holding up both hands for her to step into his grasp.

For the briefest moment, Hope felt as though she was falling, but Davis caught her expertly, swinging her down to the solid ground. He didn't let go of her until they had walked a few steps off of the trail, were out of the way of other wagons, and she had regained her balance.

"Go on, now," she told him. "Go back to whatever you were doing. What were you doing, by the way, before you were called on to rescue me?"

"Nothing."

His blush belied his words.

Hope looked back to where Davis had come from, and spotted a small knot of young folks walking together out in the grass, including Ernest and the young lady they had been teasing him about the night before.

"Hm. Making friends are you?"

He grinned. "Isn't that what you want for us?"

"Of course. Go on. Thank you, dear."

When he darted off again, and Hope was left alone, she looked around for others in her family. She did not particularly want to walk by herself, but none of her offspring seemed anywhere to be found.

So, instead, Hope sought out Maggie Kirk. Davis had been right—what she wanted for her children over this journey was to make friends. And what she wanted for herself was the same. She strode back, behind the Waterses' supply wagon, and found the other woman walking with her husband as he drove the family's wagon.

"Ah, see?" Maggie said to her husband when she noticed Hope approaching. "That's *my* friend. I told you I was more popular than you."

He chuckled and shook his head. "As it should be, I'm thinking."

"What are you up to, today?" Maggie asked brightly, turning her attention to Hope. "I don't think I saw you at the funeral this morning did I? That poor child."

"That poor family," Hope agreed. "No, I ... I confess I was a bit selfish. I stayed in bed all morning in fact, only just climbing out of the wagon a few minutes ago when I started to feel ill. The way it jerks around is hard to take for long periods of time."

"Oh no! Are you feeling all right now?"

"Of course," Hope lied. She coughed lightly, then cleared her throat. "The news about the little boy brought me low, but I'm feeling better now. I keep trying to think of some way I can ease that mother's burden but..."

"I know just what you mean. Losing a member of your family? There's nothing that can replace that."

Hope made a noncommittal noise as she fell into step with Maggie. It was strangely soothing talking about someone else's problems, giving Hope distraction from her own. As the Oregon Trail stretched westward through the prairie, away from the Kansas River, the two women filled their day with stories from back home, traded advice about raising boys, and dreamed about what might be waiting them in Oregon. In times like this, away from the pressure of her family discovering her secret, it was easy for Hope to pretend she was perfectly well. It was easy for her to envision the first big holiday dance in their new settlement in the territories, or imagine attending one of the many weddings that was sure to result from this tight community traveling together for months.

Ernest was far from the only young man flirting.

As the afternoon wore on, Hope felt her exhaustion creeping in, but she did not want to give in to it. She was having far too good of a time with her friend.

The weather, however, made a different choice for her.

The dark gray clouds seemed to roll in slowly, ominously, warning the emigrants of what was to come without allowing any reprieve.

"Those don't look good," Maggie said, her mouth set. "And we didn't have the money to get new oilskins. I should go dig out the one we have for Paul."

Hope followed her eyes up to the storm clouds that threatened. "Oh, goodness. I'll leave you to it. I'm sure my boys will be asking for their own any moment."

Though she was within only a few yards of her own wagon, Hope was unable to reach it before the sky opened up and thunder cut through the afternoon. The top of her bonnet and the shoulders of her dress were soaked through by the time she reached the back of the wagon and hurriedly climbed in while it was still rolling. Nancy was right behind her. With the clouds blotting out the sky above, the interior of the wagon was even darker than usual.

Though they were in out of the rain, there was the swaying of the wagon as it slowly inched forward to now deal with.

The rain pelted down on the emigrants almost constantly for the next two days. Hope almost forgot what it was like to not live in squelching mud with every step. Though it was nice to have the storm as an excuse to not continue to be on her feet for mile after mile, riding inside the wagon had gotten no easier than it was the day before. She fought back the nausea constantly, as the wagon swayed side to side.

The combination of the water, mud, wagon wheels and hooves of enormous animals had proved to make the trail underneath them even more craggy. The men driving the wagons had to go slowly, and each night in camp through the storm was miserable.

In the afternoon of the second day, Hope lay back on her cot and groaned involuntarily.

"Mama? Are you all right?" Sadie sat across the narrow aisle from her, where she had been talking quietly to Faith about the teacher in their company. Nancy sat at the foot of Hope's own bed, silently knitting warm socks for her husband.

"Fine. I'm fine. I think maybe the dust and mustiness of being inside the wagon for so long isn't good for me."

Sadie nodded. "I've been feeling a bit melancholy

myself. I can't think what we'll do if the storm doesn't let up soon. I'm so tired of it. I miss the sunshine."

It felt interminable, but the storm did finally let up. The next morning Hope woke slightly unsettled by the change; it took her a few moments to realize the difference was that there was no more rain pounding on the canvas top above. Instead the sounds of her cheerful family in the campsite around her signaled the break in the weather, and the rise in everyone's mood.

That evening the company made camp on the shores of a wide, shallow river. Even before most families had started supper, the captains sent around the word that they would be staying in this spot the whole of the following day. After so much time beaten down by the storm, the reprieve and rest was more than welcome.

# CHAPTER SEVENTEEN

After several days of traveling through storms, once the sun came out the company made camp on the banks of a wide, slow-moving river. It was a blessedly peaceful quiet in contrast to the torrents they had been struggling through. Hope was woken the following morning by the bustling noises of the camp all around her. The canvas wagon top did little to dampen any sound, and no one traveling on the Oregon Trail expected to be able to sleep past dawn.

She sat up in her cot, stretched and pulled her hair loose. Listening to Angus teasing Faith about how fast she was growing made Hope smile as she combed her fingers through her messy dark waves. Each of her children was precious to her, and each for their own unique selves. Even now, listening to Faith's feisty retorts to her oldest brother, Hope felt almost as though she did not deserve such wealth of love.

After braiding her hair again and pinning it up against her head, Hope climbed out of bed, changed into her clean dress, collected the wad of dirty clothes that sat at the end of the other cot and emerged into the sunlight. Though they had a full day without having to walk or make westward progress, Hope did not want to rest. She did not want to give her children any reason to suspect her health. There was certainly plenty to do in camp, and she would help.

"Good morning, Mama," Angus said. "Would you please tell your daughter she's not allowed to get to be taller than me?"

Hope smiled indulgently. Angus was rarely self-conscious about his height, even amidst his taller brothers. But Faith getting to be taller than him might be another thing all together.

"You know that girl does what she wants. It's your own fault for spoiling her. Weren't you the one who brought her sweets from town on her last birthday?" She poured herself a cup of coffee from what remained keeping warm in the coals.

Angus chuckled. "Well, on that note, I'm off to check on the horses. I don't think they've been fed yet today. You ladies enjoy your day in camp." He kissed his wife's cheek and set off.

"I'll fix you breakfast," Nancy said. "Have a seat, Mother Waters."

"Thank you, dear. But I thought I might go collect some water. Since we're here and have the river nearby, I was thinking it would be a good day to do laundry." She held up the bundle of clothing she had brought out with her. "Seems like there's always more to do."

"Faith and I have already started that, Mama," Sadie said brightly, pointing to the large tub set up a few feet from the front wagon wheels. "I was just about to make sure we got all that needs to be washed out of the wagon."

"Oh! Goodness. Thank you, dear. I appreciate that. I think Beau had a rip in one of his shirts that needed to be repaired. Maybe I'll start on that, so it can get washed too. I'll go grab my sewing kit from the supply wagon."

"Mother Waters, I'll take care of that," Nancy said, gently taking the mending out of Hope's hands. "I've already got my sewing kit out. You should enjoy your morning, and then why don't you go down to the river with the rest of the ladies this afternoon?"

"Ladies at the river? What do you mean?"

"Oh, Mama, you were still asleep when Mrs. Tenney came by this morning to tell us," Sadie said. "Since we have some time and plenty of water, Mrs. Tenney and her mother have planned a bit of a treat for the women of the company. It should be just heaven. Exactly how you should spend your day."

When she went to the Kirks' camp later that morning to ask, Maggie had already heard all about it, and filled Hope in on some of the details she had not yet learned.

"When is the last time you took a hot bath?" Maggie said, sighing happily. "This won't be quite the same as my big soaking tub was, but it's certainly better than the last time I tried to wash my hair. We'll have time for good scrub and luxuriate a bit, complete with heated water to rinse off all the soap. Goodness, I can just imagine that water being poured over my head now."

"Are you sure? You have time to take away from the boys and all the chores?"

"Not really," Maggie admitted. "But the laundry will always be there. This chance to wash my hair with hot water will not."

And so, Hope collected a towel and a small knot of soap and in the early afternoon walked down to the riverside with Maggie.

Rebecca Tenney, the young widow, and her mother Mrs. Stephens, stayed close to a campfire they had built as near to the edge of the river as they could. Mrs. Tenney fed small sticks into the fire, stoking the flames, while her mother greeted Hope and Maggie.

"Good afternoon, ladies. How are you feeling, Mrs. Waters? Mrs. Kirk?"

"Well. Lovely," Hope said quickly. "I can't believe you all are putting in so much work to do this."

"Yes, it's such a generous gift," Maggie agreed. "We will never be able to repay such kindness."

"Don't be silly. It's nothing and I trust you all will be just as generous when given the opportunity. Now, you two go on, get comfortable as you would like to. This pot is almost heated all the way through and when you're ready, we'll bring you a good pan of hot water to rinse off."

Hope looked around, from her spot on the edge of the water. A copse of trees, and a gentle bend in the river blocked the view from the camp. It was in this small pocket of privacy that at least a dozen women had given over as a changing room of sorts. There were small piles of discarded dresses, and towels waiting to be needed, here and there along the edge of the water. In pairs and trios, the women soaked in water up to their shoulders, laughing and chatting with each other.

In all the weeks they had been traveling with this wagon company, Hope had never before seen the women so carefree. In every other minute of the journey, each had seemed harried, under immense pressure to feed and care for their families all while living out of wagons. But now, even for just this afternoon, someone else was taking care of them.

"I'm so excited," Maggie whispered. She began unbuttoning her shirtwaist. "I told Paul not to look for me for at least a couple hours. Those boys should be old enough to feed themselves and not get into too much trouble in that time."

"You would be surprised," Hope said, as she too removed her bonnet, her apron, and started on her boots. "But certainly whatever trouble they get into will be their own. I'll never forget the first time my son Angus ripped a hole in his pants after he got married. My first instinct was, of course, to fix it up lickety-split. Frank had to remind me that he had a wife now to deal with that. I had done my best and it was out of my hands."

"I often think about the kinds of women my boys might marry. I'm sure they would appreciate someone who is more of a cook than I am."

"I think after these camp meals, anyone will seem like an accomplished cook."

They soon had undressed, placing their folded clothes carefully in the grass, and wading into the water. It was not nearly as cold as Hope expected for the spring run-off, melted snow trickling into rivers from the mountains miles away. Once they had reached the deepest part of the river, if they bent their legs the women could be in water up to their necks. The full submersion, with the faint currents curving around her, soothed Hope. She almost wanted to close her eyes and float away.

Maggie scratched at her scalp, letting her previously tightly bound hair fall down around her. "Goodness this feels nice," she said softly.

"With all those boys, I can't imagine anyone looks after you much, do they?"

"Well, I never have to go hunting, so at least there's that. But, no, you're right."

"We women have to look after ourselves, then."

Maggie was rubbing the slip of soap across her shoulders and upper arms. Even with this little bit of friction, the cleaned, red skin was beginning to show underneath the suds. Bright from the scrubbing, and fresh from the wash.

"Let me help. Scrub your hair and scalp," Hope instructed, "while I go fetch hot water."

She waded to the shore, staying mostly under the surface of the water, and when she drew close enough, young Nora Cole scurried to the edge of the river with a steaming pot of water in her hand.

"Be careful," the girl said. "The handle won't burn you, but it is quite hot."

"Thank you," Hope said, grateful she did not need to venture out of the river naked and barefoot. "Thank you so much for this."

The girl smiled and darted away again, off to help someone else.

Hope waded back to her friend, holding the pot of hot water high above the water to keep it from being cooled too quickly.

"Isn't this just astounding?" Maggie said when Hope drew near again. Her head was white with suds, from where she had scrubbed the soap into her scalp. "I never would have thought to do such a thing for myself, let alone for everyone else."

"Are you ready for this?" Hope asked, indicating the pot. "Lean your head back for me."

As Hope was several inches shorter than Maggie, the former had to stand up out of the water a little bit to get high enough to pour the hot water over her head. Outside of the water, the spring air was cool on her shoulders and upper chest; she was briefly glad she had not yet ducked her hair under the water as well.

"Lean back," she said again. With one hand she held the pot, pouring the hot water as slowly as she could. With the other hand, she helped separate and rinse Maggie's red-blonde hair that tangled down her back.

Maggie let out a light gasp when the water touched her skin.

"Too hot?"

"No, no. I just..." Maggie laughed. "It's been so long," she lamented. "I think I forgot how nice this could feel."

Hope continued to pour the water slowly, allowing the steam to billow up into her own face. She breathed it in, as she helped rinse Maggie's hair, hoping the steam could be healing perhaps. She took far longer to pour out all the water than she might have if she were back home in New York. Who knew when they would have such an opportunity again, and Maggie deserved the luxury just as much as any other woman there.

"All right," she said finally. "I think you're all set. Should we get more and do another rinse or... ?"

Maggie was running her fingers through her hair. The skin around her hair line was slightly pink, where the hot water had touched. "No, I think this was just perfect. Let me just comb out some of these knots and then I will return the favor."

Grateful to have a friend she could count on, Hope took the bar of soap from Maggie and set to work scrubbing her own hair. Though she brushed out her hair every morning, it wasn't often that she took the time to scratch deeply, to invigorate her scalp. Closing her eyes, Hope relished the peaceful, happy sounds all around her while Maggie went to collect hot water.

Having warm water poured over her head, washing her hair and body so thoroughly felt even better than Hope would have guessed. She and Maggie stayed in the river for more than an hour, even collecting a third pan full of hot water to share between them, just as a final treat to themselves.

"I know I am repeating myself," Hope said, as they made their way up the narrow trail that wound away from the river later, "but that was just the best thing that I have experienced in such a long time."

"Just a few more months until we are in Oregon, settled, roofs over our heads and the ability to fill up a whole tub full of hot water to do it all over again."

"Months!" laughed Hope with mock-dismay. "I don't know how we'll last months yet."

# CHAPTER EIGHTEEN

That afternoon soaking in the river was a delightful, relaxing rest. The hot water, the soap suds, the finally feeling as though every bit of her was clean, instead of just whatever corners she could get to as she had the chance. Hope slept well that night, after such unlooked-for luxury. She went to bed that evening even more optimistic that she would be able to heal from this illness, given the right circumstances. But finding those circumstances would prove difficult as long as they were still pushing west as quickly as they could.

She had even more reason to be grateful for that day —the next stretch of the trail would be the most arduous thus far.

Though most of the company relished the break, taking that time meant that they would have to push all the harder over the next few days. There were still miles and miles to go, and not one person wanted to be on the wrong side of the Blue Mountains when winter fell. The

Sullivan-Mills wagon company was set to leave that campsite just after dawn.

However, because the next stretch of trail lacked any fresh water source, they had to rise even earlier than dawn to collect as much water as they could carry away. Every bucket, tub, pan, bowl and canteen was filled with water. Animals and children alike were bidden to drink as much as they could in the time before they had to leave. Again, Hope realized they should have tried to bring more with them—pots with lids or extra canteens. The amount of water they could carry would not be nearly enough for all ten members of the family, plus the animals.

Hope tried to help collect all the water and disperse it into the family's various containers, but after lifting a full bucket to pour into the large tub that sat on the floor of the wagon, she had trouble catching her breath again.

"Mama, I'll do that," Angus said, taking the bucket from her. "Do you need to sit?"

"Maybe," she replied, as a shallow coughing fit started.

"Go. Sit."

She did not need to be told twice. Holding her handkerchief to her mouth, in an attempt to dampen the sound, Hope stumbled around the side of the wagon, away from her family, away from anyone who might see how sick and weak she actually was. She managed to keep her coughing quiet enough that she could still overhear the conversations of her boys as they hauled the water and stored it wherever they could.

Hope leaned against the front wheel of the wagon, as

her coughing subsided. Though she was afraid, she made herself look at the evidence.

Blood spots again, though she could convince herself it wasn't any worse than it had been the previous time. Hope blinked back the tears that threatened to spill down her cheeks. She had just spent the last day relaxing, doing nothing strenuous, not even making supper, and even all that rest didn't seem to be helping.

They were not even halfway to their destination. Months still to go, as Maggie had pointed out the day before.

Hope shook off her despondency.

They were not even halfway to Oregon; she still had miles and miles to go and giving up now to her disappointment would not help anyone. She refused to be a burden on her children—now or ever. She would just have to find a way to rest more without making anyone suspicious about it.

Fortunately Nancy so badly wanted to manage the entire family that Hope had already been able to give up some of the tasks she had expected to do while traveling west. The more she could encourage her daughter-in-law's inclination and servant heart, the better chance Hope would have of successfully hiding her illness until they reached the other side of the continent, even as she hated every moment of it. This was what was best for the whole family.

Even as that thought crossed her mind, she heard Nancy's voice calling out instructions.

"Ernest, bring that bucket over here, please."

She and Colin had been together so long, the rest of the boys had accepted her as family ages ago. Yes, Hope thought, Nancy was the ideal solution to the problem she wouldn't know she was solving.

The wagon company was ready to leave only a few minutes later; fortunately, Hope had recovered enough to rejoin her family without any of them seeming to worry. She considered whether or not to spare her energy and ride inside the wagon, but could not make herself do that. Such a journey would be too tedious, too much like giving up. No, she would walk across the wide plains, just like everybody else.

Walking all day under the hot sun would always be difficult, but without enough water to drink it felt nigh on impossible. The company tried to cover at least ten miles every day that they could. As the morning began, the heat was already bearing down on them. The sun's glare bounced off the white tops of the wagons, making the air shimmer with a hazy warmth. The oxen pulled the wagons slowly across the trail ruts, struggling under the weight of the supplies that needed to sustain the travelers for more than a thousand miles, including all the extra water they now hauled.

The sun crept higher in the sky, making Hope sweat as she kept pace with the wagons. Her dress stuck to her skin under her arms, and down the length of her back. She found herself trying to create spit, just for the feeling of moisture in her mouth. There was no reprieve from the sun and the heat, and even riding in the shade under the wagon canopy would be more oppressive than restful.

The only thing she could do was continue on, step after step, eagerly anticipating the small amount of water she would be allowed with supper. When they finally made camp that evening, Hope again had to excuse herself quickly to cough in private.

There was no water in this camp, no trees for her to find privacy. Instead, she walked around the curve of the circle of wagons, out into the prairie, until her own family was out of sight. Her throat already felt raw from the lack of water, and the forceful spasms of her coughing only made it worse. She felt the eyes of some of the other women following her, but every other immigrant was so consumed with making their own camp that no one checked on her well-being.

The sun was low in the sky, and her sweat from earlier in the afternoon had dried, but Hope knew she did not have water to spare to wash any more than her face. When she felt as though she had been gone too long—someone might worry—Hope hurried to make her way back. By the time she returned, a fire had been built and Nancy and Sadie were coordinating the family's supper.

"Where'd you disappear to?" Colin asked, as Hope took a seat in the circle around the fire.

He didn't seem interested in a reply, but Hope caught her husband's eye and intuited that he guessed where she had been.

She looked up at the sky, darkening after sunset. "I wish I knew more about the stars," she said, apropos of nothing. She knew she was grasping at straws, trying to keep her family in the dark about her illness. But she would do anything to distract them. Even talking nonsense. "Does anyone know what constellations are up there?"

Frank caught her eye again and shook his head a tiny bit. He saw right through her.

"I don't know, Mama. Supper is almost ready," Colin announced, as he approached the circle of his family around the campfire. He carefully carried a bucket, with a dipper in his other hand. "I don't suppose any of you all would like a drink, would you?"

A small cheer went up throughout the Waters family. Hope laughed. As poorly as she felt after that long day, sitting here with those she loved best was a balm. She needn't have tried so hard to change the subject—she could have just brought up the thirst that had consumed them all day.

Colin began passing the bucket around, person to person. From her right side, sitting around the campfire, Faith handed her mother the share of water that the family was drinking from. Hope took the bucket and dipper and sipped the tiniest amount. It was barely enough to wet the inside of her mouth, it felt like, and her entire body cried out for more. But she quickly handed the bucket on to Davis, who sat to her left. She felt her husband's eyes on her, and she smiled brightly at him. The last thing any of them needed was complaining or bemoaning what they were lacking.

Everyone wanted more water, and everyone knew they still had days to go before they could get more.

Later, when she was saying her goodnights before crawling into bed, her husband followed her to the wagon and held out a canteen for her.

"You haven't had enough to drink today," he said in a low voice. "Have more. Please. Don't make me worry about you."

"We need to conserve this, Frank," Hope said. "You know that if the animals don't get enough water, we'll be even worse off than we are now."

"That's true, but I also know that my wife is struggling to stay healthy herself. Let one of our big strong boys give up their share before you give up yours."

"You know me better than that," she scoffed. "A mother is never going to take something from the mouth of one of her children."

He looked at her for a long hard moment, before sighing. "You know... Maybe Nancy will be a match for your stubbornness. I have half a mind to tell her what you're doing and see if she can make you see reason."

"That's not funny. Though, I will admit that I had the thought today that it is such a blessing that she is willing and eager to take on so much. I might try letting her do more of all of that."

"You should!" he said excitedly. "Please do. I am far more inclined to keep your secret if I know you are doing more to take care of yourself."

"Very well. I'll see what I can do. But! Without raising suspicion. You can't tell them, Frank."

He nodded. "We are going to have this conversation again."

"I know." She sighed. "I know. It's not getting better. But not yet, please."

He just shook his head and walked back to the campfire. After a moment watching him, Hope climbed into their wagon alone and was asleep in minutes.

# CHAPTER NINETEEN

The treacherous journey continued the next day, each member of the company parched and unable to think about anything other than the next chance they would have to drink water. Hope isolated herself from her family and from Maggie. The struggle of trying to walk all of that distance under the unrelenting sun with no water to speak of made it far too difficult for her to hide her recurring cough. Instead, she wandered out, at a distance from the trail. She could still clearly see the long line of white-topped wagons, but she was far enough away that she was unlikely to be spotted unless someone looked for her.

It was a lonely few days, but Hope knew if she was to successfully keep her illness from her children, this was the sacrifice required. When they saw her at supper, she was questioned lightly about her day, but none needed to look any closer.

After several days of parched, unrelenting travel, the wagon company reached the top of a low hill that overlooked the Platte River Valley. Stretched out in front of them was the wide, shallow river, curving north and south for miles. Hope crested the hill, seeing the valley they were to cross, and then made her way back to her own family's wagon.

When she reached the caravan, she was far back in the line of wagons and sped her steps a bit to catch up to her own. Frank was driving the supply wagon that day, and she settled in to walk alongside him as the trail wound down the other side of the low hill to meet the water.

"That's the Platte?"

He turned when he heard her voice, and smiled at the sight of her. "It is. I'm not sure if you can see from here, but the trail follows the curve of the river for a few days, before we get to the best spot to cross it."

"But thank goodness we have water. I vow to never take it for granted again," she said with a laugh.

"Oh, my love, I'm sorry. I thought you knew. That water isn't drinkable. You can almost see from here how muddy it is, and whatever silt is in it will give us stomach cramps. There might be some springs along the way, but they won't be much."

"No water? You mean... Frank, you're telling me I have to walk alongside all that water and not be able to quench my thirst? How did anyone ever make it to Oregon this way?"

"I'm sorry," he said again. "Maybe you should think about riding in the wagon again, to conserve your energy."

She didn't answer; she hated to admit she was tempted.

In the end, Hope's pride was too strong to let her give in to that small luxury of riding within the wagon. Low sand dunes stretched wide on either side of the river, and as long as she stayed on the side of the trail opposite the water she could mostly convince herself that she was fine. Though the family's water supply was running low, the two youngest boys spent an entire day venturing wide of the trail, away from the caravan and the rest of the company, to find the springs and small trickles that fed into the Platte River. It was never enough. Hope was perpetually thirsty. But it did help some.

When the day finally arrived that the trail crossed the Platte, Hope thought she was more than ready.

"It's about time," she told Frank as he double-checked the oxen's yoke before leading them across. "We need to be going west."

"Did you tell Captain Mills that?" he teased. "Maybe he needs the reminder."

"I should," she retorted with a grin.

Beau had just led the family's lead wagon into the shallow water, with Ernest helping on the other side. The river was not even as high as his knee, but with as muddy and thick as it was, the danger of getting stuck was imminent. Angus waited to help his father guiding the second wagon.

Hope looked behind them, feeling a bit sorry for all the families that did not have this wealth of labor, this strapping corps of strong men that would ensure the safety of them all.

Once the second wagon had begun its slow crossing, Hope began her own. She held up the hem of her skirt high above the water and stepped in. Her boots were soon stuck tight to the muddy bottom. She took a deep breath and continued on, step by step, struggling with every foot. The current was not all that strong, and the water was only as high as her knee, but it required all her strength and focus to keep moving.

By the time she reached the other side of the river, her breath was heaving and she was struggling to cover her cough.

"I've got you, Mama," Davis said, appearing at her side and wrapping his arm around her waist. The young man was at least eight inches taller than her, and all but lifted Hope off her feet completely when he propped her up.

She could not even get out the words to thank him, as the coughing continued.

"Let's just get away from the shore," he continued, guiding her a few more steps. "Then we'll rest."

Even as her coughing stopped, Hope felt tears well up. Everyone was being so kind to her, looking out for her, taking time out of their day to make sure she was all right, even without knowing the full extent of what she was suffering from. What lengths would they go to if they knew?

"Thank you," she whispered, though she wasn't sure he'd heard. He stood with his back to her watching the wagons crossing behind them.

"You let me know when you're ready to walk again," he said over his shoulder.

She slowed her breathing, stifling more coughs, until she felt almost normal again. It took several minutes, but finally Hope was ready to continue on. The caravan was continuing on, past the Platte, as they still had a few miles to cover that day before stopping for camp. When they finally caught up with the rest of the family, Ernest was telling some of the others what he had heard that day.

"I was talking with Martin Jameson earlier, and it seems we're going to have a dance tonight."

The faces of Sadie, Angus and Faith all lit up. Hope and Davis fell into step with them, listening to the conversation.

"Mama," the young girl said, "can I go? Please?"

"I don't know… It will probably mostly be older folks, won't it? Are you sure you want to go?"

"Yes! Of course. Even if no one asks me to dance, it will such a sight. I'm so tired of the dust and the grass and the backsides of oxen."

Beside her, Angus chuckled. "We'll look after her, Mama, if you're worried about that. Maybe we'll even drag Beau along too, and Faith can have at least one dance."

Accordingly, not long after supper the sound of Martin's fiddle floated through the air. The sun was setting, and many of the families with children were turning in, but for the young adults of the Sullivan-Mills wagon company the night was just beginning.

"Come on," Sadie said, extending her hand to her husband. "I told Rebecca we would be her chaperone."

"Rebecca…? Tenney?" Hope asked. "Is that the young widow?"

Sadie nodded. "She's sweet. I think she was only married a few months before her husband died, and I have the impression this trip west was meant to be made with him."

"Oh, that poor dear. It must be hard to be going through all of this without him."

"Hopefully a little diversion tonight will do the trick."

Accordingly, just after supper Angus, Sadie, Beau, Faith, Ernest and Davis headed off together, leaving Colin and Nancy behind as they chose.

Hope sighed contentedly.

As she watched her little brood walk away into the twilight, Hope's heart swelled with gratitude. Frank came to stand by her side, watching the same. She slipped her hand into his and rested her head against his shoulder.

"We've done pretty well for ourselves, haven't we?" he murmured. "I would offer to take you dancing, but I think maybe you're better off resting."

"Do you know that I have not had to do laundry since we left Independence?" Hope chuckled. "It certainly seems like we have done something right."

"They love you. They want to take care of you just as much as you've taken care of them."

"But they also love each other," Hope insisted. "And to me that is just as important. Think about how awful this journey would be if the eight of them didn't get along, or if there was resentment from any corner."

"Well, I don't think we would all be making this move together if there was animosity."

"That's true... I suppose I'm just ... I'm proud and I'm grateful. I'm afraid of messing something up to ruin this beautiful balance. Everything seems to be working out so well."

Frank cleared his throat, before turning to face his wife. He put a hand on each of her shoulders and all but forced her to look at him. "You know what might ruin it, don't you?"

"Frank, stop—"

"I won't. It's all I can do to let this be your decision and not tell them about your illness myself. But I refuse to stay quiet between the two of us. You are playing with fire, my love. The longer you keep the secret the harder it will be when they eventually all learn the truth *and* learn you were keeping it from them."

"We don't know that they will ever have to learn the truth. It could be that this is all just the pneumonia hanging on and I'm getting better?"

"Do you really believe that to be true?" he asked somberly. "Or are you just living up to your name, full of hope, regardless of reality?"

She swallowed hard. "That's unkind."

"Is it?"

He dropped his hands to his side again and turned back to the family's campsite, where Nancy had enlisted her husband to help dry the dishes and pack them away after supper.

"What I see," he continued quietly, "is a woman who so desperately wants to hang on to what she has always had that she won't face what is coming ahead."

"That's not—" A cough tickled Hope's throat. She stifled it—mostly.

Nancy and Colin looked up at her with concern, pausing in their work.

"Can I bring you the canteen, Mama?" Colin called across the distance.

"They are going to find out," Frank said quietly. "You have to think about this. Do not let the situation get beyond your control."

"No, darling," Hope called to her son. "I'm just coming now."

Without looking at her husband, Hope walked away from him, determined to shut out his dire warnings and disappointment.

# CHAPTER TWENTY

The next morning, Hope tried to pull details out of her children about how the dance had gone the night before. Angus made some reference to the schoolteacher, Miss Atkins, that made Sadie and Faith laugh, but she wasn't able to extract any useful details. But, Hope supposed, this was how it should be. They were all grown, or nearly so, and entitled to their privacy. Even if she wasn't told details, the Waters children would look after each other and she had nothing to worry about.

That was the thought she kept returning to: she had nothing to worry about in regards to her offspring. They were all smart and capable and making their way in the world. She should be very proud.

The one thing she did have to worry about—the nagging cough—she preferred to ignore.

And so, after breakfast had concluded and the camp all put away, she turned her attention to the trail ahead. It would be a shorter travel day for the wagon company, as they had two large obstacles to get passed before making camp that night.

After her long days walking alone, far away from the trail so none of her family could overhear her cough, Hope wasn't sure she could do that again. She missed her family. She even missed her friend, Maggie. She was far too social of a person to withdraw from community for days on end. She would just have to find another way to hide her developing illness.

On this side of the Platte, their water supply had again become more reliable, but that was about all that could be said for this stretch of the trail. They wagon company didn't get more than a few hours on the trail before they had to stop again to address the hazard in front of them. Hope had been walking with Sadie and Angus, when the lead wagon slowed to a stop, halting all progress behind as well.

"Well, this is going to be fun," Angus said, as he peered at the terrain ahead.

Hope followed his gaze, around the dozen or so wagons ahead of them. At first she wasn't sure what she was looking at, but then the view snapped into focus. The ground ahead of them and seemingly all around looked like something not of this world. All over the earth, and some dug halfway into it, were rocks, stones, boulders of all sizes littering the trail. The rocky terrain stretched to what seemed like the horizon in both directions. There was no clear way to get around it, nor was there a definitive trail cut through it.

"How on earth are we going to get through that?" Sadie asked her husband.

He shrugged. "I'm going to go see what I can do to help. You ladies going to be okay?"

"Go on, then," Sadie said, as her husband trotted away toward his brother driving their lead wagon.

"I don't suppose there's anything we can do, is there?" Hope asked. "You would think that with as many companies as have come through here someone would have found a better way."

"That's what I would have thought. It seems that every day there's some new reason for me to marvel that anyone ever made it to Oregon with a wagon full of their life. It seems so brazen sometimes. I don't know that I was cut out to be a pioneer," she concluded with a laugh.

Hope scanned the horizon, looking for Nancy and Faith. All the Waters men were consumed with the careful steps and delicate movement they would need to weave their animals and wagons through the stony terrain.

"Should we make our way through?" Sadie asked. "We can wait on the other side for them."

"I suppose we'd better. I assume Faith is with a friend somewhere, though I worry about Nancy trying to take on too much. Is that her with Beau?"

Sadie looked where Hope pointed. "Looks to be. I hope she knows what she's doing and doesn't get hurt, though you know she did read the guidebook front to back several times. Maybe she has helpful suggestions for the men."

"Maybe."

Making a wide arc to stay out of the way of any of the wagons carefully being brought through, the two women picked their way between the rocks and around the bigger of the boulders. And they were not alone. Most of the women and all of the children were doing the same thing. The way the wagons had to get through this landscape seemed extremely dangerous, and having fewer people in the way the better.

While the stones were too close together to allow a wagon easily through, walking proved far easier than it looked. Hope and Sadie continued for the dozens of yards until they were clear of the rocks and waiting for their wagons.

Once on the other side, the way was clear, though it did not seem that much safer. The two women headed in that direction, where the first of the wagons was just approaching. The trail wound away from the boulders and uneven terrain, before seeming to disappear down into a gorge. While the various river crossings had been difficult and the uneven ground had been a hazard, this descent into the ravine seemed the most perilous so far. When she looked down the trail, Hope felt herself sway on her feet, grateful she would not be expected to get a wheeled vehicle down that incline.

"You feeling all right, Mama?" Beau said, appearing at her elbow as though from nowhere.

She looked at him in surprise. "Why wouldn't I? And why aren't you back there with your brothers?"

He only looked at her, waiting for her answer.

"We've been fine," Sadie said, answering his question. "Easiest just to stay out of the way. Are the rest of you all getting through?"

Beau answered Sadie succinctly while Hope stewed. She resented whatever her son was implying. Even as she did so, however, she recognized that was unreasonable when she was otherwise so willing to let her children take care of everything around camp.

She looked back down into the gorge, eyes tracking where the first wagon was beginning to descend.

"It's awfully steep," she finally said, changing the subject. "How are we all going to get down there safely?"

Beau looked at her for another silent moment before finally answering her. "We are going to chain the wagon wheels, so they don't spin out of control."

"Will that work?"

"It's the best option. The captain will leave some gaps between wagons to allow the women and children to descend safely. You two should head down the first chance you get."

Hope nodded, taking in his advice.

"And then at the bottom, we'll make camp," he concluded. "You sure you're feeling all right?"

"Beau Waters, I will tell you if I am feeling poorly."

Though even as the words left her mouth, she was reminded of the coughing she had successfully hid from the rest of the family just that morning while she was washing her face. But that was over. She was telling the truth at the moment, at least. She did feel fine.

He reached for her hand. Though she hesitated briefly, she gave it to him. He squeezed gently, tipped his hat, and turned back to where his brothers were in the midst of delicately guiding their wagons through the stones scattered in every direction.

"Well," Sadie said. "I don't mind saying I will feel a lot more comfortable once everyone is safe and sound in camp tonight. I can't imagine how we will all get there without some accident or injury, though."

"Oh, don't say that," Hope pleaded. "I couldn't stand another funeral."

"Are you ladies ready to head down?"

They turned to see Samuel Findley looking at them expectantly. He was Captain Mills's right hand, and his family was always just behind the Mills family in the wagon caravan.

Gesturing to the trail at the top of the ravine, he said, "A few women and children are walking down now, and I'll wait 'til you're all at the bottom before I lead my own wagon down, but you have to go now."

"Right you are, Mr. Findley," Sadie said. "Ready, Mama?"

"Wait for us!"

Mrs. Kirk, Mrs. Benedict, and the two young Benedict girls were hurrying up from behind.

"Goodness that was an adventure, wasn't it?" Maggie said with bright eyes. "I'm sure Paul told me about it when he was going through the guidebook, but I had no idea what to expect. It looks like the kind of place that would have been made up for a story."

"From what I've read about the west," Mrs. Benedict said, "there are miles and miles of terrain that seem as though they cannot be real. Did you all read anything from the journals of Captain Lewis?"

Hope and the other shook their heads.

"Well. I didn't read it myself, but I heard from my brother who heard from a friend at college that there are lakes of boiling water that smell like hell itself. And giant stones taller than the tallest buildings in New York City."

"How is that possible?" Hope asked in wonder.

"Oh, but some of that we'll be passing right by, won't we?" Maggie asked. "The descriptions of Chimney Rock and Scott's Bluff in the guidebook sound awe-inspiring."

"I will just be happy to get to the other side and see the ocean," Sadie said. "Do you know in New York we lived only a couple hundred miles from the Atlantic Ocean and never visited? I told my husband, I don't care if it takes us an extra week, but we are going to see the Pacific Ocean."

"A couple hundred miles is no easy matter," Maggie said.

"Easier than the thousands to Oregon," Sadie responded.

"Well, you do have me there," Maggie concluded with a laugh.

# CHAPTER TWENTY-ONE

Once all the wagons, families and animals had made it successfully to the flat bottom at the end of the steep trail, Captains Mills and Sullivan decided that the company would stay in this camp for another full day. They had water, they had trees, and they had several days of difficult passage to recover from. At least four of the wagons required repairs.

When Hope heard the news, she felt a pang of worry that they were taking too much time. But more than maybe anyone in the company—aside from perhaps Mrs. Van Anda, who was expecting her first baby sometime between here and Oregon—Hope Waters was ready to rest.

But even on a day set aside for such a break, there was still plenty to do. As soon as the wagons were in place, Hope grabbed two of their buckets. If she knew Nancy, all the Waters family's laundry would be done by the end of the day, and getting the water heating as soon as possible would be a big help. As Hope made her way toward the spring, following the trickle of women on similar missions, she caught up with Maggie Kirk.

"How's all your boys?" Hope asked. "They get the wagon through all those rocks all right?"

"They did, yes, but I think a few of the families behind us had trouble. Did you hear? A wheel broke. What a nightmare."

"I can't even imagine. We've been so lucky so far, compared to some other families, haven't we?"

"So far," Maggie said cheerfully, as the two women joined the queue of others waiting their turns to fill their buckets. "Lord willing it stays that way." She glanced down, indicating the buckets Hope carried. "You all doing some big cleaning this afternoon?"

"My daughter-in-law certainly has some kind of plan in mind, though I don't know for sure what. But water is always useful. With as many boys as we have there is always laundry to do. I thought I could at least get this started."

"I'm sure I've said it before, but I envy you that daughter-in-law. What I wouldn't give for just one of my boys to be able to make them all biscuits now and again." Maggie chuckled. "I hope you never take that woman for granted."

"I try." Hope grinned. "That's why I'm here trying to do my part."

After they had gathered the water they needed, and said their good-byes, Hope carried the heavy buckets back to her own camp. There, Davis was in the middle of building the campfire, while Angus and Beau were taking care of the animals.

"There you are!" Nancy exclaimed, hurrying to take one of the buckets from Hope. "You didn't say where you were off to. We were worried."

Hope felt a flash of irritation; she was a grown woman and should not have to report her every movement. But she pushed it down, remembering what Maggie had said. She was lucky to have Nancy. Hope knew that.

"I'm sorry to worry you. I didn't realize I was gone long enough for it to be an issue."

"It's not how long." Nancy took the second bucket, from where Hope had set it at her feet, and poured it all into her big pot. "It's that we didn't know where you were in case something happened."

"I'm sorry," she said again, watching Nancy bustle around importantly. "Would you like me to go get more water?"

"No, I'll send Ernest when he returns from gathering fuel for the fire. Thank you, though."

Hope watched her a moment longer. Nancy was adding a handful of dried grass to the flames, coaxing them higher under the pot of water.

"Is there anything else I can do?"

Nancy looked up at her then, a kinder expression on her face than before. "No, thank you, Mother Waters. I have everything in hand here."

Hope nodded, feeling superfluous and out of place. She had just turned away, looking for something to occupy her time, when Nancy called out again.

"While you were gone, Pastor Montgomery came by to let us know he would be holding a church service here tomorrow night."

"Oh, are we staying here that long?"

"Two nights. The rest of today, and all day tomorrow." Nancy shook her head. "I worry about taking that much time, but, then, I'm not in charge."

Nancy was beginning to sound like her mother-in-law. Hope too was worried, but didn't feel as though encouraging the other woman's fretting would be productive.

"Should we go to the pastor's service?" Frank asked. "How long has it been since we've sung a hymn with a group of other Christians?"

"I would love that," Hope gushed. "Even surrounded as we are by people all the time, it doesn't feel as though we have really been able to connect. And I miss it."

He kissed her cheek. "We'll walk over together after supper, then."

Not all of her children chose to join them that night, but after supper Frank, Hope, Colin, Nancy, Ernest, Davis and Faith all made their way to the open spot near the water that the pastor had designated as their meeting spot.

Most of the emigrants gathered were finding seats in the grass, though there were large rocks and boulders here and there that could serve as chairs as well. Hope walked with her family, picking through the growing crowd, looking for a space large enough that they could all sit together.

A tiny movement caught her eye, and Hope noticed the doctor's wife waving at her. Hope smiled and waved back as Colin led her to a rough seat on a large stone.

"Who was that?"

"Oh, just—" She hesitated, unwilling to draw attention to her illness. "I met her right after we left Independence. But with everything going on, I had completely forgotten, since her wagon is not near ours."

Colin looked back at the woman, who Hope now saw was standing with her husband.

"Isn't that the doctor standing with her? That must be his wife, then, Mrs. Martell? Why didn't you tell us you had met her?"

"I forgot," she said, not putting voice to the thought that she had deliberately not thought about it. "But, you're right, I should go seek her out sometime soon. Maybe the next time we are stopped for a whole day. It must be terribly useful to be friends with a doctor."

Colin looked at his mother curiously, nodded, and turned his attention to getting his wife situated.

Hope sat alone on the stone, while the rest of her family spread out on the grass all around her. In the lull before the pastor began, she watched the interactions of the families—mothers pulling small children in to sit still and behave, fathers finally sitting at all after a day on their feet. A worship service in the middle of the Oregon Trail might sound completely impractical, but for some of these hard-working men and women it felt essential.

After a few minutes, Pastor Montgomery moved to the front of the crowd and called for their attention.

"Greetings, friends. All day today I've been praying for a joyful and peaceful night together, and the Lord delivered. I'm so grateful you're here," the pastor began. "If you would all rise, let's begin with a hymn."

Hope stayed seated, as the rest of the community stood to sing with Pastor Montgomery. She closed her eyes and let the music wash over her; it was not unlike her afternoon in the river, when Maggie had poured hot water over her head and let her relax into the feeling of being taken care of, being able to just float away.

She wasn't sure how sick she was. In fact, it wasn't until that moment that she had even remembered that there was a doctor in their company. Eventually, she knew, she would have to consult with the doctor. But she wanted to put it off as long as possible.

Hope threw herself into the singing with gusto, determined to demonstrate she felt perfectly hale and hearty.

---

As the wagon company left the camp at the bottom of the ravine the following morning, the trail slowly climbed out of the ravine. The depth of the canyon kept the emigrants in the shade for much of the morning, as they continued their ascent back up to the flats of the prairie.

They were now well into June, and Hope realized they were coming up on a full year since she had first seen spots of blood coughed up in her handkerchief. As each day passed and her coughing became more and more frequent, she was having a more and more difficult time convincing herself that she was getting better. There was optimism, she knew, and there was outright denial. And Hope knew she was swiftly tipping into the latter.

But there were still days and weeks and months of the Oregon Trail ahead of them, and to Hope there could be no difference in facing her illness now instead of later. She kept her secret, pushing it to the back of her mind as much as she could.

# CHAPTER TWENTY-TWO

After another several days pushing westward as fast as they could, the Sullivan-Mills wagon company was set to leave early in the morning. They had many miles to make up from all the previous delays and rests. The Waters family ate breakfast—some sat together near the fire, some took their biscuits and bacon with them as they rounded up the oxen. As their wagons were generally near the front of the caravan, the Waterses needed to be ready at any time.

But the time for the wagon company's departure from camp came and went.

Hope was listening to Faith tell her about the rag rugs she was helping Abby Mills make, when she noticed Captain Mills hurry by their wagons in the opposite direction of his own.

"Wonder what that's about?" Faith said, her gaze following the captain as well.

"I don't know if I want to think about it. Have we ever seen him that perturbed?"

They didn't hear anything more about the delay or what had the captain hurrying as he did. Within another thirty minutes the lead wagon pulled out of camp, guiding the rest of the caravan away from the campsite and out along the trail again. To Hope, the lack of information seemed ominous, but she reassured herself that this sort of thing was precisely why they joined a company like this: so someone else could worry about problems.

Whatever the problem was, it could not be too terrible, or they would not have left camp at all. Or that is what she told herself.

Over the course of that day, Hope felt reasonably strong and well enough to walk next to the wagons. They were getting into summer and the sun was relentless, but at least outside of the wagon she had a chance of a breeze, and fresh-smelling air. The horizon stretched out ahead of them, tall grass in all directions. Occasionally she would spot movement—perhaps a prairie dog or rabbit getting curious about this long line of strange creatures cutting through their home—but for the most part the landscape was quiet and serene.

The company did not stop for midday break, presumably because they had gotten a late start, but as usual Nancy had it all taken care of. She had baked two extra batches of biscuits that morning, and brought a cold one to Hope without even being asked. After thanking her daughter-in-law for her thoughtfulness, Hope decided what she needed most that day was a distraction. Her children were scattered throughout the company with their own friends, and Hope could be too.

And so, as she swallowed the last bite of her lunch,

she ducked back along the line of wagons to find Maggie, who she found walking alone through the grass. Her oldest boy, Judah, drove the Kirks' wagon and the rest of the boys were nowhere to be seen.

"Have you been abandoned?" Hope asked, as she approached.

"Unless I am actively handing them food, yes, it is safe to assume I have been and will continue to be abandoned," Maggie responded with a laugh. "But at least I know they will always come back to me. How are you?"

Hope fell into step with her friend, regaling her with stories of all the ways her daughter-in-law was making this journey so much easier. "It really is a pity your boys were too young to marry off before you left for Oregon," she teased. "I'm not sure there's anyone in the company as lazy as I am now."

As the afternoon wore on, the two women walked in rhythm, feeling the packed dirt underneath their feet where hundreds of emigrants had come before. They fell into a comfortable silence.

"Do you think Oregon will be what we expect?" Hope asked after a bit. "It seems as though this journey is both not as difficult as I had expected, but also much harder than I prepared myself for."

"I know. Even with having two funerals already, I still keep expecting something tragic to happen every day." Maggie shook her head. "I know we did not have much of a choice but to try for a fresh start, but I still wish this all could have been easier. The callouses on my hands have never been so rough."

"I think maybe..." Hope began slowly. "I'm not sure how to word this, but I wonder if maybe that feeling of dread comes from us not really having the home and stability that we have been used to in life until now. I'm sure that when I had the idea to come west I only thought about the end result. I gave no thought whatsoever to this long stretch of day after day of walking, with little water, barely enough to eat, dirt and dust and—" She coughed lightly, interrupting herself.

"Isn't it strange to think that every step we take is the farthest we have ever been from home?"

"But also each is a step closer to our new home. It's just these in-between days that are unsettling. And they do seem to stretch on forever."

Approximately mid-afternoon, Maggie's youngest boy, Norman, ran up to the two women as they were walking.

"Ma, do we have any more biscuits?"

Maggie sighed. "You're still hungry?" As an aside to Hope, she said, "Growing boys and limited food supplies is a harrowing combination."

"You have my sympathies."

"Ma?"

"Yes, Norman. Since we were delayed for whatever reason this morning I had time to make more. Look in the grub box in the wagon. Should be on top there, unless your brothers already ate them."

"Oh, that delay was because of the Sullivans," he said.

"What?" His mother frowned. "How do you know that? Did you know that?" she asked Hope.

Hope shook her head and looked to the boy, only twelve years old but already taller than her and nearly as tall as his mother.

Nathan seemed surprised that they didn't know.

"Oh, actually, Junior Sullivan told Billy Whitson who told me."

"You're kidding. Do you hear that, Mrs. Waters? The not quite grown boys are more gossipy than we are." Hope laughed. "Now, Norman Kirk," his mother continued, "you've been holding out on us. What was the delay about?"

"One of the Sullivans is sick. The youngest, Jeremiah. Apparently the doctor thinks it's measles."

"Measles," Hope gasped. "Measles in our camp? Is no one afraid it will spread?"

"I dunno," Norman responded. "I only know what Billy told me. I guess there was some talk about making the Sullivans stay behind, so the measles didn't come too, but that didn't end up happening."

"Oh that poor family," Maggie said. "Of course they don't want to be left behind, and then be on their own out in the middle of the wilderness, but it must be such a risk to the little boy's health. Have you ever tried to spend the day riding in the wagon?"

Hope nodded. "It's awful. If he's very ill, I don't know how he will be able to stand it."

"Can I go?" Norman asked. "The boys are waiting."

"Go on," his mother said. "But if you hear any more about this, you let me know."

"Yes, ma'am."

"That poor family," Maggie said again, to Hope. "This is exactly the kind of development I had been half-expecting."

Hope stayed quiet, thinking about what it meant to that family that one of their members was sick. They could have been left behind. They could have been abandoned in the middle of the prairie without the manpower or community they needed to protect themselves. They could have lost everything.

Though Hope didn't think consumption was as contagious as measles, she still dreaded what might happen to her, to her entire family, should knowledge of her illness come to light. In the best case, she would be forced to stay inside, resting in bed all day every day. In the worst case, it was not hard to imagine that her family may be asked to leave the company.

Though not likely, such a circumstance was not impossible. Hope knew that.

And Hope also knew that she needed to do everything she could to keep her frailty under wraps as long as she possibly could. She could not put her family at risk like that.

When the wagon company left the trail to make camp that evening, Hope was just about to say her goodbye to Maggie and return to her family, when Norman ran up again.

"Ma, you said to tell you—"

"What happened?"

Hope held her breath. The boy looked from one woman to the other.

"He's gone," he said softly. "Jeremiah died not long ago. I guess the doctor told Mrs. Sullivan that the journey was too much for him, or maybe he was sicker than they realized. I don't know."

Hope let out a strangled cry. That poor woman. One more mother grieving. One more family who had to leave a member behind.

"Thank you for telling us," Maggie told her son. "We'll have to see what we can do for them."

"I need to go tell my family," Hope said. All she wanted to do was hold her children close.

Maggie nodded a brusque good-bye and turned back to her son, as Hope hurried to her own wagons just ahead. Frank and Ernest had just gotten the vehicles in place in the tight circle the company still used for protection as they traveled through Indian territory. Beau had collected two buckets and was about to go find water when Hope approached.

"I've just heard the worst news," she announced to the group as a whole. The story—as much as she knew of it—poured out of her in a rush. "And just the thought of yet another death..." She trailed off, unable to finish.

"And another funeral in the morning, most likely," Frank added softly.

"The poor family," Sadie added. She looked at Angus who reached out for her hand.

"I think... It's been a long day. I'm going to lie down until supper."

Feeling a cough coming on, she climbed into the wagon, awkwardly, banging her knee on the wooden side at the back as she tried to cover her mouth with one hand and hold on with the other. Once she was well inside, she sat at the foot of her cot, covering her mouth and trying to dampen the sounds of her coughing. Her knee throbbed where she had hit it, and she hoped the bruise would not affect her ability to walk the next day.

"Mother Waters?"

Hope looked up guiltily, to see both Nancy's and

Colin's worried faces in the gap between the canvas flaps at the rear of the wagon.

"Mama, what's wrong?"

"Nothing," she responded hurriedly. "Nothing. I'm just feeling a bit faint. A little tired, the news of Jeremiah just makes me feel..."

But she could not finish her sentence, as another fit of coughing overtook her.

"Mama, here, take the canteen. Have some water."

Hope nodded, still coughing, and reached for the offered drink. In doing so, she noticed the look of suspicion on Nancy's face.

"It's just such a terrible thing to learn," Hope choked out. "Another little boy and his poor grieving mother. It's hard for me to wrap my mind around, and I suppose my body just..." She shrugged, cleared her throat and took another sip of water. "Thank you, both. I'm fine. I'll be fine."

After they left, however, Hope could not get the curiosity and dubiousness of Nancy's expression out of her mind.

# CHAPTER TWENTY-THREE

For the third time in just a couple months, the Sullivan-Mills wagon company gathered for the funeral of one of their own. This was not just another death, but the death of another child. And not just any child, but the youngest son of one of the company's captains. No one was safe from the dangers of the Oregon Trail.

As the emigrants crowded around the tiny grave, Hope stood with her husband. She bowed her head, listening to the pastor say kind, hopeful things about Jeremiah Sullivan. But even Hope noticed that this funeral was being conducted perhaps a little more quickly than the previous ones.

How swiftly they had all become jaded by the perils of this journey.

Not ten minutes after Pastor Montgomery concluded his prayer over the small grave, Captain Mills was ready to leave camp. Junior Sullivan and a couple of his friends piled rocks on top of the disturbed earth where his brother was buried, to protect the body from wolves or other scavengers. But that was the last act of kindness they could do for Jeremiah. His family had to leave him behind. There was no time to delay, no room to mourn. The emigrants had more than a thousand miles still to go and the time to do so was dwindling. Though it was difficult to think about the dangers of snow when they were in the hottest part of June, the deadline of winter was on everyone's minds.

The wagon company left mid-morning, heading west as quickly as they could. Day after day, rising with the sun and finally making camp long after most of the families would have made supper. The sun set late at this time in the summer, and they used every hour of daylight they could. For several days they traveled like this, the flat prairie stretching in all directions. Each day felt the same as the last. There were no variations in the landscape, save the periodic sad, lonely tree some miles from the trail. The flat earth seemed like a shallow bowl, the horizon curving all around, with the stark blue sky stretching overhead.

For the most part, Hope alternated between walking with one of her children and walking with Maggie. Occasionally, the weight of the secret she held so tightly made her feel too guilty to bear conversation with anyone, and she walked alone. During these solo hours, Hope let her mind wander distractedly to thoughts of settling in Oregon. They would need to build a home before winter. They would need to build all new furniture. They would need to think about the spring vegetable garden and learn what they could forage in the Oregon forests. All these concerns were months from being something she needed to worry about, but anything was better than trying to decide how and when to tell her children how ill she was.

As they traveled through the wide-open prairie, Hope tried to rekindle the feeling of excitement and adventure that had so consumed her when she had the initial idea for this move. She had been so enamored with the idea of building a new home for her family in Oregon that she had prepared an entire speech about it. But now, nearly a year later, exhausted and stressed, she could not remember even a word of it.

Perhaps once each day, a large bird of prey flew overhead. At first, Hope was interested, watching it circle overhead, occasionally diving for the prairie rodents that scurried just out of the sight. But after a few days of that, even her interest in watching the hunt waned.

The Oregon Trail asked too much of her. It was all she could do to keep going.

As the wagons rolled on, occasionally a discarded piece of furniture or moldy side of beef popped up on the side of the trail. Carcasses of fallen oxen weakened by the lack of water and extreme demands placed on them appeared, dragged off the trail to the side before being feasted upon by the scavengers of the great plains. A heavy, wood trunk that had clearly been a beloved heirloom once, now sat abandoned, pulled off the side of the trail out of the way of passing wagons. Hope peeked inside before continuing to walk. It was mostly empty— whatever it had been storing must have been unpacked —but the bottom of the trunk held at least a dozen books, a small set of children's wooden blocks, and a single boot missing half of the sole. The trunk now sat in the grass, subject to the wind and the rain of the wilderness.

The furniture had been abandoned for a reason. Every ounce of weight carted across the continent meant more of a burden on the animals that pulled their wagons. Whether that weight is made up of life-giving flour and bacon, or more frivolous luxuries like a hand mirror or jewelry, made no difference to the oxen. But when one of the animals could not go on any longer because of that weight, decisions need to be made.

Though Hope often felt as though her family would be at a disadvantage when they reached Oregon because of the strict, pared down nature of their belongings, when faced with this alternative she was grateful. They had made the most difficult choices back in New York, when they had clear heads and plenty of food in their bellies. To be faced with the same emotional choices now, when they were tired and often hungry, could lead to disaster or even starvation. Every step was hard, but Hope knew it could be much harder.

She chose to believe it would all be worth it in the end.

To Hope, a string of days in which nothing terribly exciting or dramatic happened was to be treasured. She was tired of the deaths, tired of the injuries and risks taken to get the wagons through the terrain. She was tired of her own coughing and what that reminded her of. As day after day passed in which the most interesting thing that happened was a horse overturning a bucket of water, she felt herself relaxing a little more.

After several days of monotony only occasionally broken up by hawk sightings or Mr. Benedict's singing, something new appeared on the horizon. Hope and Maggie had been walking parallel to the trail all morning, closest to the Waters family's supply wagon, when Maggie halted her steps and squinted ahead.

"Do you see that? It's awfully small, still, but I think that might be some kind of rock formation. Finally." Maggie laughed and continued walking. "I've been waiting for something else to look at other than just grass and dirt and more grass and dirt."

She pointed and Hope followed her gaze. At first she didn't notice anything different on the horizon. It all looked flat, plain and the same as it ever did. But after a few more steps, scanning carefully, Hope noticed what Maggie had seen first. There, in the distance, was what looked like two big rocks, alone in the middle of the flat plain. As the days passed and the company drew closer to it, Hope felt a sense of wonder at the majesty of these natural formations.

Nancy, who had practically memorized the guidebook, told the family over supper that it was called Courthouse Rock, named after the county seat in Missouri, and it was just the first of several enormous formations they would be passing over the next few days. Now that she saw it, though, Hope felt the word rock in its name was insufficient. This landmark seemed to rise out of the landscape thousands of feet like a sentinel, sandstone walls standing perpendicular to the ground. This was no mere rock.

When they finally reached the foot of the monument, Hope felt awe, along with a mild curiosity, wondering how such structures even came to be. But ultimately she decided to simply enjoy the sights. She didn't need to understand everything to appreciate it.

A few days after they passed Courthouse Rock, the wagon company reached Chimney Rock, a similarly enormous monument, though thin like a spindle. A few days of travel after Chimney Rock, and the wagon company made camp at Scott's Bluff, another granite landmark that dominated the skyline.

Each day that the wagon company spent in the shadows of these enormous monuments, Hope was reminded of what Lewis and Clark had reported back after their Corps of Discovery returned to the east coast. Such sights would have sounded unreal only weeks ago, but now the emigrants were rewarded for their bravery and setting off into the unknown. None of their friends or family back home would believe such things existed, and here they were camping mere feet away.

When they left the rock monuments behind for the time being, the next destination the emigrants had to look forward to was the first fort of their journey. It would be a place to hopefully acquire new supplies and repair wagons. It would also be the first sign of civilization since they had left Independence weeks earlier, and Hope, for one, could not wait.

When they were still a couple days' journey from the fort, Hope was walking with Frank when they heard several of the men up ahead let out a joyful whoop.

"What...?" Frank chuckled. "Someone just got some good news."

The wagons slowed to a stop, and even from this distance it was clear there was some kind of commotion going on at the head of the caravan.

"I hope everything's okay," Hope murmured.

They didn't have long to wonder. Soon, Daniel Mills, the captain's son, was riding swiftly down the long train of wagons shouting instructions and calling for the men.

"Making camp here," he explained, when he was within shouting distance of the Waterses. "For the rest of the day. Buffalo has been spotted. We're going hunting!"

# CHAPTER TWENTY-FOUR

The men frantically gathered their rifles and ammunition and rode off toward the north, toward the herd of buffalo that had been seen on the horizon. The hum of activity was over quickly, though, once the wagons were drawn into a circle and the hunting party left. The camp fell into a quiet, lazy afternoon. A number of the women settled in to get a head start on laundry and baking—any chance to be in camp for longer than just a meal needed to be taken advantage of. A far larger number of the women and children who remained in camp, however, let the lethargy of a too sunny afternoon tempt them. A lull fell over the campsite; even the animals seemed happy for an uneventful afternoon.

Hope was torn—though she knew she should try to nap or rest when she had the chance, she really did not want to. If her friend Maggie was searching for wildflowers in the prairie, then Hope wanted to be there too. If another woman was perhaps perfecting her pie recipe with dried apples, Hope didn't want to miss it. There was almost nothing she hated more than hearing about some fun adventure after the fact, and this could be an entire afternoon of something other than work.

"Mother Waters, why don't you have a seat? I was just about to make some coffee." Nancy returned to the Waterses' camp with two full buckets of water. "I thought I might also wash some of the bedding. All of it if there's time. If you want to give me your quilt, I'll see that yours gets done first."

"Oh, you marvelous dear. I'm sure I don't know what I would do without you. Let me know how I can help you, please."

Nancy offered her a half-smile, which Hope took to mean that the younger woman agreed with her but was too polite to say so. Laughing to herself, Hope reflected that Nancy was born to be a manager. It was people like her that made Hope sorry that women could not hold public office. Perhaps when they finally settled in Oregon, she would find the position and opportunity to best suit her skills.

Not long later, Hope was enjoying a fresh cup of coffee, with just half a spoonful of sugar in it. They should be rationing some of their less essential supplies, like sugar, but just as an afternoon nap was the luxury of choice for many of the women in the company, a sweetened treat was Hope's idea of a delightful day on the Oregon Trail. Such luxuries were few and far between, and Hope would relish this. Nancy had started boiling water for the laundry, while Sadie and Faith half-heartedly tried to focus on Faith's schoolwork.

Hope seemed just about to nod off in the sun when

she heard what almost sounded like thunder. Looking up into the clear blue sky in confusion, Hope sat upright, confused.

Nancy stood, and looked to the north. "Are those horse hooves? Are the men back already?"

The bright yelp of an Indian war whoop soon told them the truth.

Hope gasped so deeply it kicked off a coughing fit.

"Indians!" Nancy said. "With all our men gone!" She stood, looking toward the sound, every muscle tensed.

"They must have known. They must have seen all of them ride off and were just waiting for this moment," Sadie said, frantically gathering up Faith's workbook and slate that had been spread out all around her. "We have to hide."

"Where can we hide?" Nancy asked. "They're coming, and there's nothing we can do. Is there even a gun left in camp or did the men take them all?"

"I'll check," Faith volunteered, running to the family's supply wagon.

Through all of this, Hope tried to get her coughing under control but the excitement combined with her general weak constitution made that difficult.

Before Faith returned, the grating sound of something heavy being dragged across the ground arrested their attention. Hope stood, finally, walking a few steps out into the middle of the circle of wagons, and noticed immediately where that sound was coming from.

When the company had made camp that afternoon in advance of the buffalo hunt, the men had pulled all the wagons into a tight circle for security as they always had before. A handful of men stayed behind to keep watch, but it was clear now, not all the steps had been taken that Captain Mills and Captain Sullivan had decreed all those weeks earlier.

Someone—from this distance Hope could not decipher who—had neglected to chain their wagon's wheels to the next wagon over. This created a small gap, the barest hint of vulnerability, that the attacking Indian tribe was now taking advantage of. Half a dozen of the strong warriors had dismounted and pulled two of the wagons apart, creating a gap several yards wide through which the rest of the attacking party could enter.

Dozens of bare-chested, dark-haired men armed with bows and arrows poured into the circle of wagons, spreading out in all directions.

No one was safe. No wagon was secure.

A single gunshot rang out—one of the men who had stayed behind had begun their defense.

"I found this," Faith called.

Hope turned back around to see her fourteen-year-old daughter holding a rifle nearly as big as she was above her head.

"Can any of us shoot this?"

"Doesn't matter now," Sadie said. "Get in the wagon. Mama, come on. Climb in. They're coming. They're coming!"

Hope glanced over her shoulder once more to see four of the Indians break off and head in their direction. She turned back toward her wagon and ran, as fast as she could, climbing in just after Faith.

"Shh, now," Nancy said. "Maybe they won't be thorough. If they don't know we're here, there's a chance they'll ignore us."

"Do you really think so?" Faith asked, sitting on the cot across from Hope, with the rifle on end between her legs.

"I don't know." Nancy shook her head.

Hope was on her own cot, huddled against the back of the wagon, as though the difference of a few feet from the entrance would keep her safe. In her panic and her running, she had begun to cough again, a little at first.

"I wish Angus was here," Sadie whispered.

"I wish any of them were here," Faith whispered back.

Hope cleared her throat, stifling a cough.

All the women held their breaths.

They heard footsteps around the side of the wagon. Something heavy knocked against the side, making them all jump. Was he going to their supply wagon?

They could lose everything.

She could not stop coughing.

"Mama, please," Faith whispered in agony. "They'll hear you."

Hope lay down, rolled over in her bed and drew her knees up so she was as small as she could make herself. Bending her head down, under her arms, close to her lap, she continued to cough, the muscles of her abdomen aching with every convulsion. So focused was she on herself, on her cough, on using every muscle she had to stop the coughing, that Hope almost didn't hear the intruder.

After another heavy knock on the side of the wagon bed, the tie holding the flaps of canvas closed was cut through unceremoniously. Hope heard Sadie gasp, and rolled over to see what had happened. Still coughing lightly, unable to catch her breath, still covering her mouth with both hands, Hope watched as strong, brown hands grasped the edge of the wagon and hauled the man inside.

He was tall, stooping to fit under the wagon bows, and wore an expression of bored disdain. It was clear at a glance that this warrior found such plundering beneath him, and did not really expect this wagon to hold anything of use. He glared at each of the women in turn, his dark eyes smoldering.

Hope continued to cough, and when his eyes fell on her, he furrowed his brow. That attention sent a shock of fear through her, and her coughing worsened. She could not get her breath. She could not get a handle on herself. Against all her instincts of safety, Hope was forced to take her eyes off of the man, as she doubled over in coughing.

As she struggled to catch her breath, Hope kept her eyes closed, her focus on her body and what she needed to get control of it again. She heard some more thumps, felt the wagon sway a bit, but the coughing consumed her. When she finally recovered and sat back up again, the man had left and her daughters all stared at her.

"He's gone," Faith said in wonder. "He left without taking anything."

"Did you see the way he looked at Mama, though?" Sadie asked.

She felt three pairs of eyes on her.

"What is going on?" Nancy asked in a low voice. "Mother Waters?"

# CHAPTER TWENTY-FIVE

All of that stress and excitement of the Indian raid had positively depleted her. Hope stayed in bed, even after the attackers had left. Her coughing fit had taken so much out of her, she didn't trust herself to do more than sit in one place anyway. Though the sounds and voices weren't completely clear, she could hear enough outside the wagon and throughout the campsite to assume that there had been injuries and thefts. Several women were crying just within earshot of Hope, and she wondered what the final damage was.

"Mama, would you like some tea?"

Sadie stood at the rear of the wagon, holding a steaming mug out for Hope to take. It required a small effort, but she managed to sit up and scoot to the end of her cot where she could reach the mug.

"Thank you, dear. That's thoughtful. How is everyone getting along out there?"

"It's hard to say. Everything is still a bit chaotic. My friend Rebecca's brother got shot by an arrow; Mrs.

Mills is still trying to count how many head of cattle they have left. I think the pastor's wife hurt her ankle pretty badly. I'm sure there's more that I just haven't heard about yet."

"And the food? The supplies? Are the families all right?"

"I don't know." Sadie looked stricken. "I... It's bad, Mama. We don't yet know how bad, but I think if the men don't come back with some meat there will be families in this company that will really be hurting."

Hope nodded, sipping her tea. "I wish I knew how to help. Maybe talk to Nancy about rationing our own food better, in case things get too bad in the coming weeks for others."

Sadie nodded. "We've already talked about it. But, you know, Mama, we had some of our supplies stolen too."

"I expected this. Do we know yet how much?"

"Nancy and Faith are going through it now. Fortunately with the way Nancy had the wagon packed, the bulk of the food was harder to get to, so hopefully it was mostly left alone."

"I'm sorry that I brought you all out here," Hope said, reaching forward to pat her daughter-in-law's hand. "I'm not sure any of us realized what we were getting ourselves into."

"Maybe. But we'll make the best of it. And we have each other, right?"

"We do. I love your heart, Sadie. Angus is very lucky."

She smiled her thanks. "I'll let you rest, and go see

what help Nancy needs. You just stay off your feet for now, Mama."

When Sadie had left her alone again, Hope sipped her tea contemplatively. Telling Sadie that she had not realized what they were getting into was an understatement, but like the secret of her illness, Hope did not know what choice they had now. The best they could hope for was to not starve or lose anyone else before they reached Oregon.

After another couple hours of drifting in and out of sleep, Hope was startled to full consciousness by sounds of yelps and horse hooves coming from elsewhere in the camp. The men had returned.

Hope considered getting out of bed to meet her husband and sons, but she was too afraid that the coughing would return. And then what would Frank say? No, her daughters would just need to explain why she was still in bed—after the severe shock they had undergone, no one should be surprised. She lay back and closed her eyes, listening as her husband and tall sons called out their concern and surprise the closer they got to camp.

She didn't have long to wait before one of them came in to check on her.

"There you are." Frank climbed into the wagon and sat on the edge of Hope's cot. She stayed lying back, watching him. "Do you want to tell me what happened?"

"Someone neglected to chain their wheels and an Indian tribe took advantage of the lack of security. I don't think you needed to come in here to learn that."

Frank was quiet for a long moment, staring into the middle distance. He was quiet for so long, in fact, that

Hope worried she had been too flippant. Maybe she had run through his streak of good humor. She sat up, letting the quilt pool around her waist, while her feet remained on the bed, behind her husband.

"Didn't the girls tell you what happened?" she asked, more seriously.

"They did. In fact, they told me quite a bit. But I wanted to hear it from your point of view."

"It was so scary, Frank. I don't know who to blame— I know the captains would never have left us unsafe and vulnerable if they had known, but to see all those strong, warriors, all with weapons, bearing down on us—"

"No, I meant I want to hear about what happened in here. When you were hiding, or trying to."

His gaze seemed to pierce her, and she hesitated. He already knew, that was apparent. And he wanted something specific from her... An admission? An apology? She could not read his expression.

"I— I don't know what you mean."

"You do," he said softly. "Tell me please. We never keep things from each other."

"Well, I..." Her voice shook. "I, um... I had an attack of coughing, probably from the dust and the running. All the excitement. And I tried to stifle it so none of the attackers would hear me, but one of them came into the wagon anyway and... The girls, well, they were worried about me, of course. It was a lot of coughing. But in the end it might have been the suggestion of my illness that made the Indian leave without bothering us anymore."

"The suggestion of illness?"

"Yes, well, you know..." She bit her lip, worrying over how much to say. "There wasn't any blood, I don't think," she concluded in a low voice. "What did the girls say? Do they know?"

"I don't know if they know, for certain, but they certainly suspect. I overheard Nancy saying that they should keep an eye on you, make sure that one of them is always with you."

"Treating me like a toddler who cannot take care of herself? They can't do that. I won't allow it. The suggestion is absurd. I brought them into this world, and it is my decision whether I sit around waiting to die or not."

"Hope, she has a point. You are not taking care of yourself. You seem to forget on a regular basis that not only did Dr. Jansen specifically instruct you to rest, but you have also gotten sicker since that happened. I just... I don't understand how you can justify this all to yourself. If Nancy and the others realize how ill you are and further realize that you have kept that secret from them, well, I cannot predict how that will all sort itself out. Every day that passes that you keep up with this pretending is another day that you are hurting the people that care most about you."

"The pretending isn't hurting anyone but me. Are you angry?"

"Of course I'm angry," he said hotly, though still trying to keep his voice down. They both knew quite well how easy it was to eavesdrop on other people's conversations in this cramped campsite. "You are not taking care of yourself, and when things escalate far enough, the burden of that is going to fall on me. Or our children. I know you think that you're protecting them, trying to keep their lives free of worry, but Hope... My love. My heart. My whole life... You are *hurting* them.

You are hurting Sadie and Nancy and Faith who all have been doing the tasks that you would otherwise be doing, and when you get too sick to help at all, when you are so weak that you *are forced* to stay in bed all the time, who is going to be the one to bring you food, to help bathe you, to take care of you? I don't know how else to make this clear to you. I'm just..."

He threw up his hands in frustration and stood abruptly, though in the small space under the wagon's canopy he could not even straighten to his full height. Hope had never seen him actually angry. Up until now he had always held his tongue, kept his temper, done his best to be patient and understanding with her flightiness. Though she knew that some of her impulses were trying for him at times, she had never realized how vexed he was.

"I'm sorry—"

"I don't want you to be sorry, my love. I want you to do what you know you need to do. I want you to take care of yourself. No one else can do this for you."

"I know—"

"Do you?" He turned to face her then, though still standing, head bent at an awkward angle under the wagon's bows. "I don't know if you truly recognize what you are doing to this family. In fact, I hope you don't. If I thought that you were being deliberately selfish..." He took a deep breath and rubbed his eyes. "The way this is going, my love, there's still time. We have months ahead of us, and you could stay off your feet for most of it. Nancy has already taken charge of most of the cooking. I know that resting is anathema to you, but I promise if you do not make some changes... We might reach a point of no return."

A light joke sprang to Hope's mind, but she bit her tongue. She may have made light of it in the past, but she could at least recognize in this moment that she should be listening, and showing Frank she was taking it all seriously.

"I'm sorry," she said finally.

He shook his head, and exited the wagon, leaving her alone with her thoughts and her guilt.

Hope could admit to herself that she was running out of time. There was a chance any day that she would be found out, that she would not be able to get out of bed, or that the bloodstains would be identified. Frank was right, and she needed to figure out how to be honest with her children.

# CHAPTER TWENTY-SIX

The next morning, the company left camp just after dawn. Not only could they not afford to take any extra time, but no one wanted to stay at the site of their attack any longer than necessary. Most of the women and children who had been in the camp were still petrified, wondering if the tribe would return to seize or destroy more of the few belongings they had. Hope had heard at least one crying child in the middle of the night, some poor soul who had likely been woken up by a nightmare. Even the men who had been out hunting when the attack occurred seemed jumpy, on alert, and angry with themselves that they had not been able to protect their families.

After Nancy and Faith had assessed the damage, it was clear the Waters family had lost some of their supplies. There had been no one in or near their supply wagon when the Indians had raided, no one to guard against theft. It was a mere stroke of luck that Nancy and Sadie had reorganized the wagon only a few days earlier, tucking the most valuable items deeper in the space and leaving the heavier, more unwieldy things closer to the opening.

Whoever had robbed the wagon had made off with a hundred-pound bag of flour, half a bushel of dried apples and most of the sugar they had left. All the meat, however, beans and rice had been left untouched, somewhat hidden behind the trunk stuffed full of blankets and winter clothing.

So many other families in the company had lost so much—flour strewn through the dirt, fine cast iron pans carted away, broken wooden chairs tossed aside. The boon of the fresh buffalo meat had been essential in keeping everyone's spirits up, and everyone's bellies full after the tragedy. It was only the reminder that they would reach Fort Laramie in a few days that kept many of the emigrants from panicking over their stolen supplies.

The Sullivan-Mills wagon company left the site of their attack and headed straight for the fort, and the promise of not only food to purchase, but also American soldiers to offer some measure of protection.

Fort Laramie had been purchased by the United States Army only a few years earlier, with the intention of stationing soldiers there as a way to help protect all of the American citizens who were passing through this wide-open stretch of territories. It had originally been a trading post, and still served as a site where emigrants could stock up on food, ammunition and other supplies. The selection was limited, and the cost was immense, but necessities were necessities.

The caravan arrived at the fort in the early afternoon

a couple days after the attack; Hope had been riding on the wagon seat, still self-conscious about what her children might suspect after her coughing fit in front of the Indian warrior. But that meant that from her elevated vantage point, she saw the fort as soon as it appeared on the horizon.

The walls around the fort were about fifteen feet high, built around an empty square that could serve as refuge in the event of an Indian attack. There were two guards posted at each corner, keeping an eye on all directions for emigrants seeking assistance or any attacks from the tribes that lived in this part of the country. The fort was rough, small and seemed haphazardly thrown together, but this was still a taller wall than Hope had seen in months.

The cheerful, rich baritone of Mr. Benedict singing was heard across their section of camp, as the Waters boys maneuvered their wagons in place and looked after the animals.

"I'm going to check out the store. Is there anything we need?" Frank asked Hope as he helped her down from the bench.

"You know that Nancy is the one to ask about that. She—or even Sadie—knows far better than I do which foodstuffs we might be running low on. Although—" she added, calling him back. She lowered her voice, keeping this detail just between them. "I could use some more handkerchiefs. If they have any, or fabric for some. The ones I have are…"

"They're stained, aren't they? And you don't want to put them in with the rest of our dirty clothes for fear Nancy will see them."

"Please, just... look for me? Please. I promise I am figuring out how to tell them, but we don't want it to be a surprise in the laundry, do we?"

"No, you're right. I'll see what I can find."

He strode off to consult with Nancy and Sadie about any food or other needs the family had, and Hope was left to her own devices. She stood, watching uselessly as her children took care of everything.

"How can I help?" she asked Angus, as he walked past her to grab something out of the supply wagon. "What do you all need?"

"Since we are here for the rest of the day," Angus suggested, "why don't you go see Dr. Martell about that cough?"

"My cough?" she asked, rounding on him. "Why? What did Sadie tell you?"

Her oldest son raised his hands in defense. "Nothing, Mama. Nothing specific. Just that you had what seemed to be a difficult fit the other day in camp. I know that the stress of the attack was probably a part of that, but it's still worrisome, don't you think?"

"Is that what you all think?" She looked from Angus to Sadie to Faith, who were nearby waiting for Angus. As Hope looked around their small campsite, she realized the other boys were avoiding her eyes. Angus looked at her quite frankly, though. Almost impertinently, she thought.

Hope took a deep breath and looked out to the prairie, the open landscape past the fort, past the wagons, past any hint of civilization. The deeper she got into this, the harder it would be to extract herself without disappointing someone. Maybe this small concession could buy her more time before she had to break all their hearts.

"Fine," she said, turning back to her oldest son. "You're right. I should talk to the doctor. See if he has something different to say than Dr. Jansen did."

"Thank you, Mama," Angus said, kissing her cheek. "Want me to walk with you?"

"No. I'm fine." She waved him off dismissively. "I'm not quite the invalid you all seem to think I am."

"And Dr. Martell will probably say the same thing," Angus said with a grin. "Let us know the verdict."

Hope nodded, frustrated, feeling as though she had been cornered. But there was nothing for it now. Her children were not wrong that she should see a doctor about her cough... She just did not want to hear what the doctor had to say.

She fetched her shawl out of the wagon and as she wrapped it around herself, she set off across the campsite in the general direction of where the Martell wagon was. They tended to be in the last half of the caravan, so she looked for other families who would be nearby. When Hope finally spotted the wagon that was the Martells, she slowed her steps as she approached.

"Hello?" she called. "Dr. Martell? Mrs. Martell?"

The doctor's wife came around the far side of the wagon, carrying a bucket of water. "Oh, I'm so sorry," she said when she noticed she had a guest. "I hope you haven't been waiting long."

"Not at all, no. Is the doctor here?"

Mrs. Martell deposited the bucket near the embers of her campfire that had died down to a low warmth. "No, I'm afraid not. Is there something I can help you with, or I can send him to see you the moment he has a chance?"

"I'm not sure. I..." She worried at the edge of her apron, rubbing her finger over the hem stitch. Now that she was here, the impetus she had had to face the truth had deserted her. "Do you remember when I fainted, when we first met a few weeks ago?"

"Of course. Have things gotten worse?"

"Perhaps. That's what I wanted to talk to the doctor about. I've been feeling weak, still, and cold when no one else is. It's nothing too terrible—I don't want to waste the doctor's time."

"You do look a little pale, especially for someone who has been outdoors every day for the last several months. Are there any other symptoms that have worried you?"

"Um." She cleared her throat. "Yes?"

Mrs. Martell looked at her with an encouraging smile, waiting for Hope to elaborate.

"I, um... I've been coughing a bit more than usual, I suppose. In fact—" Now that she had come to it, all the words came out in a rush. "My children have been a bit worried about my cough, so they insisted I come see the doctor today."

"And how long have you had the cough?"

Hope reiterated the same thing she had told Dr. Jansen the previous summer—that this seemed to be a lingering effect of the pneumonia of the previous winter. She knew perfectly well that she was leaving out the most concerning symptom, but she could not bring herself to say it out loud. Not until the doctor's wife asked directly.

"And when you're coughing," Mrs. Martell inquired, "does anything come up? Does it feel like a dry cough?"

Hope took a deep breath. "Blood," she said in a low voice.

"I'm sorry?"

"Blood," she stated, louder this time. "Not every time, and not a lot, but I have ruined a couple handkerchiefs coughing up blood in the last few weeks."

The expression on Mrs. Martell's face shifted from one of interested concern to one of sympathetic worry.

"I see." Mrs. Martell looked thoughtful, gazing off into the center of the wagon company's campsite, toward where men and women were bustling around. She turned back to look directly at Hope. "What about fever, or chills? Lack of appetite? Any other symptoms you can think of at all?"

"No. Well, perhaps a lack of appetite. It's difficult to judge my true appetite with the circumstances we're in, isn't it?" She laughed lightly, hoping the doctor's wife would laugh with her, lighten the mood and help her feel less worried. "All this walking. My boys are eating everything they can get their hands on."

"Mrs. Waters," she said gently. "We need to talk about you. Not your boys. I think you might have consumption."

"Oh," Hope responded in a small voice. Suspecting she was so sick, and hearing someone else say it out loud were two very different things. As much as she had thought she was prepared to hear that sentence, she knew now she was not.

"Of course, it's my husband that is the doctor, and I can send him to your wagon as soon as I see him, so he can look you over and give you an official diagnosis, but—"

"No. No, thank you. That's fine. I don't need to waste his time. I'm sure you're right." Hope stood. "Thank you for your time, Mrs. Martell."

"You can sit, stay awhile. You should be resting as much as you can—"

"I'm fine. As I said, you must be right. I'll go right back to my camp and rest now. Please do not send the doctor to me."

"But, Mrs. Waters—"

"Please." She heard the fear in her own voice, the utter desperation she felt at wanting to keep this all a secret still. "Please, I don't need to take up his time. And please don't mention this conversation to anyone."

"Your family—"

"I will inform my family when the time is right," she said. "Please, Mrs. Martell, can we keep this between us?"

The older woman frowned, watching Hope carefully. "If that's what you want," she said finally.

"Thank you. Now, I must be getting back. Thank you again for your time."

"Please take care of yourself, Mrs. Waters."

"You sound just like my husband," Hope responded airily as she walked away.

# CHAPTER TWENTY-SEVEN

"You're back!" Angus said, as his eyes fell on his mother making her way back to the Waters family's campsite. He and Sadie sat close to the campfire, chatting. "That was quick. Is everything all right?"

"Of course. I didn't learn anything new. It's just as we have been talking about—I should rest more." Hope shrugged, and sat across the campfire from her son. "Though I don't know how to do that, exactly, and still do my part in getting us to Oregon."

"Mama," Angus said, with a scolding tone. "You know that Nancy already has everything under control. You have no excuses. We don't want to hear you cough any more on this journey, do you hear me? All of the rest of us will bully you into staying in bed if we have to, but whatever this sickness is you have to beat it. Wouldn't you rather be better by the time we get there?"

Hope felt a wave of relief wash over her. Maybe she would never need to tell them the whole and complete truth. Especially if she could actually be better before they reached the territory. Maybe she could simply accept the opportunity that Angus was offering. She told herself this could count as telling her children; surely Frank would understand why she had not wanted to name the dreaded disease out loud.

"Thank you," she said to her son. "I'm trying. But I do appreciate how much all of you have taken on. It makes me feel downright lazy."

"Getting better from pneumonia is not lazy, Mama," he said absently, as he fed a little more fuel to the fire. "Get that thought out of your head right now."

Before Hope could respond, she heard her husband's hollered greeting to the family. Looking up, she spotted Frank returning from the fort, with Nancy and Colin in step behind him. He carried a small, filled crate, while Nancy and Colin each had a large sack in their arms.

As soon as they got near enough, Nancy split off to the supply wagon to store the bag of flour she had been carrying.

Hope looked to her husband, but he caught her eye and shook his head subtly.

"The general store didn't have everything we wanted," he said to the group at large, "but we did manage to get more flour, as well as some rice, and salt in case the boys are able to go hunting. Oh, and some extra fishhooks. Hopefully one of more of these rivers we have ahead of us will be stocked. That should at least make up for some of the food that was stolen."

"I'll take that," Nancy said, appearing again. She accepted the crate from her father-in-law, before taking it to the supply wagon where she disappeared inside.

"Did other folks get what they needed?" Hope asked.

"Some. The shelves will likely be bare by the end of the day. But the soldier keeping shop there did tell me that every fort we stop at between here and Oregon has served as a trading post of sorts, so there should be more opportunities in the weeks ahead."

"And even if it's not buffalo, some of us can go out hunting over the next few days," Colin added. "To supplement what we have here. I don't mind going, but maybe Ernest and Davis would prefer to."

"Davis will do anything to not have to drive the wagon," Angus said with a laugh.

"I imagine you'll have to roam pretty far out, won't you?" Hope asked. "If the shelves here are bare, that means that all the wagons that stopped here before us would also be looking for meat or some other food to supplement what they brought. What would that be? Hundreds of emigrants come through here?"

"We'll see," Colin said. "It's just an idea right now. But it's better to plan ahead as we need to."

Hope smiled to herself. Colin was only ever Colin: level-headed, planning, and serious about both. "I'm sure you'll handle it all efficiently and completely as you always do," she told him.

———

After leaving Fort Laramie the next day, the company had another long stretch of trail without any water. They needed to cover at least fifteen miles of trail every day, in order to get to the next source of fresh water before they all ran out of their stash. In the morning just before they were to leave, Nancy oversaw the Waters brothers hauling bucket after bucket from the river nearby, and made sure that every canteen, pot or remotely water-tight container was full.

"I think maybe this is the way to convince me to stay in the wagon," she said to Frank as they both stood back out of the way. "The idea of walking in the sun without water again is enough to make me cry. And that's me standing here with a full canteen that I can drink as much as I want from before we leave."

"Well, I don't care what it takes. I will go days and days and days with as little water as possible if it means you will stay off your feet."

"Yes, you've made that clear."

He looked over his shoulder to make sure none of their children were near enough to hear. "Aren't you worried that the doctor will inadvertently share your secret?"

"I'm trying not to think about that possibility. I'll tell them. I will," she insisted. "When the time is right. I asked Mrs. Martell to keep it between us, but I don't know her that well. I hope I can trust her."

"The time is never going to be right, Hope, and the longer I am abetting you in this secrecy, the more angry they are going to be at me as well. Don't do this to me, Hope. Don't do this to our family."

"I *know*, Frank."

With that, she walked off, taking a long swig from her canteen as she did so. She did not need to listen to any more of his haranguing. But she did climb into the sleeping wagon for at least the first part of travel that day. Walking under the sun without water to tide her over was more than she was interested in putting herself through that day.

The wagon company rolled out of camp, but it was only a few hours before they were delayed.

"Hold up!" someone shouted from behind. "Halt the caravan!"

Even from where she rested in her cot in the wagon, Hope could hear the desperate cry from somewhere in the rear of the caravan. Underneath her, she felt the wheels roll to a stop, and when her wagon was at a standstill, she poked her head out from between the canvas flaps to investigate.

They had stopped just next to the site of another enormous piece of furniture discarded on the side of the trail. A gorgeous, old cherrywood desk, with intricately carved legs and a wide, smooth top. Hope took in the sight, her heart breaking for whatever family had left home back east with such optimism that they could make it to Oregon with this treasure in tow.

Angus and Sadie made their way toward the trail, toward the wagons, from where they had been out walking in the prairie grass.

"What do you think the hold-up is?" Angus asked, craning his neck to see around the Kirks' wagon. "I hope no one else is hurt."

"Let's go see," Hope said as she climbed out of the wagon. "I need to stretch my legs anyway. We'll stay out of the way if we need to, or maybe we can help. But waiting here for who knows what is wearing on me."

"You sure you don't want to stay here, Mama?" Angus asked. "I can go back and check and you can rest while we're stopped."

She shook her head. "I'm too antsy. You know me. I'm no good at resting. I won't be able to think about anything else until I know, so I might as well go myself. You're welcome to come with me, of course."

Her oldest son grinned and offered her his arm. "Shall we?"

She took his arm, grateful for the assistance. It was increasingly distressing the way her body was unable to keep up with what her heart and mind wanted to do. They walked parallel to the caravan, as each of the wagons slowed to a stop, to account for whatever development had occurred. They had not gone far at all when Hope spotted a cluster of folks surrounding the Gladwell family's team of oxen.

"Oh, no," Angus said under his breath. "I don't like the looks of this."

Even as he said that, the crowd parted briefly and Hope saw what they had all been looking at. One of the Gladwell's oxen had fallen in its yoke. It seemed as though Mr. Gladwell and Mr. Ulmer had moved fast enough to unhitch the fallen animal so it did not bring down its yoke mate with it. From this distance it was difficult to see if the ox on the ground was still breathing or not, but even Hope knew that even if it was still alive at this moment, that could not last.

She shook her head. "Goodness, what will they do now?"

"Maybe borrow a cow from one of the other families? Or, maybe they'll just empty out their wagon as much as they can so the weight is less on the animals remaining. I don't envy them, though."

"Take me back, please," she said in a low voice. "I can't look at this anymore."

As mother and son walked slowly back to their own wagon, Angus talked animatedly.

"I was just telling Sadie the other day that it feels as though our family has been uncommonly lucky on this journey so far, don't you think? No deaths, no terrible injuries or repairs needed. Even the Indian raid left us better off than many others. Your cough is worrying, but that is far preferable to what some of these other folks have had to go through. No, I don't envy them one bit."

Hope kept quiet, wondering if Angus would still think the Waterses were as lucky if he knew the extent of what she was hiding from them.

# CHAPTER TWENTY-EIGHT

The carcass of the Gladwells' ox, pulled to the side of the trail to rot, was not the first such death they had witnessed, and it would be far from the last. There were times along the trail, in fact, when Hope and one or more of her children walked way out into the prairie grass, far enough away from the trail that they could no longer smell the stench of the rotting flesh. There were other days when the wagons rolled passed sun-bleached skeletons of animals that had perished in years past.

It was days like this that Hope was struck by how truly wild this country was. The community around her, the structure of the fort, along with all the treasures from home they had on hand, helped her forget for long stretched at a time. But the truth was, in deciding to move to Oregon, they were choosing to live side by side with the threat of starvation, loss and deprivation. Death was all around them, wherever she looked.

In this context, Hope thought she could be a little

bit justified in trying to ignore the death that might be lingering inside her.

The trail from Fort Laramie was stark. Though Hope still often suffered the effects of motion sickness from riding within the wagon, it was better than the alternative. There was so little water in this part of the country that even the grass and shrubs native to the terrain seemed to be barely hanging on, and what water remained in her canteen needed to last her as long as possible.

At various times, some of the men would lead their wagons out farther into the terrain. They traveled still parallel to the trail, but could do so without the dust and debris kicked up by the wagon in front of them obscuring sight and hindering breathing.

One afternoon when Hope was riding inside the wagon, trying to focus on the sweater she was knitting— the same one she had begun over winter—she overheard Faith asking her father something as they walked with the oxen. Though Hope did not hear everything, the hint of fear in the girl's tone piqued her curiosity. She put her knitting to the side, and peeked her head out of back of the wagon. Only just in time to see the back of another wagon, heading in the opposite direction.

She frowned, and called to her son, Beau, who was driving the family's supply wagon not far from her.

"What— No, *who* was that?" She pointed to the receding cloud of dust, as the unknown wagon continued heading east, back to everything they had already left behind.

"Turnarounds. Didn't recognize them. Must be from another company."

"Turnarounds? You mean they... They're going back? But, they've made it this far, how can they give that all up to go back?"

Beau shrugged. "Not everyone is willing to give up this much," he said simply.

She nodded, thinking, and returned to the relative quiet of the interior of her wagon.

This journey was far more difficult than she had expected. She wondered if she would have still chosen to come to Oregon if she had known what she was truly in for, especially with her illness only getting worse. It pained her to realize that she sympathized with the family who felt driven to turnaround and go back. That would just be one more secret she kept from her children—it had been her idea to come to Oregon in the first place, after all.

———

"We're almost there," Faith said excitedly, bouncing on her toes. "Maybe by mid-day?"

Hope was walking with her daughter next to the sleeping wagon, the team led by Angus. Nancy and Sadie walked nearby, just off the trail. Even though Hope was feeling her exhaustion in every inch of her, she had been so tired of riding in the wagon that she was forcing herself to complete this last half mile on her feet.

They had almost reached Independence Rock, one of the last of the huge granite monuments that marked the Oregon Trail through the territories. All through the morning the humungous boulder loomed on the horizon, drawing them forward like a magnet.

"Well, we're a few days late, but it could be worse," Angus said, good-naturedly. "What's today, the eighth?"

"We were supposed to reach Independence Rock by Independence day," Nancy pointed out. "Those four days could mean life and death when we get to the end of the trail."

"We can't do anything about that right now," Angus said, trying to soothe his sister-in-law. "So we should just enjoy this afternoon, don't you think?"

Nancy pursed her lips but didn't respond. As Hope listened to this conversation, she felt pity for Colin's wife. The woman was only ever trying to do her best for everyone else in the family, and was working with very little, not to mention the whims of forty other families she was forced to travel with. Not for the first time Hope wondered if she and Colin regretted leaving New York.

Once they reached the base of Independence Rock, the wagons settled into place. The company made camp for the rest of the day, though it was still early afternoon. There was fuel and a small river nearby, so the emigrants could once again have as much water as they needed. That alone was worth the small delay of a few hours.

After one of the most grueling, soul-crushing stretches of the Oregon Trail, camping at the foot of Independence Rock seemed a luxury. There was water and grass, shade in at least some places, and a long afternoon in camp to rest and recover as best they could. In fact, many of the young people in the company seemed to get a burst of energy, the moment they arrived. The wagons were all pulled into their protective circle, the animals were unhitched and watered, and then a stream of young men and women, and some of the older children, trickled toward the rock itself.

From where her family's camp had settled for the day, Hope looked up at the top of Independence Rock wistfully. She could admit that she was in no fit state to even hike to the base of the rock, let alone climb all the way to the top, but it was the kind of adventure that she would have loved in her youth.

As she stood there, watching the silhouettes of young people carefully picking their way across the broad, flat top of the monument, her husband came to watch with her. He wrapped one arm around her waist and held her close to him.

"Do you remember the time we found that cave?" she asked, not taking her eyes from the awe-inspiring sight. "And you almost got stuck when we tried to explore it?"

"You would have left me there," he said with a chuckle. "Don't try to deny it."

"I was just going for help!" she insisted. This had been an on-going disagreement their entire marriage, though it had long ago settled into comfortable teasing. "You weren't moving, so I thought I should."

"I wasn't moving because my shoulders were too wide for that passage."

"Excuses excuses," she said with a smile.

They stood in comfortable silence for a few moments before Frank continued.

"Thank you for resting more," he said quietly. "I know how hard it is for you, but it means a lot to me that you are taking care of yourself."

"Just because I'm not about to go climb up on the

top of that rock doesn't mean that I'm resting all the time," she teased. "I can't even tell you how nice it is to be out of that wagon, have some fresh air for the rest of the day. I can't keep doing that day after day."

He cleared his throat. "And I can't keep doing this, Hope. I need to go. I'm getting too angry to have this conversation yet again."

With that bald statement, her husband walked away from her, back toward the camp, toward the wagons.

Frank had always been so indulgent of Hope's whims, and even of her stubbornness. Even throughout this entire journey he had been understanding, if begrudgingly. She had never before seen him outright refuse her.

For the first time, Hope wondered if perhaps she was going too far, that she was making this all too hard.

But, then, she did not know how to find her way back. It seemed as though she was in the middle of a dark tunnel and just had to keep going until she reached the other side. There were no detours or shortcuts. She had gotten this far without telling her children the complete truth, and each day that passed made the revelation that much more intimidating.

It was early enough in the afternoon that her own children had not yet darted off to their adventures. Angus and Sadie were collecting water, while two of the other boys were wrestling by the wagon. She called out to Davis, telling him she was going to rest in her cot, but she wasn't sure he heard her at all.

And, to be honest, she wasn't sure it mattered either way. Though Frank still thought it was not enough, Hope felt as though she had been spending so much time in bed lately that if her family did wonder where she was, the first place they would look should be the sleeping wagon.

After all her excitement over this big adventure coming west, her whole world had shrunk to the four feet by fifteen feet of the interior of the family's wagon.

Hope removed her shoes, unpinned her braids, and settled into her bed. Though she had originally thought she might try to get more finished with this seemingly interminable sweater, her brain felt a little foggy, and she thought a nap would likely be a better way for her to conserve her energy. She could always get up again if she didn't fall asleep.

Closing her eyes, Hope sank into the warm respite of the July afternoon. Her family had scattered; the wagon company was settling in for the day. She overheard more conversation outside the canopy. It sounded as though a friend had come to visit; Sadie and this other woman sat near the campfire and chatted for a while. The affectionate murmurs reminded Hope that it had been days since she had been able to visit with Maggie Kirk. What must that woman think of her?

She would try to be a better friend.

But that would have to wait until later, when she was less tired.

Hope dozed off in the warm afternoon. The last thing she thought of before she was unconscious was to wonder if this was what the rest of her life would be like —listening to other people's conversations because she was too sick to participate in any.

She emerged for supper, but was asleep again even before Pastor Montgomery's church service began that evening.

# CHAPTER TWENTY-NINE

When the wagon company left Independence Rock the next morning, Hope felt no more rested than if she had spent all of the previous day on her feet. She had, instead, spent it napping on and off in the wagon, but her body seemed to require even more rest. Always more rest. It took some willpower to put on a brave, cheerful face for her family when she rose for breakfast. If she were to admit how much she was struggling, it would only be a small step from that to them learning she had been keeping this enormous secret from them.

As she walked slowly with the animals, following along as the caravan left the lush campground at the foot of Independence Rock, Hope looked around and noticed expressions of expectation on so many of the faces around her. While she had been trying to rest and recover, other members of the caravan were successful in doing so. The adventure and relief of reaching Independence Rock seemed to have energized many. The oldest

McKinnon girl, one of Faith's friends who had come by this morning to walk with her, even seemed to have a bounce in her step.

Hope, on the other hand, felt nothing but discouragement.

Feeling trapped between the fact of her illness and the possibility of hurting her children resulted in a kind of despondency she had not experienced in more than twenty years. That occasion had been during a family tragedy in which she felt utterly helpless, as though she had done everything she could do and it was still not enough. It had been so long ago, she almost forgot what it felt like, but even a small reminder brought all that heartache rushing back.

It had been about a year after Colin was born. Hope and Frank's next baby had been so wanted, so anticipated, but it was not to be. Frank Junior had been born two months too early. He lived only long enough to be named and held by his parents, born and died the same day. After the child's death, Hope felt broken. She spent several months in bed, rising only to feed her other children, and even then she missed more meals than she made. Her husband did his best to support her grieving, never saying a harsh word or expecting more from her than she could give.

She had been in such a dark place, and saw no way out.

With time, though, she began to feel more herself, more capable of taking care of her family. Occasionally, she was spurred on by the sheer necessity of her small children's very survival, but that was enough. The loss still burned a hole in her heart, but the edges of that hole felt less raw. She still had three little boys who needed her. The first time Hope washed her hair after the baby's death, it had given her a feeling of such release that she promised herself to not let so much time go by without doing that again.

But even now, as she compared that personal hardship to what she now faced in her struggle westward, she could not fool herself about the differences between the two circumstances. There was not some easy small step she could take that would pull her out of the despondence. Then had been pure heartbreak, knowing that there was nothing she could have done differently. Now, however, even if she did not have Frank's accusing expression to remind her, every time Hope tired herself out from walking she knew she could have chosen differently.

She should be choosing differently.

And even as she knew this, even telling herself this, and hearing her husband's voice in her head telling her the same, Hope was not sure she could actually make the change. The fear of breaking her children's hearts was too strong, and supported by Hope's fear that they would insist on going back.

She did not know how to get out of this hole, between this rock and hard place as she had found herself.

To distract herself from these thoughts, Hope needed to get away from her family, away from the reminder of her own duplicitousness. When she looked back to the Kirk family's wagon, trailing behind her own, she didn't see her friend Maggie. But, then, it had been so long since she had talked to Maggie that for all she knew the other woman could be injured or sick as well.

Hope felt as though she was failing everyone in her life—including herself.

The flat sameness of the Great Plains was behind them, and though the trail itself was still difficult, the change in scenery was a welcome distraction. The landscape shifted to low, rolling hills, with a slow climb in elevation toward the mountain ranges in the west. Low scrub bushes, perfect for the desert climate, blanketed the ground in all directions. The shift was slow and subtle, but Hope found herself a bit cold in the mornings again, layering on a second shawl if she was going to be outside of the wagon.

A few days after the trail began to climb into the foothills, the sound of a celebration was heard from the wagons ahead of them.

Frank was barely speaking to her, particularly when he saw that she was walking with the trail instead of resting. Hope had been walking with Beau, who drove the family's supply wagon. This allowed her to stay close enough to their sleeping wagon that she could at least go rest when she felt as though she needed it.

But when she heard the enthusiastic yells, she was glad she was outside and not missing whatever the excitement was.

She looked to Beau, who shrugged without saying anything.

From behind them on the trail, a trio of boys Hope recognized as Kirks ran past.

"Where are you going?" Hope called after them. "What's happening?"

"It's the Continental Divide," Joseph Kirk yelled back to her.

They didn't stop to talk, though, and Hope had to turn to her son to interpret.

"The Continental Divide is where the split is between water flowing downhill toward the east and water flowing toward the west," he explained. "Sounds like we're crossing over it, so all the water we come across from here will be heading west to the Pacific Ocean. Should be about halfway there, now. That's why they're all celebrating."

"Halfway?" Hope tried to smile, tried to be cheery at the news of the milestone, but the idea that they still had so far to go all but defeated her. "And we're... three months into the journey. At this rate, will we even make it over the mountains before the snow?"

"We will, Mama," Beau said calmly. "We'll make it."

She nodded and again tried to smile at her son. "I know. We will. We will. You know, I think I'll rest in my cot until we make camp tonight."

She disappeared back into the wagon, and left the young folk to their celebrations.

There were still three months of traveling to get through, and she did not have an ounce of energy to spare.

Their next source of water would not be until they reached Pacific Springs, still a couple days ahead. The promise of fresh water and sweet grass for the animals kept each man, woman and child putting one foot in front of the other, day after day, trying to only look ahead instead of looking back.

Hope crawled into her cot, pulling her quilt over her. When she closed her eyes, all she could think about was the relentless trail ahead.

# CHAPTER THIRTY

One morning soon after, Hope woke up shivering. The trail was climbing higher, and even though it was still July, the mornings were chilly. She pulled on an extra pair of stockings, wrapped a scarf around her neck, and layered on three shawls. When she emerged from the wagon, a concerned Sadie immediately handed her a cup of coffee. The steam curled up into Hope's face in the frosty morning.

"You feeling all right, Mama?"

"A mite cold, but otherwise the same as ever. Do I not look all right?"

"Same as ever," Sadie responded with a smile. "A little pale. But there are some other folks in the company who have come down with some kind of sickness, and since you've been feeling poorly we just were worried about you. But you're on your feet, and that's more than any of the sick ones. Is there anything you need?"

"Well, you could always make me coffee, and do all the cooking and cleaning so I don't have to. Oh, wait, you're already doing all that." She patted her daughter-in-law gently on the cheek. "You're doing more than enough. The only other thing I might need right now is to steal my husband's heavy coat, but I think it's deep in the supply wagon, so I might just have to do without for a little bit."

"I'll ask Nancy. We'll find it for you before it gets too much colder."

"Thank you, dear. I keep hoping I'll finish knitting that sweater any day, and that could keep me warmer, but haven't found the energy. Tell me about these other sick folks. Does the doctor know what's wrong?" She sat close to the campfire, letting the warmth thaw her fingers and toes.

"Well, mind you this is all secondhand. Buck Robinson came by this morning, asking if any of the boys could be spared. The doctor calls it Mountain Fever—it's apparently common at higher elevations like this. I think John Harper, Ruth Goldman, and I don't know how many other folks are laid low. Fever, headaches, body aching. Sounds just miserable. I hope none of us come down with it."

"When Mr. Robinson asked about the boys being available, that was...?"

"Because so many people have fallen ill, there's almost not enough labor to go around. Otis Van Anda has taken ill and there's no one to drive their wagon. John Harper's delicate, New York socialite sister is driving their wagon now, for example, though I think she finally found something else to wear than one of her tattered silk dresses."

"Are any of the boys helping?"

"Angus and Colin are talking it over this morning. I think Colin still wanted Davis and Ernest to go hunting, but we'll see what they all decide. If other folks need them more, I'm sure they'll do the right thing. I'm just glad that you aren't feeling any worse."

"Thank you, dear."

Her gratitude was short-lived, however. It was only later that afternoon that the wagon company learned that one of their captains, William Sullivan, had also taken to bed with Mountain Fever. But despite all of this, Captain Mills continued to push the company to cover as many miles as they could every day. If Mountain Fever was a result of the high elevation, staying in these hills as short a time as possible was essential, even as a dozen men, women and children lay sweating out fevers in their wagons.

During these long summer days, the wagon company had far more daylight hours available to travel west. It made for exhaustion at the end of the day, but with the sun setting so late, the emigrants were grateful they did not need to make camp after dark, at least. Instead, each person was so famished by the time they finally did make camp that suppers were often rushed, consuming whatever odds and ends were easy to get at. It was only Nancy's forethought that gave the Waters family substantial meals on these nights.

That particular evening, a mere two hours after the news of their captain taking ill, the company finally rolled into camp, where more bad news spread through the families. Little Ruth Goldman had died, passing after losing consciousness as she had ridden in her family's wagon. She had been only four years old, and too weak to handle the immense physical demand of both emigrating across the continent, and doing so while ill.

Hope did not know how the poor child's mother could go on after that. She didn't know how any of them could go on. Grief seemed to saturate every word, every action, on the Oregon Trail.

But go on they must. It was either move forward or move backward, and Hope had no intention of doing the latter.

Day after day they pushed westward, and Hope barely saw her family, so focused were they on helping the families of the sick. She worried over their continued good health until she realized that the irony.

Only a couple days later, though they had been instructed to be ready to leave camp at dawn, the appointed time came and went. Hope leaned against the back of one of their wagons, staying off her feet as much as she could until the very last minute. But as they were now so late into the summer, the delayed start worried her.

"We should go," she said, to no one in particular. "I hope nothing too terrible has happened. Why haven't we left?"

Lewis Jameson appeared at the edge of their camp, his hat in hand. "Mr. Waters, sir?"

"What is it, son?" Frank crossed to the young man. "Would you like to sit?"

"No, I'm sorry but I'm here with bad news. Um... There's no easy way to say this, sir. Captain Sullivan has died in the night."

Nancy gasped, and covered her mouth. "No..."

"Yes, ma'am." He nodded at Nancy. "That's why we

haven't left yet. Pastor is going to hold the funeral in about an hour, I think. We'll be getting a late start, of course. And again I'm sorry I have to tell you folks all this. If you'll excuse me."

The young man nodded his good-bye and headed to the next camp over to break the difficult news to the Pierces.

"That poor family," Hope whispered. "First the little boy and now the father. And with no time to grieve, either." She reached for her husband's hand, seeking his comfort. Frank reached for her in return, his expression anguished.

"And they lost him so quickly, with no warning," he said gently.

"Stop," she whispered. "I know, all right. I know. I'm trying to figure it out."

"We should pay our respects," he said after a moment. "Grab what shawls you need and we'll walk over."

A short while later, Hope stood near the front of the crowd gathered around Captain William Sullivan's grave. After so much death, so much loss, she almost felt numb. They could not possibly take any more, and yet they still had months ahead of them. Anything could happen. Any number of illnesses or accidents or deprivation.

No one in the gathered crowd had dry eyes as the pastor began his eulogy.

"William Sullivan wasn't just a friend, a husband, and a parent. He was a leader of this company," Pastor Montgomery said. "He looked after each and every one of us.

He wanted every member of this party to get to Oregon. We can't let him down."

Hope darted her gaze to the widow—Mrs. Sullivan kept her eyes down, fixed on the wrapped form of her husband in the shallow grave. The rest of the pastor's words were lost as Hope watched the pained expression dance across Mrs. Sullivan's face.

All she could think of was her own Frank's heartbreak if this illness were to take her. That pain was what Hope wanted to spare her family from, but as each day passed that possibility seemed to get smaller and smaller.

She was stuck.

# CHAPTER THIRTY-ONE

The company continued heading west, the mood somber after such a loss. The death of one of their wagon captains would have hit the members of the wagon company hard, regardless of any other circumstances. But Hope, for one, could not stop thinking about that poor man's wife. She had already lost her youngest son just a few weeks earlier, but now had to put that grief aside to both mourn her husband and attempt to fill his shoes in leading her family.

The next day, the remaining captain led the caravan to make camp a little bit earlier in the afternoon than usual. He then called a meeting for all the heads of household. Without the benefit of Mr. Sullivan's wisdom and decisiveness, Captain Mills would solicit the opinions of the men.

"Pop, I know you're the one who gets the vote," said Colin as he ate his supper standing by the wagon's rear wheel, "but I'm going with you."

"Do we know what the vote is going to be on?" Hope asked.

Her husband nodded at his middle son, before turning to her. "We have a couple options for the next stretch of trail. And Nancy can correct me if I'm misremembering, since she certainly knows the guidebook better than I do. But we can go straight across the desert. There's a cutoff that will shave miles off of the journey, but going that way would be risking another few days without water or grass, and without stopping by Fort Bridger."

"Goodness, that sounds awful. What is the alternative that this is even a question?"

"The alternative," Colin spoke up, "is taking a full week longer to go around. We would go south a bit, west and then back north. There would be grass and water the whole way, and the fort, as Pop mentioned."

"But it's seven extra days," Nancy said, shaking her head. "After everything we lost to the Indians, I don't know that some of these families can spare the time, let alone the risk of winter upon us."

"But the extra time will take us by Fort Bridger," Frank insisted. "And they can purchase more supplies there."

"Hopefully," Colin said darkly. "But maybe not. There's no telling what the fort will have in stock or if the families that need it will have the funds."

Hope listened to this debate with interest, wondering how it would pan out when the men gathered together to discuss it. "So you think you will vote for the longer route?" she asked Frank.

He glanced at Colin, and then around the campfire

at the rest of the family. "I haven't decided. And we can talk about it, of course, but I tend to think that is the safer option. We can make up the time in other ways, but if we risk going without food for the animals we will not be able to replace them should the worst happen."

The men left just after supper. Angus joined his father and brother, but he did not seem to have as strong of an opinion as the other two. As Hope watched them walk away toward the captain's camp, she turned to Nancy.

"Are so many families really in that much danger? I had not realized."

"Some are worse than others. The Kirks, you know, have had to send the boys out foraging nearly every day to supplement the little they have. I've tried to help as I can, but we don't really have anything to spare either."

Hope was struck with guilt—she had not known how badly the Kirks were faring. She had not had the energy to seek out Maggie in the last week or so; the last time she did Hope realized she had not asked her friend a difficult question at all. She had been too concerned with distracting herself from her own troubles that Hope hadn't thought to ask her friend about her own. With a flush of shame, Hope searched desperately for something—anything—she could do.

"Is there anything... I know you just said we don't have the food to spare, but I'm wondering if there's any other way we can help the Kirks, or anyone else."

Nancy shook her head. "Maybe if one of the boys bag a big enough game, we can share in that, but... an extra week on the trail could be a matter of life and death for some of these families if something doesn't change. But this time of year, after coming down the trail after hundreds of other emigrants..." She trailed off, as if unwilling to speak such pessimism out loud.

Hope sighed, and looked across the packed dirt to the Kirks' campsite next to their own. Paul Kirk had gone off to the meeting with the rest of the men, but Maggie stayed sitting by her campfire. From this distance, Hope could not be sure, but it seemed as though all her dishes were still out from supper, and that Maggie was simply sitting and watching the flames in contemplation. "I wish there was something we could do. I wish there was something I could do."

"Maybe if you were feeling a little stronger, you could help with the animals or drive a wagon to free up a man to go hunting," Nancy suggested. "Plenty of women have had to step into that role, unfortunately. But with as cold and weak as you seem to be lately, I would worry about you being able to go more than an hour or two without collapsing."

Hope looked carefully at her daughter-in-law, wondering if she imagined the coldness in the other woman's tone. "You're right, though. I'll think about other ways that I can help our neighbors. Especially if I start feeling better."

Nancy nodded, and turned back to kneading the loaf of bread she was making. Hope felt dismissed, though she supposed that was her own fault. Nancy was not wrong to suggest that Hope was not pulling her weight on the journey thus far.

Not quite an hour after they had left, the three men were back, serious expressions all.

"We voted to take the longer route," Frank said without preamble.

Hope, Nancy, and several of the rest of the family had been waiting anxiously to hear what the verdict would be. In Hope's mind, either option seemed fraught with risk. As she was in no state to do anything about any of it, she would just have to go along as cheerfully as possible.

Her husband came to sit next to her at the campfire as they continued.

"I don't like it," Colin murmured. "It seems utterly irresponsible to take even more days to get to Oregon, when so many among us are already stretched thin."

"Well, I'm sorry you don't have your own wagon, then, to go off and make your own way, if you know so much better," his father snapped at him. "Take the cutoff by yourself and I suppose we'll just meet you in Oregon."

"Pop, that's not what I'm saying—"

"I'm sorry we didn't buy extra supplies to feed everyone in the company. I'm sorry you're stuck with us."

"Frank," Hope began.

"Colin," Nancy interjected.

"The only way—and I mean the *only* way—we are all going to make it to Oregon as healthy as possible is if we stay together, help our neighbors, and take care of the animals that are the whole reason we are able to go on this journey at all. When your mother came to me with the idea to move all of us to the other side of the continent, my first thought was that I would not want to go without you all."

"Well, yes," Colin said, "but I still think that adding that much time to the journey is a far bigger risk than the chance that any of the oxen won't make it a few days without grass."

"And your opinion was heard, Colin. But the men voted. It wasn't just me. Blame me if it makes you feel better, but a majority of the men in this party think the same way I do."

Hope could read the pity and compassion in Frank's expression, but she wasn't sure her son saw the same.

"Colin," she began gently. Her son did not look at her when she said his name, but she continued on. "I love your heart, and your sense of responsibility. It speaks well to who you are as a man."

"Thanks, Mama," he muttered, still not looking at her.

"As your father says, though, we have to all stay together and do our part to help when we can. And perhaps that means that you range out even farther to hunt so you can be sure to come back with something substantial. Or perhaps that means we all ration a bit more. Nancy can take an inventory of what we have left and how long it will last us."

"Right, so, my wife and I will be the ones to carry this whole family, is that it? I will go out miles into the wilderness alone to hunt for food, while Nancy does all the cooking and cleaning for ten people, rationing as needed, doing whatever calculations to keep us all healthy." Colin looked at his mother finally, his eyes flashing. "After all your insistence and your enthusiasm, I would have thought you would be more involved in our welfare than spending hours in bed every day."

"Do not speak to your mother that way," Frank said.

Hope held her son's gaze, taking his criticism and resentment for the truth it was. "No, I need to hear this. I don't want any secrets between us."

She felt her husband's intense gaze on her at that, but didn't take her eyes off of Colin.

"You're right; I haven't been much help at all for a while. And I... I'll change that. I'm sorry if I've let you down. Let both of you down," she added, acknowledging Nancy. "I don't want to get in the way, so if you two could just tell me how best to contribute, I can do that now."

She stood.

"Hope," her husband said softly.

"I'm going to go collect some water," Hope said. She felt a tiny bit light-headed when she stood, but it was not so much that it affected her balance. "We can always use water. And you're right that I should be doing more to get us to Oregon since it was my idea in the first place."

She walked away from them, feeling their eyes on her back as she picked up the two buckets and walked into the dark.

# CHAPTER THIRTY-TWO

In a delightful surprise, considering the circumstances, bringing two full buckets of water back to her camp had not depleted Hope as much as she had anticipated. The bigger hurt, the more pressing concern, was the anger and frustration from members of her family. Though Sadie and Faith had not spoken up, they too had plenty of reason to complain about Hope's inaction. When she returned to camp, and set the water near the fire, Faith had taken over, assuring her mother that what she had done was helpful, but why didn't she rest now.

Hope did not have the energy to argue, especially when she noticed that Colin and Nancy seemed to be deliberately avoiding her. Though it was still early, she climbed into the wagon and into her cot, alone and a little cold. As she pulled the quilt up to her chin, Hope stared at the wooden bow that curved overhead, the delicate structure that was used to hold up the entire canopy.

So often the things that did the most work, the

people that provided the most support, went long unnoticed, like that same bow. Hope had never intended to take Nancy, or any of the other children, for granted, but she had to face the fact that she likely had.

Hope had a decision to make. Though she had tried her best to avoid being cornered like this, she now realized that she had run out of options. She could choose to finally be honest with her family about the seriousness of her illness, and make it clear that this was far different than her just being tired. Everyone was tired. That could no longer be her excuse.

But the alternative would be for her to push through her exhaustion, perhaps to the point of actively worsening her illness, in an attempt to help more and carry her own weight. And if she did that, there was only a partial chance that she would be able to successfully hide her illness the rest of the journey. There were still months ahead of them.

The murmuring around the campfire gave way to laughter. Hope could pick out the low chuckle of Beau, the animated storytelling of Angus, the shy giggles of Faith. It sounded as though the tense disagreement of the family's earlier conversation had dissipated. Not for the first time was Hope grateful for how close her family seemed to be.

She couldn't break that up. She couldn't heap more worry on them, on top of the deprivation and exhaustion they were already feeling.

Tomorrow she would get up early and make breakfast—or help make breakfast. Navigating Nancy's natural tendency to manage might make for some growing pains, but Hope would not hurt that woman for the world.

She drifted off to sleep listening to her children getting along.

Adjusting the schedule to account for the extra week they would be traveling meant that the Sullivan-Mills wagon company now needed to leave camp at first light every day. Rising before the sun the next morning, Hope had a new resolve. She would not be dead weight on this family. She would take care of her own children and not leave that for her daughter-in-law, and with whatever extra energy she could scrounge up, she would see about what she could offer Mrs. Kirk, or any of the other families who did not have the wealth of labor that the Waters had.

She quickly made herself presentable in the pre-dawn dark, and found Nancy in the family's supply wagon, gathering up what she needed to make a quick breakfast.

"I can help, dear. Here, I can take some of that from you?" Hope offered her empty arms. Nancy seemed surprised, but she didn't comment on it, instead handing her mother-in-law the coffee and stack of tin mugs. "Do we need water?"

"Faith should have brought some back, I think," Nancy said, continuing to paw through the wagon. "But if you could get the coffee started, that would be a help. I don't know how we're going to get any food in those boys at all with as soon as we need to leave."

Hope got right to work grinding the beans they needed for that morning. All around her, the boys were packing away their blankets and tents, and hitching up the animals to be ready to leave. Nancy had not been overstating it when she lamented how little time they would have in the morning. She appeared moments later, hurrying to fry up enough bacon so the two men who would be driving oxen all day would have something warm in their bellies to get them through.

As soon as the coffee was finished, Hope doled out the cups, taking them to where her boys were with the oxen or the horses. It took her several trips to make sure each of the six men had what they needed, and then she made the rounds again to collect their empty cups. There was no time to wash them, and she was still making her way to the supply wagon to pack them when the caravan began to move.

When she heard the captain call out the command to move, Hope looked around and saw how much there was still to clean up and put away. Faith, Sadie and Nancy all had hands full, working as quickly and efficiently as they could. Seeing such need, Hope could not believe that she had let herself be so lazy. She had not had a true coughing attack in weeks, and yet she had let herself lay about, resting in the wagon, while the people she loved most worked themselves to the bone.

No more, she told herself. No matter how Frank might protest.

As the other women carried the dishes and supplies back to the wagon, Hope kicked dirt over the last of the campfire. She could do that. She could help. With hands still full of tin cups, she followed Nancy and Sadie to the wagon. Everything got put away in the small moments before Ernest called the team of oxen to move.

That day, after the vote, the trail turned south,

around the desert stretch and away from the cutoff. There were still members of the company laid low from Mountain Fever, but for the most part they seemed to be recovering. John Harper was back on his feet, so his sister no longer had to drive the wagon. Otis Van Anda had recovered sufficiently that Ernest was no longer needed for their wagon. As each day progressed, they had received news of improved health of the members of the company, as well as seeing their oxen be able to eat their fill of the fresh, sweet grass that stretched on either side of the trail.

After the death of William Sullivan, this seemed like an unexpected change of fortune. After two days even Colin seemed to acknowledge that taking the longer route might not be as dire as he had predicted.

But then there was another death.

Louisa Hudson, the loud, capable spinster who was traveling with her unmarried sisters, had not been able to regain her strength after taking ill with Mountain Fever. She had poured all of herself into getting her family out of Virginia, heading toward Oregon where the youngest sister had a groom waiting. After all she had done and given and sacrificed, Louisa had not been able to withstand the illness.

Hope avoided the funeral.

She could not force herself to suffer through another one, as guilty and un-neighborly as that made her feel.

Louisa Hudson's story reminded her far too much of her own, and Hope was simply not ready to face the possibility that her own body might give out on her before she reached Oregon. She refused to consider it.

When the wagon company was ready again to keep

traveling, Hope cheerfully looked ahead, walking through the grass with Faith and only allowing herself to think about the blessings and opportunities ahead of them. On this stretch of trail, there was water and grass enough for the animals—if nothing else, hopefully those blessed creatures would be able to regain some of their muscle and strength after so long hauling wagons.

And they had Fort Bridger to look forward to.

A week into the detour, the company reached Fort Bridger. The fort was surrounded on all four sides by a tall, sturdy wall, protecting the interior against attack. Though it didn't have the watchtowers or bevy of soldiers that Fort Laramie had boasted, just the sight of a stable, finished structure was enough to boost the emigrants' spirits. It seemed to be hunkered down, close to the ground, holding steady against the chaos of the wilderness.

Near the wide front gate, a narrow stream offered water and a clear place for the wagon company to camp for the night. They arrived in the middle of the sunny, August afternoon, and would stay there until the following morning.

Davis and Angus had been driving the wagons that day, and they made camp quickly. The emigrants were all excited to have a slow afternoon.

"Who's going to the fort for supplies?" Hope asked, as her boys maneuvered the wagons and unhitched the animals. "I'm happy to go and help carry things back."

"Ernest and me will go as soon as this is all settled," Colin said. "Nancy is making me a list. Don't feel like you need to come, Mama, but if you're up for it you're welcome."

"Of course I'd like to come," she said cheerily.

Maybe it was the sight of something like civilization, or maybe it was simply her confidence knowing that she was trying, but Hope felt more energetic than she had in weeks. She truly had no concerns about whatever effort she was signing herself up for.

# CHAPTER THIRTY-THREE

With her sons Colin and Ernest, Hope made her way between other campsites to the wide, fortified front gate of Fort Bridger. There were at least a dozen other men and women, members of the company, streaming in ahead of them. Each person seemed eager to add to their supplies as much as they could, as soon as they could; there was a comfort in having enough, especially after the journey they had been on. After the raid by the Indians left many families depleted, and then all the necessary delays for funerals and repairs, many of the families were down to rationing their food already.

Even a few pounds of flour or beans would help them get through the next month or more before they reached Oregon.

Hope walked a few steps behind her sons, intending to let them do the negotiating and choosing. It wasn't easy for her to be passive in situations like this, but Nancy had made her husband a list, and Hope was merely there to be whatever support she could be.

But the trio had not even made it to the door of the fort's store before they were stopped. Mrs. McKinnon passed them, out the front door, stalking back to the campsite with an expression of terror and despair. She did not seem to see them, even as she walked within feet of the Waterses.

And her arms were empty.

Hope watched her go with concern, and when she turned back to her boys, they were questioning Mrs. Mills, who had also just exited the store.

"The shelves are bare," the woman said bitterly. "And I gave that shopkeeper a piece of my mind, never you fear. But that won't fill anyone's bellies."

"How can the shelves be bare?" Colin asked.

"There was a shipment that overturned in the Kansas River before it could get very far," Mrs. Mills said angrily. "I just don't know what we're going to do now. But, excuse me, gentlemen. I need to go inform my husband so we can make whatever plans and adjustments are necessary."

As she walked away, Colin and Ernest exchanged expressions of bewilderment.

"Well..." Colin said helplessly. "I guess we should go back too? If there's nothing there for us."

"Are you... angry?" Hope asked. "I know you advised against taking this route."

Colin shook his head. "To be honest, I'm too stunned to be angry. There are families that are on the verge of starvation, and I don't know what they are going to do. I don't think I ever believed that things could get this bad."

As they stood in the fort's inner yard talking, more of

the men and women from their wagon party passed them, some going into the store with hope, others leaving empty-handed. Hope felt as though she were in the middle of a school of fish, everyone around her having purpose and direction, while she merely floated with the current.

"We have to do something," she insisted, thinking of her friend Maggie, and the woman's five growing boys. "Is there anything, anything at all we can do? I wish I knew better what our own supplies are like…"

Ernest looked thoughtful. Hope reached for his hand, taking comfort in the strength and steadiness of her tall son. "Let's go back to camp, assess, talk to the others, maybe?" he said. "The stream we are near might have fish; it seems deep enough. Or, I could roam out a few miles see if there's any game. Since we have horses and other families don't, that might be the best bet."

Hope and Colin both nodded, turning back to leave the fort. More and more men and women passed them, heading to the store hopefully, but Hope did not have the heart to tell them what they were walking into. She kept her eyes cast down and did not engage as they returned to the Waterses' campsite.

Faith, Beau and Frank had all dispersed, off to entertain themselves however seemed fit on that summer afternoon, but the rest of the family were still nearby. While Colin explained to his wife and the few others still around the situation, Hope surreptitiously watched her friend Maggie at the campsite just next to them. They were too far away for her to hear what was being said, but she noticed Paul saying something in a low voice to his wife, and then caught the expression of panic on Maggie's face.

Hope's heart broke for her friend. She may not know exactly what Paul had said but she could make a fair guess. She looked away, not wanting to spy on Maggie in this moment of vulnerability. The situation was too dire already without Hope's unwanted attention making it more difficult.

But even without reaching out to the Kirks, the family had their chance to help a neighbor even as early as that evening. Beau returned to the camp for supper, with the young widow Mrs. Tenney in tow.

"I told her we might have... something to spare," he said delicately.

A flash of panic crossed Nancy's face, but it was gone in an instant and she offered Mrs. Tenney a welcoming smile. "I'm sure there's something. Have a seat. You can sit there with Mother Waters."

Hope patted the space in the grass next to her. "It's so nice to see you again, dear. And I'm so glad you took Beau up on his offer. I was so worried to learn the fort did not have any food. I didn't realize your family was one of those so affected."

"I can't thank you enough," Mrs. Tenney said in a low voice. She looked around at the numerous Waterses. "It must take mountain of food to feed this many of you, but Beau said— Your son, um, Mr. Waters told me there would be plenty and I didn't know what else to do. We haven't... That is, my family... " She trailed off, embarrassed.

"I'm not sure I'd say we've had plenty since we left back east," Hope said with a self-deprecating laugh, "but

Beau is certainly correct that we have enough. Please don't worry about it. And we have more than others. I don't think any one of us would hoard anything in the face of letting a neighbor go hungry. We take care of each other, Mrs. Tenney."

Even saying that, Hope felt a flush of shame, knowing what she was keeping from her children. Knowing she was keeping them from taking care of her the way they might want to. But with this immediate opportunity to help someone else, to share in their meager supplies, Hope could let herself forget that. For now.

# CHAPTER THIRTY-FOUR

Leaving Fort Bridger took the company almost due north, into the Bear River Valley. Nancy and Colin had assured the rest of the Waters family that this stretch of trail promised to be green, lush and verdant. There should be plenty of water, plenty of grass, and likely even plenty of game that the company could feast on. Hope was almost afraid to believe it. Such bounty seemed utterly foreign to their journey on the Oregon Trail thus far.

But as the trail crested the hill before plunging into the valley, Hope was thrilled to see that the guidebooks had been completely right. Even from this distance, it was clear that the Bear River Valley was an oasis compared to what they had been through. Because Hope knew she would struggle to walk up the hill into the valley, she had spent the day thus far riding on the wagon seat, up at the front instead of within. Her husband was driving the team of oxen for her wagon, and when she gasped in delight at the sight of the green valley, he looked over his shoulder at her.

"Not bad looking, is it?"

"It's beautiful," she said. "Surely we should be able to find enough food in this promised land for everyone."

Hope was not the only member of the company who had that thought. After weeks of pushing the caravan to cover as many miles as possible, as soon as the Sullivan-Mills wagon company began crossing the Bear River Valley, their speed slowed considerably. Captain Mills seemed to recognize how badly his people needed this respite, and so they took several days to travel across, stopping early in the evening and getting a late start in the mornings.

On their second day crossing through the valley, Hope didn't want to rest any more. In fact, what she wanted most was to run and play and feel her hands in the earth as she had before she got sick. But for now, she thought, walking through the grass would be good enough.

They had stopped for a mid-day break, giving everyone a chance to eat their fill of the game they were hunting or the fruit they were foraging. As Davis brought the team of oxen to a halt, Hope called down to her other son who had been walking parallel to the trail.

"Angus, help me down, please. I'm so tired of riding in the wagon all day. I need to stretch my legs."

"And what better place than this beautiful valley," Angus said encouragingly. He offered her his hand, a steady support as she climbed down.

"It really is beautiful." Hope looked around with wide eyes. "I tell you, there have been times on this journey when if you had told me we would be in a place like this I simply would not have believed you. Imagine if the entire trail was through landscape like this."

"If that were the case, I'm sure the Oregon Territory would be all full up with people already," Angus said with a laugh. "You know, if you feel like walking today, I could use a hand."

"With what?"

"Sadie was going to come hunting with me, and help me carry things back, but then she and Faith took Mrs. Tenney out foraging instead. If you feel like stretching your legs I'd love if you took her place. Just you and me. I'll take a rifle and you can help carry whatever I bag."

"Yes, let's do that. Put me to work."

"I don't know that I said that," he said, "but let's go."

Grateful for time with her oldest son, Hope deliberately kept quiet all of her thoughts of being tired or concerns that they were getting too far from the trail. She and Angus tramped through the grass and forest nearby, going deep to find any untouched part of the valley where he could have the best luck. As they walked, Angus told his mother all about what he and Sadie were planning for their home in Oregon.

"Near you and Pop, of course, but with as much wide-open space as there is sure to be in the territory it might not be all that close."

"That sounds perfect, dear," she said, struggling to catch her breath.

He peered at her. "You look a bit peaked. Maybe this walk was too much."

"No, I—"

He stopped her by holding up a hand. "Doesn't

matter, Mama. I don't want you to follow me anyway. Stay here, take a seat on that log over there, and I'm gonna go up ahead a few yards where this game trail leads. I'll call you if I need you."

She smiled and nodded, accepting his instructions without complaint. Having her stay farther away from where an animal might hear or smell her was smart whether she was feeling weak or not.

He strode on ahead, disappearing into the brush.

She coughed a couple times, and tried clearing her throat to end the slight tickle. But it didn't help. Coughing a little harder as she walked forced Hope to pause and lean against the closest tree trunk.

"Mama, you all right?" Angus called from up ahead on the trail.

She tried to say 'fine,' but couldn't get the words out. Pulling a handkerchief out of the sleeve of her dress, Hope tried to contain her coughing as best she could. This was as bad as, if not worse than, the coughing fit she suffered when their camp was under attack. She could not get her breath, and felt as though her legs were going to collapse underneath her.

She heard her son's footsteps returning to her through the undergrowth.

"Mama?"

"I'm fine," she croaked out, not looking at him. "Just a little out of breath, I think." She beamed at him, trying with all her might to counter the look of concern on his face. "Let's keep going."

"I don't know. Maybe I should take you back, so you can rest. You've been a lot more—"

"I'm fine," she said again, more forcefully. Though the next coughing fit belied her words.

"Mama!" Angus exclaimed, hurrying to her side. "Sit down, at least. Until this subsides. We don't have to go any farther until you're ready."

But even as he said that Hope was wondering if she would ever be ready. After her weeks of trying to rest, and making Nancy resent her, she would have hoped that such a sacrifice would have at least made some kind of difference. But here she was, barely twenty yards away from her own wagon, weak and coughing so much she was thwarting the entire hunting excursion.

She could not even get the words out to say any of this to him.

"Mama," he said again, this time a concerned whisper. "Let's get you back. You don't have to do this."

"But I want to," she managed. Still leaning against the tree trunk, she looked up at her son with a pained expression. "I want to be able to do this. I want to help."

"All right," he said calmly. "But not now. I'm going back to the wagons, and I suggest you come with me."

Hope wiped her mouth, the streak of blood a stark red against the white. She took a deep, shaking breath, grateful that it did not set off another fit of coughing.

"Mama," he said in a low voice, his gaze intent on what she held. "What is that?"

# CHAPTER THIRTY-FIVE

"Mama," Angus said again, his voice cracking. "What is that?"

Hope began to shake, so great was her terror at her secret being discovered. Her mind seemed to go blank, and she had no answer for her son. There was no excuse she could come up with that would make any sense at all.

"Oh, I…"

Would he believe that she tripped and fell? That she bit her lip? Tore a cuticle? She felt as though any lie would be better than the look on Angus's face at that moment, a mix of fear and accusation. Hope could not think of the right words to make everything better for him.

"Come on," he said, wrapping his arm around her waist and hoisting her to standing. "We're going back. You are not going to argue with me. I will carry you bodily if I have to."

Hope burst into tears. "I'm sorry."

"We'll talk about it when you're settled. Save your strength."

Hope knew her son. She had seen Angus through every stage of his life, every pain and every joy. She could tell just from his tone how hurt and angry he was, even if, true to Angus's character, he was being kind about it for the other person.

She struggled along with him, but managed to keep her feet under her. When they returned to the line of wagons, it was already continuing on for the rest of the afternoon and they had to catch up with the rest of the family.

"This is what is going to happen," Angus said, as they slowly made their way up the caravan. "You are going to spend the rest of the afternoon resting in the wagon, and when we make camp for the night, when the whole family is around, you are going to tell us the truth. *All* of the truth."

"Please don't, Angus. Please, let's just forget— I'm fine. I'll be fine. We can just—"

"This is not a conversation, Mama," he said, sadly. "The time for conversations seems to have passed, and for whatever reason you decided not to take advantage of that window of time when it might be easier to... I don't want to talk about this right now. I have to think. Here's our wagon."

He nodded, indicating the closest vehicle, the Waters family's supply wagon that Colin was driving. Angus helped his mother past that team of oxen to the family's sleeping wagon just ahead of it. The caravan was moving slowly, but not slowly enough for Hope to be able to climb into the wagon in her current state. Angus banged on the side of the wagon bed to get his brother's attention.

"Davis!" he called ahead. "Hold up a minute."

The wagon drew to a slow stop, and Angus all but lifted his mother up and over the back of the wagon. She stumbled against her cot, her legs weak and still having a difficult time catching her breath.

"I'll see you at supper," Angus said through the canvas.

He banged on the side of the wagon again, letting Davis know to continue, and left his mother alone.

All afternoon, Hope lay in her cot, inside the stuffy wagon. On one of the few days when they were traveling through a beautiful, flourishing landscape and she was stuck inside, in the near dark with all the dust and mold of months of travel. It was a fitting punishment for what she had done, keeping this important secret from her family.

She had not seen Frank since she and Angus returned to the wagon. She wondered if he knew, if he had said anything. She wondered how angry he was at her.

Her mind was in chaos for hours, all afternoon as she finally faced her own shame at the situation she had gotten herself into. The truth would have been so simple, but it was too late for that now. All the things she had been afraid of happening could still happen, and she had the betrayal on top of all of it to make up for.

When the wagons stopped for camp for the night, Hope hesitated in climbing out of the wagon. Minutes passed as she tried to summon the courage to face her children.

Finally, Hope heard Angus's voice calling to her through the canvas.

"Mama, do you need help getting down?"

"No, no, I'm coming."

He was waiting to help her down when she peeked her head out between the canvas. "How are you feeling?"

Hope felt like melting into a puddle of gratitude. He could have been cold or cruel, even, but here was her sweet son asking how she was feeling despite his own anger and frustration.

"I'm better," she answered meekly.

"Everyone's here," he said softly.

He dropped her hand, letting Hope make her own way, alone, to the campfire where her husband and all her children, along with their spouses waited to hear what she had to say. She turned the corner around the side of the wagon, and felt her knees go weak when she saw all those faces she loved so much looking at her expectantly.

"Angus said you had something you want to talk to us about," Colin began. He looked around at his siblings for confirmation.

Hope could not remember the last time her entire family had been together like this, all focused on the same thing. Too often when they stopped to camp for the night, each person was distracted by their own tasks or wanting a break from the crowd. Even if they were in the same place physically, their minds were elsewhere.

But now they had a single-minded purpose: to listen to what their mother wanted to tell them.

"I... um..." She looked around at them all, both wanting to cherish their faces and expressions before they were too mad at her, but also wanting to avoid their eyes as she told them the truth. "I don't know what Angus said—"

"I didn't say anything," he interjected. "Just that you seemed to have something you wanted to say to us."

She nodded briskly, steeling herself for the next words that needed to come out of her mouth.

"I..." She cleared her throat and looked down at her hands. Though she had not realized it, she was still clutching the handkerchief she had coughed into earlier that day. It carried the rinsed-out stains of previous coughing attacks, previous blood brought up from her lungs. And now the dark, copper-red stain from earlier this day.

She had tried so hard to keep this piece of evidence secret, even to washing it separately, on her own and away from prying eyes. And yet it held the signs of weeks—months—of illness. The blood stains, though small, overlapped, indicating multiple attacks, numerous chances she had to show her family the truth, and had not.

As Hope held the small piece of fabric, looking at it in wonder, Nancy spoke up.

"Mother Waters..." Nancy's gaze was trained on the white—and red—handkerchief that Hope held. "What is that? Are you hurt?"

But even in asking that question, Hope could hear the accusation in her daughter-in-law's tone. She seemed to know perfectly well that Hope was not hurt. She met Nancy's eyes silently. Nancy only looked at her, also without saying anything, but the expression on her face spoke volumes.

"I... well, Dr. Jansen, um... Or, I guess, Mrs. Martell said... Um."

"Mama," Colin said.

"Mama, what is that?" Faith asked, all innocence and confusion as she saw how her mother and sister-in-law were fixated on the thing in her hand.

"Hope..." Frank stood from where he had been leaning against the wagon and came to stand by her side. "Tell them. Stop being so evasive."

She cleared her throat.

"I think I have consumption," she finally stated, in a whisper. "That's what the doctor's wife says, but I've been coughing up blood and been weak and pale since we left New York, so I have no reason to doubt her. I'm sorry I didn't tell you before."

Hope kept her eyes cast down, merely listening to the reactions of her children all around her. Even without seeing their expressions, she could sense their dismay, hear their upset. Her heart was breaking at the thought that she had hurt her children so much, but Frank was right—she couldn't do this anymore. She couldn't hide it from them. She could no longer pretend she was just tired.

It was all over now.

She would get better or she wouldn't but at least her family knew the truth.

"What does that mean?" Faith asked, putting voice to what the rest of them were likely thinking.

"I don't know," Hope said. "I'm so sorry, my love. I just don't know what happens now."

Conversations—adamant, angry, and confused— broke out all around her. She could not follow what all of them were saying, let alone feeling. Even in the midst of those she loved best, Hope felt alone again.

And through all of this, Hope finally saw what she had been putting her children through. Frank had been correct; she had not been protecting them, she had been lying to them. By not being clear about what she was going through and what lay ahead, she was being deliberately unkind to these people who she loved most in all the world.

Keeping the secret had done nothing more than let her pretend to be comfortable for a few extra months. And it crashed down on her now.

# CHAPTER THIRTY-SIX

After the chaos that had been unleashed in the Waters family with the revelation of Hope's potentially fatal illness, she found herself trying to downplay the reality of the disease while at the same time defending her choice to keep it secret. She over-explained, deflected, apologized profusely and tried to regain control of the situation. All while her exhaustion weighed heavily on her as the family continued to struggle westward.

Each of her children handled the news more or less how she could have expected it of them, some with quiet anger, some with confusion and hurt, some with denial.

But the reaction that cut most to Hope's core was that of Colin and Nancy. Those two, more than any of the others, felt the most betrayed, felt the most as though they had sacrificed and worked for a reality that was not true.

In the moment, Nancy said nothing in reaction to

Hope's confession, but for the first time in the nearly twelve months since the family had all been traveling together, she walked away from supper. Sadie finally jumped up when she smelled the bacon burning, to take over what needed to be done. Nancy was nowhere to be found for the rest of the night.

----

When the Oregon Trail climbed out of the Bear River Valley, the emigrants and their animals were well-fed, well-watered and well-rested—as much as they could be in the few days that they were among such abundance. Many of the families had been able to hunt and fish, salting the meat for the future. The next stretch of the Oregon Trail wound out of the valley and through the high desert, where tall, shade-providing trees were a thing of the past.

The trail headed north, through the scrub brush and baked earth for two days before reaching Fort Hall. The elevation of this part of the country had stunted all the growth and vegetation the emigrants had experienced elsewhere, even though it was near to the rushing Snake River. Through these foothills, there was barely any grass for the oxen, and many families had to supplement their feed with oats from the wagons' stores.

The fort itself was two stories tall, built from roughly hewn logs and windowless. It was little more than a box, sitting in the middle of a virtually barren landscape. But for the emigrants who had come so far and needed so much, it was the respite they needed.

Fort Hall offered some supplies, though not many of

the emigrant families could afford to pay the prices required. This far into the journey, some of the wagons were close to empty. The thousands of pounds of food they had acquired back in Independence had been eaten, stolen, spoiled or were otherwise gone, though they still needed enough sustenance to make it another several weeks of travel.

When they made camp outside Fort Hall, Hope had been resting inside the sleeping wagon, on her cot. The short time in which she had tried to exert effort again, to ignore her illness, was over and in the previous two days, any time she had set foot outside the wagon to walk with the animals, she had suffered the anger and rejection by her children.

She stayed in the wagon when she heard them making camp, waiting for a moment when she could step outside without running into one of them right away. As it happened, once the campsite went relatively quiet, Hope stuck her head outside the canvas and was surprised to find Frank right in front of her.

"I was just coming to check on you," he said. "We're here for the night. Do you need help down?"

"Is anyone else around?" She offered Frank her hand and he helped her stay steady as she climbed out of the wagon.

"Beau went to the fort. Sadie and Angus are here. Nancy is baking biscuits, and Colin stayed with her but everyone else has gone off somewhere."

"None of them are speaking to me," Hope said despairingly. She peeked around the corner of the wagon to where Nancy was working over the campfire.

Frank looked at her with dismay. "Are you actually

surprised by that? Hope, you kept the truth from them for months."

"But I was just trying to—"

"Stop," he said gently. "Please stop justifying it. If their reaction now is not enough for you to recognize you made the wrong choice, I don't want to hear about it. I'm so..." He sighed. "I'm just disappointed, I suppose. I know all the reasons you told me—you told yourself—that keeping the secret was the right thing to do, and I am tired of hearing about it. You gambled that you would be able to manage and manipulate their perception of you, and it did not pay off. This is the consequence."

"But what if they stay mad at me?" she said, despairingly. "What if they never talk to me? How can I... ?" She trailed off, completely overwhelmed at the thought that she could be estranged from her family forever.

"I don't know."

"Are you telling them to stay angry? It's been days; at least one of them should have forgiven me by now."

He looked at her in shock and anger. "Do you think I would do that?

"Well, I just can't think why they would be so obstinate otherwise," she retorted stubbornly.

"I can't have this conversation with you," he said, taking a couple steps back. "I don't know how many other ways I can try to make you understand. I'm going to... I don't know where I'm going, but I can't do this right now."

He strode off toward the other side of the camp before Hope could say another word. Her mouth hung open in surprise. Frank had always been supportive of her, had always been patient and understanding. And yet now, when Hope was at her lowest, he would not even stay to comfort her.

A flash of frustration coursed through her; angry tears sprang into her eyes. She was sick. She was alone, more or less. How could he desert her like this?

Hope had been watching Frank's back, but turned away from him quickly. Too quickly. She was forced to put a hand out, bracing herself against the wagon to maintain her balance. Sadie and Angus sat about ten yards away, leaning close to each other and talking. They glanced up when Hope appeared around the side of the wagon, but neither moved to help her. She wanted to tell herself that she saw pity in their expressions, but when they turned away from her, the frustration bubbled up again.

There wasn't much more she could do to try to bring them around to her point of view. She had given them every argument, every reason she had why she had kept the secret from them. Now, Hope supposed, all she could do was wait for her children to forgive her.

If they were going to.

All around her, members of the Sullivan-Mills wagon company were settling in, making camp for the night.

With a final look back at her oldest son and his wife, both deliberately ignoring her, Hope stalked off to find one of her friends. Surely Maggie Kirk would be sympathetic to her plight. She had children of her own she wanted to protect above all else.

Hope made her way to the Kirks' campsite, which

was near enough that she would still have Angus and Sadie in view.

"Maggie, please tell me that glorious smell is coming from your pot," she said cheerfully, trying to ignore the hurt that still cut to her core.

The other woman looked up as Hope approached. "This?" She laughed, and sniffed the air exaggeratedly. "Must be the wild onions you smell. Your Faith brought me a handful when we were in the valley, and I've been saving them until we had something substantial to cook with them."

"What a wonderful idea; what did you get?"

The Kirks had been struggling more than most of the other families in the wagon company. The fact that they had five growing boys to feed was problem enough in keeping their food supply stocked, but the raid a few weeks earlier had greatly depleted the stores they had on hand as well. As far as Hope knew, all the Kirks that could were out hunting and fishing every day they could to supplement the supply.

"This is the last of the rabbit that Nathan caught. It's a little too salted—I couldn't risk having it spoil. But with the onion and the last handful of rice, I'm making a big pot of soup. Hopefully the water will help with the saltiness." She stirred the pot and raised her spoon to her lips to taste it. "Mmm. Still a bit strong, but we're getting there. You're welcome to stay for supper if you would like."

There was nothing Hope would like more than to stay here with her friend who clearly cared about her, eating some of this meal that smelled delicious. Any chance to avoid the accusing looks of her children was welcome. But doing so would break one of the unspoken rules of life on the Oregon Trail—she could not take any necessity from another person if she had enough of her own.

And she did. Of the many things that Nancy was doing for the whole family, keeping their food rationed and consistent was one of the most welcome. With Davis and Ernest roaming out to hunt periodically, the Waters family was one of the few in the company that always seemed to have enough to eat.

Not a lot, but enough.

"I would love to," Hope said, "but I told Frank I wouldn't be gone long."

"Another time then," she said airily, just as though she were inviting Hope to tea. "And how is Frank, and the rest of your brood?"

"Oh." Hope chuckled a bit, determined to not let her true concern be revealed in her tone. "They're all mad at me. For once all of them are agreed upon the same thing."

Maggie chuckled. "Children do surprise you in some of their likes and passions. What are they mad about?"

"Oh, I haven't been feeling well and I didn't tell them all about it immediately." Hope waved her hand, dismissively. "Frank wanted me to tell them months ago. He has valiantly refrained from saying I told you so, but the thought is apparent in his expression every time he looks at me."

"You're sick?" Maggie clarified, as she leaned over her pot to check on the soup's progress. "I'm so sorry. Do you want to tell me what's wrong?"

"Um, I…" Saying these words out loud to her family

had been heart-wrenchingly difficult, but perhaps saying it again would help the entire situation feel more normal. "I have not exactly gotten confirmation from the doctor, but Mrs. Martell says it sounds like consumption."

"You have consumption?" Maggie's eyes widened, now all attention on Hope. "And you kept that from your children? Did you know before you left back east?"

"I suspected. But, I wasn't sure."

Maggie blinked rapidly in confusion, standing to her full height and letting the soup simmer. "You suspected that you have a potentially deadly disease, and not only did you not share that with your family, but you convinced them to travel with you thousands of miles without knowing all of the information?"

"Well, but, I... You understand, don't you? As a mother. Don't you? I didn't want them to worry or coddle me. They shouldn't be making decisions for their life based on whether or not I am sick. It was better this way. They haven't spent the last several months worrying about me for no reason."

"I..."

Maggie turned away from her briefly, and Hope could not see her expression. Whatever it was, however, this was not how she had imagined her friend reacting.

When she turned back to Hope, her expression seemed both tired and falsely cheerful.

"I'm sorry, I don't mean to be rude, but I really need to get to my chores. It's just a bad afternoon for me to be social and gossiping like this. You understand." She gestured away from herself, inviting Hope to leave.

"Oh. Yes. All right." Hope took a few steps back

toward her own camp. "Of course. I hope your soup turns out well."

Hope had never felt more alone. She had never felt more rejected, but at the same time she did not know how to get out of this hole.

# CHAPTER THIRTY-SEVEN

"Absolutely not," Hope declared. "I won't do it. You can lecture me until you are blue in the face, but I am not going to stay inside the wagon, not being able to see what is happening around me, when we are this close to a cliff."

"You will get worn out from the walking and end up in the wagon eventually," Frank told her. "Why not save your energy? We won't have any water until we make camp later, and you need to rest."

"I would spend the entire time fretting about what was happening that I could not see. I'm walking. I will live without water if I have to."

"Fine."

It had been nearly a week since the Waters family had all learned about the severity of Hope's illness, and still only her husband would have conversations with her. And even knowing how isolated she was, Hope could not just roll over and let Frank tell her what to do. While Faith and Beau seemed to be thawing, offering her acknowledgement occasionally, the rest of her children seemed even more determined to punish her with their silence. Even Frank seemed reluctant to give her much more than the bare minimum.

If Hope had at any time thought that her illness would make her family more conciliatory to her than they had been before, she was being proven wrong.

But as each day passed and she felt more and more isolated, Hope also began to feel more repentant. The very act of surviving on the Oregon Trail took much of her time and energy, so she was able to push away the suspicion that she might have made a mistake most of the time. She hated to admit she was wrong, and for several days had absolutely refused to. There had always been the assumption that her children would understand and be grateful that she had been trying to spare them. When that had not come to fruition, Hope looked elsewhere for explanation.

When Frank had left her to her devices, Hope walked along the trail, just between the two Waters wagons. Her son Ernest drove the supply wagon, and trailed only a few feet behind her, but by this point she knew better than to try to talk to him. The trail was cut partially into the rock high above the Snake River. At times the landscape opened up on one side, to flat rock and hard-packed dirt. The other side, however, was simply a drop straight down to the rushing water below.

She had already crept to the edge of the gorge and looked down to the river once, but the height and the speed of the rapids made her dizzy. Now she made sure to walk several yards away from the edge; she could hear the river, but not see it.

As the wagons slowly rolled down the narrow trail, Davis came to walk with his brother, and Hope could overhear their conversation, though she was wise enough to not try to join in.

"All that water so near and us not able to drink it. Seems cruel," Davis said.

"Maybe some future wagon train will figure out how to get down to the river," Ernest replied.

They walked in silence another few steps before Davis spoke up again.

"I'm going down. Give me your canteen. I've been looking at the rock face every thirty yards or so and I think there are enough hand and footholds that I can climb down and back up with water."

Hope went cold with fear. This was a nearly vertical drop of hundreds of feet her son was talking about scaling.

Ernest chuckled. "If you bring me a full canteen of water, you'll be my favorite brother."

"Oh, good," said Davis sarcastically. "I've been waiting for that chance."

As Hope watched, Davis punched his brother lightly on the shoulder, accepted his canteen from him and crossed the trail to the edge of the ravine. He assessed the climb down, moving a few feet to his right, before he turned around and cautiously began his descent.

"You can't climb down there," Hope exclaimed. "It's not safe. Davis Waters, you get back up here. Please."

His legs were already over the edge, and he was holding himself up. Despite the distraction, he looked directly at his mother, and for the first time in a week,

Davis spoke to her. "Just pretend you don't know, Mama. Didn't you decide that's better than worrying?"

The shock of her son's impertinence silenced Hope. He had disappeared down into the gorge before Hope could come up with a response. She cautiously crossed to the edge and looked down; Davis was already about ten feet down the side of the rock. She wanted to call out to him, to demand he come back up, but she did not want to be the reason he lost focus.

Hope felt helpless.

As Ernest led the family's supply wagon past her on the trail, he met her eyes with a bit of defiance.

"Why did you let him go down there?"

But Ernest turned deliberately away without answering, looked ahead and murmured to the ox closest to him.

The wagon train continued its slow progress, and Joseph Kirk led his family's wagon past where Hope stood watching over Davis. Maggie walked next to her son, and when she met Hope's eye, she waved pleasantly but said nothing and didn't stop to see why Hope was at the edge of the trail.

Hope and Maggie had not spoken since that afternoon at Fort Hall. The look of confusion and horror on Maggie's face had done more to make Hope doubt herself than any conversation with Frank had done. In that doubt Hope felt too ashamed to try to continue the conversation at a later time.

At the time, Hope had told herself that Frank just did not understand because he was not a mother. He did not have the same inclination to nurture and shield their children from hardship.

But when Maggie seemed to agree with him, Hope had to at least entertain the possibility that her secrecy had not been the best option.

She looked down again, and saw that her son had reached the rocky bottom. There was little space for him to stand, and all of it was rocks and boulders that made up the side of the river. As she watched, he squatted at the shore of the Snake River and lowered two canteens under the surface to be filled. Even without the danger of the climb back up, she worried he could slip on the wet rock, injure himself, possibly get stuck down there.

Hope walked away from the edge again. She couldn't watch.

The wagons continued past her, the Benedict family, the Ulmers, the Gladwells, who were borrowing a cow from another family to help pull their wagon after their ox had collapsed. Most folks smiled at her, but none stopped to see why she was standing at the edge of the trail.

Hope looked down into the ravine again, both relieved and petrified to see that Davis was beginning his climb back up the sheer cliff.

"Be careful!" she called down.

He did not acknowledge her.

Was this how everything would be from now on? Hope shut out of her children's lives—the good and the bad—because she had shut them out of hers? She stood over the edge of the crevice, watching her son, hoping that he had steady hands, was able to find all the necessary footholds. If anything happened to him, at least she would know, at least she could go get help.

She was worried and anxious the entire time watching, but what else could she do?

Davis made it to the top of the ravine again, awkwardly climbing up over the lip while two canteens hung off his body. Hope hurried forward to offer him a hand, but he did not accept it.

"Are you all right? Oh, goodness, I'm so glad you made it back up. Please don't do anything like that again, Davis. Please."

"I'm not sure I'll be telling you much of what I do, Mama."

He turned away from her, running a little to catch up with Ernest and leave her behind.

# CHAPTER THIRTY-EIGHT

The following day, the Sullivan-Mills wagon company continued along the trail that ran the length of the canyon, parallel to the Snake River. Word of Davis's exploit had circled through the camp and reception was mixed. Another half-dozen men and boys vowed to attempt the same. Mothers who did not have a strapping, adventurous son to climb down and fetch water consoled themselves that at least they did not have to worry about their children performing such a feat.

Just the one day walking along the trail had been enough for Hope to give in to Frank's admonishment. Yes, she needed to rest, and needed to not push herself any more than necessary. But she also could not face another day in which her children actively ignored her.

Instead she curled up in her cot, tried to ignore the swaying of the wagon, and settled in to knit as much as she had the energy to do. The sweater she had been knitting on and off since leaving New York was still only three-quarters of the way done. She had allowed so many other things to distract her and take up her time; hiding her cough from her family had been more consuming than she had realized. But now she had not much else to occupy her, as she tried to grow accustomed to being alone.

Early in the afternoon, however, she felt the wagon slow, stop, and then when it began again was led off the trail. It seemed far too early to make camp, so when they stopped again, Hope emerged from the wagon full of questions.

"What's wrong?" she demanded of Angus, who had been driving the family's supply wagon and was the first face she saw.

He glanced up ahead and called out. "Pop!"

"What is it?" Frank appeared around the side of the wagon, and noticed his wife climbing out. "Let me help you."

She batted his hand away as she climbed out. "I'm fine. But it's too early to make camp. What's wrong?"

She glanced at her son, but Angus continued to focus on his team of oxen, seeming to ignore his mother and their conversation completely.

"Well," Frank said somberly. "Bit of a busy day. Good news is that Mrs. Van Anda's baby is on the way, and the doctor asked that we stop if possible. Make it a bit easier on the new mother."

Hope gasped in delight. "A baby! What a brave woman. I hope she's all right."

"And ... I also have bad news. John Harper fell," Frank continued. "Climbing down into the ravine to get water. He... The Jameson brothers have agreed to collect the body."

Hope was stunned. "He tried to climb down to the river? Like Davis did?"

Frank nodded. "It's a real shame. I think Davis feels bad he set that example. I don't know if Harper just slipped, or wasn't quite strong enough but... He leaves behind his poor sister, an orphan and now trying to get to Oregon completely on her own."

But all Hope could think about was if it had been one of her own children—if not Davis then any of the others. She knew quite well all of her sons were reckless or confident enough to try the same misguided feat.

And what if Davis had fallen yesterday? What if he had been lost to them, because she hadn't known he was going down, because he had kept a secret from her? Though it meant facing all of her choices that led her to this point, Hope was beginning to see why her children were so upset with her. She had apologized, and she had meant it, but she didn't know how else to make it up to them.

How could she regain their trust?

All that afternoon she stayed in the wagon, avoiding her family and trying to find a solution. She was beginning to think that time might be the only thing that would connect her children to her again, but she was increasingly afraid that she might not have that much time left. Her coughing was more frequent now, and though it did not always bring up blood she knew better than to assume she was healing.

John Harper's funeral was held the following morning, before the company left for the day, but Hope stayed in bed. She could not face it all over again. Leaving behind another grave was both utterly demoralizing and far too common for the emigrants to be able to mourn deeply. It seemed as though the same tragedies kept finding them, that no matter what they did, how hard they worked, the suffering was unavoidable. Hope's heart broke for the man's sister, now left all alone in the world, in the middle of the wilderness.

But she had plenty of her own problems to worry about; there was no energy to spare for another person she did not know very well.

When the caravan began moving that morning, continuing along the trail that ran parallel to the Snake River, Hope stayed in her wagon. The motion still made her ill, but she was getting weaker and weaker every day and was loath to put herself in a position where she was so weak she needed to ask one of her children for help.

Even as she was beginning to understand just how hurt and dismayed her children were, Hope did not know what she could do beyond apologize again. She could not go back and do it over, even if she wanted to. So, instead, she avoided the situation all together and tried to sleep while the journey continued.

The trail descended to water level, little by little, getting out of the high desert and still parallel to the river. The Snake River had turned almost due west, and the trail would follow for days until they needed to cross again. By the end of the day the roar of a waterfall could be heard in every part of the caravan. Shoshone Falls was thought to be the largest waterfall this side of the Mississippi. Hope realized she missed hearing Nancy talking about what they could expect next on the trail.

It was already dark when the company made camp near Shoshone Falls, but the thundering sound echoed through the night. They would stay at this campsite through the next night, allowing the emigrants to take advantage of the cool, deep pool at the bottom of the falls.

After breakfast the following day, Hope tried again to make conversation with Nancy and Sadie, but the latter only glanced at her while the former pretended as though she did not exist at all.

She was waiting around at a bit of a loss, when she noticed Frank returning from elsewhere in the campsite and gathering Angus and Colin to speak with them. She could not hear what they were saying from where she was, and she did not think she could stand the rejection from her sons if she were to try to insert herself into the conversation.

Hope was spending much of her time now just waiting. Waiting for someone to pay attention to her. Waiting for their anger to thaw. When Frank and Colin climbed into the supply wagon, she found herself waiting to learn what they were doing. If she were to ask directly she would likely be rebuffed again.

But when they exited the wagon again, arms full of the family's belongings, she could not keep quiet any longer. Colin walked past his mother without looking at her.

"Where is he going with my sewing box?" Hope asked. She stood and called after her son. "Colin!"

But he kept walking, ignoring her. She seized her husband's arm.

"Please, just... tell me what is going on."

"I will, but you need to stay calm. It won't do for you to upset yourself."

"I am calm."

"Yes, now, but when I tell you—"

"Frank."

He licked his lips and began. "This morning there was a meeting with the captain. As you probably know, we're on Shoshone land, and every day that it takes us to cross it is another day that game and resources are scarce for that tribe. We are disturbing their entire way of life by being here. They are allowing us to cross unmolested, but they require a toll from each wagon company."

"What kind of toll?"

"Their first demand was twenty dollars in cash from each family, but Captain Mills convinced them that asking that of poor travelers was unreasonable."

"So... So, I have to give up my sewing box? I just don't understand."

"We had to give them something. Things that are useful, and might be difficult for them to get otherwise. Seeing as you have not used your sewing kit since New York, we agreed that of all the things that we still carried this far into the trek, that was what we could most spare. Colin is taking it to Captain Mills as our contribution to the toll."

"But— How could he do that without asking me?"

Frank looked at her, waiting for Hope to make the connection. "Hope..."

"Oh, come, Frank. This is not the same thing at all. Keeping an illness from someone because you don't want to worry them and giving away something another person owns without telling them are very different."

"They are," he allowed, "but in this case, given how little you have used the sewing box, and the fact that is own wife Nancy has been doing all of our garment repairs with her own sewing supplies makes a difference. And given that you were asleep when the meeting happened and we needed to contribute something, I have to admit that I can sympathize with his choice."

"I just... Well, you're right that I wasn't using it, and..." She shook her head, as despair threatened to overtake her. "I honestly don't know if I will ever feel strong enough to do that kind of focused work again, but I still should have been consulted."

He gave her a tight smile. "And I imagine that is what he thinks about your illness. You know that."

"I know," she said in frustration. "All right? I under-stand now. How long will I be punished for this?"

"I don't know," he said softly. "They love you, but you hurt them deeply."

"I just want to make it right," Hope said. "Building our home in Oregon won't be the same without our chil-dren around."

# CHAPTER THIRTY-NINE

The Shoshone tribe accepted everything—from the large ornate mirror the Hudsons offered, to the single pound of coffee the Kirks provided—and allowed the wagon company to continue through their land, with the understanding they would move as quickly as possible. The Americans were more than happy to oblige. The knowledge that there was an entire tribe watching them, just out of sight, kept much of the company on edge. That afternoon, camp was packed up again and the wagon company was on the move.

The Oregon Trail curved away from the falls, out into the flats, before turning back toward the water. Where the trail curved back toward the river, it ran straight into the dead end of a rocky ravine before rising again. The incline out of the ravine was so steep, it would prove a trial getting all of the wagons up out of the depths. With the extreme incline where the trail climbed out, that most of the wagons had to be doubled up—twice as many draft animals yoked together to haul two wagons up at a time, to ensure the proper support was present.

"Mama?"

Hope had been riding in the wagon, though occasionally poking her head out to see what the progress was. The bottom of the ravine created a bit of a bottleneck, and the progress was slow. The Waters boys were hitching their two wagons together to haul them up the trail, when Hope heard her daughter calling for her.

"Faith?" In her excitement, Hope almost tripped getting out of the wagon.

"Mama, you should walk up with me," Faith said shyly, in the first words she had uttered to her mother in more than a week. "Pop doesn't want you to ride in the wagon, just in case there's an accident, and he sent me to come get you."

"Your father did that?"

Hope had a million questions—including what had changed in Faith that she was willing to do this, that she was not only open to speaking to her mother, but also in helping make sure she got to the top of the ravine safely. But, she knew better than to look a gift horse in the mouth. She was afraid what Faith's reaction would be if she voiced any of these questions.

"Thank you," Hope said. "I saw how steep the trail is. I was afraid I wouldn't be able to get all the way to the top by myself."

Faith smiled tightly, the awkwardness almost palpable between them, and offered her arm. "There's a break in the wagons. We should walk up with the rest of the ladies now."

Beyond simply the degree of incline, so many of the

oxen and mules were malnourished and exhausted that it wasn't certain how easily any of them could drag the wagons up. Every consideration was made—they were too close to Oregon now for any accidents. Even though many of the families had just given up what they could spare to the Indian tribe, they were again faced with carefully considering the worth of each and every ounce packed away in the wagons.

Just as Hope had seen at many places along the Oregon Trail, at the bottom of this ravine, even more belongings were discarded.

Hope accepted the arm, and let her daughter lead her to the foot of the trail. All around were more discarded items—empty barrels, moldy pork, a short stack of well-worn books—that were simply too much weight for the depleted animals to manage. The two Waters women joined a cluster of a dozen or so women and children all using the gap in the wagons to climb to the top.

Within only ten feet, Hope was already feeling short of breath.

"We can go slowly, Mama," Faith said, noticing her mother's struggle. "No one is going to run us over. I don't think."

Hope chuckled, which then turned into a cough.

"I'm sorry!" Faith said.

Hope had to stop walking for a moment while her cough subsided. Though she kept her head down, she felt the other women passing them on the trail.

Suddenly, from her other side, Hope felt a strong arm around her waist, all but holding her up. She looked up to see Beau, bracing her and making sure she had all the support she needed to get to the top of the canyon.

"I've got you, Mama," he said.

Hope could have cried with relief. Whatever anger, whatever hurt, whatever trust she had broken, it seemed that finally her children were starting to forgive her.

"Thank you," she croaked, after getting her breath again.

Hope felt happy tears course down her cheeks, but she didn't wipe them away. She did not want to draw attention to how emotional this small gift had made her; she was too afraid of alarming her children, that they would again retreat if she made too big of a deal about it.

Step by step, Faith on one side and Beau on the other, Hope made it up the trail, out of the canyon to where the caravan would regroup and continue on to Oregon. Somehow this short walk, supported by family despite the overwhelming struggle, felt like the entirety of their journey in a nutshell.

Hope was overcome with gratitude.

When they reached the top of the gorge, only a handful of wagons had made it up before them. Hope could not catch her breath, and began to cough, but she couldn't stay where she was. Too many more people, animals and wagons were coming up behind her.

"I've got this," she heard Beau say to his sister.

Faith wavered, but hung back and let Beau handle everything. He guided Hope to the side, away from the stream of emigrants making their way out of the gorge, and found a small boulder for her to sit on.

"I'm sorry there's no shade," he said, as he handed

her his canteen. "But you should be able to rest here until our wagons are up."

Hope continued to cough. She wanted to ask him questions, she wanted to talk to him. It had been so long since they had had a conversation. She could not let this precious moment slip through her fingers, in case it was only temporary.

But it seemed as though Beau read her mind, and forestalled any further exertion.

"Just rest, Mama," he said. "I'm not going anywhere."

She nodded, still coughing, her entire body weak.

"You know," he continued, "I am still disappointed you didn't think you could tell us what was really going on with you. But..."

Hope met his gaze, as well as she could while trying to get her coughing under control.

"But I don't want any more time to pass without talking to you. I realize now we might not have that much left together."

Although that was precisely the fear that Hope had been avoiding for months now, hearing Beau say the words out loud brought her a sense of peace she would not have expected.

"Thank you. I'm so sorry."

"So," he said, "I need you to take care of yourself just as much as you have always taken care of us."

"You sound like your father."

"And does that surprise you?"

"No, my love. I appreciate you."

Her son leaned down—he was more than a foot taller than her—and kissed the top of her head. "I'll be back for you. Just rest now."

He ran off, back down the trail to where dozens of families still needed assistance getting their wagons out of the ravine. Hope stayed where she was, watching, waiting, resting, and thinking over what she needed to do to reach out to the rest of her children.

After the wagon company had climbed out of the gorge, Beau was as good as his word. He collected his mother from where she sat, and helped her back into the wagon before the caravan left again. They continued on, for several hours before they were able to make camp for the night. It had been a long day, and they only had more long days ahead of them.

The Oregon Trail followed the curve of the Snake River farther west, until the wagons would need to cross the water to get to Fort Boise a bit north. For the full three days, the Sullivan-Mills wagon company traveled along the river. Every day, the emigrants threw together a quick breakfast so they could leave with the sun. Every evening, they made camp exhausted and hungry, trying to find any small grain of time in which to make the food they needed to continue.

Day after day, each person was under so much stress, so weary and fatigued, that the strain was beginning to show. The Waters family was not the only one in which family members were barely speaking to each other. Hope had not heard Mr. Benedict sing in weeks.

But Hope kept trying to connect with her children. Beau and Faith had warmed slightly, and once she even got a smile out of Ernest, but it seemed an uphill battle, especially considering how weak and dependent Hope already was. Being shut out of her children's lives was not something she would ever get used to. So each morning she rose, joined her family for breakfast, and tried to mend the trust between them that she had so destroyed.

They had come so far, and still had far to go. The emigrants were now into September, the month that many of them had hoped would see them settling in the Willamette Valley, but instead they had miles and miles to go, through foothills, across rivers, up into mountains and down the other side.

Hope's cough persisted. She liked to believe it was not getting worse, but as she had been hiding it for so long from everyone else, there was no one outside of her to confirm this. Though she was no longer trying to disguise her attacks from her family, neither did she want to constantly remind them she was an invalid.

# CHAPTER FORTY

The Oregon Trail turned north to cross the water at a spot known as Three Island Crossing. The Snake River curved to the west, and the wagon train needed to get to the north shore. There was only a small window of the year in which the water was shallow enough and slow enough to allow fording at all, and with all the previous delays, the Sullivan-Mills wagon company was cutting it close. In this particular stretch there were three sand dunes, one after the other, that provided small respite as a man led his team and wagon through the water. It would take the caravan two days to get all fifty wagons across, but it was the last of the large rivers they needed to get across before Oregon.

Hope had reached such a point of illness that the idea of trying to ford the river almost defeated her. Even if it was shallow, the strength and energy required to walk against the current would be beyond her abilities. There was no question that she would remain in the wagon while one of the men guided it across. Even so, she could not help but watch out the back, in between the canvas flaps, to where Colin led the supply wagon across behind her.

The water seemed dangerous, the current too fast, but Hope's husband and sons were more than capable of getting their wagons across. After watching cautiously for a few minutes, she settled back into her cot, trusting herself to their hands.

The Waters family's luck held—other folks in the caravan suffered damage to their wagons, or sustained injuries, but all emigrants were over the water by the end of the second day.

After leaving the Three Island Crossing behind, the wagon company spent another couple days heading northwest toward Fort Boise. There they could rest next to the river, feel safe near the soldiers stationed there and possibly supplement their supplies. It would be the last such fort they visited before reaching Oregon, so all in the wagon company were pushing hard to get to that camp as soon as possible.

They arrived early in the afternoon. Fort Boise was made up of just a few small buildings behind a stockade wall, but its placement on the Boise River afforded an idyllic location for the Sullivan-Mills wagon company to camp for half a day. Though it was so late in the summer, the stores had not yet been picked clean. Fort Boise was close enough to the ports on the west coast that food and stock could be brought inland from ships that sailed around Cape Horn, instead of brought overland from New York or Boston. The families with the funds could increase their food stores, ammunition, or other necessities they might need in these final weeks.

Frank and Colin ventured to the fort with trepidation, but returned triumphant. They had secured enough rice, beans and cornmeal that the Waters family should have sufficient—though not abundant—food until they reached Oregon.

Hope tried to stay out of Nancy's way as the young woman made the family's campsite: building the fire, starting a batch of biscuits, and even finding the energy to repack the supply wagon. Of everything the family had set off from Independence with, they had lost, eaten and given up so much over the previous few weeks, that there were now wide-open spots in the wagon. The organization had been neglected, and Nancy only ever wanted to make things more efficient. Hope considered offering to help, but after how angry her family had been by her not taking her illness seriously, she did not want to rock the boat. She needed to take care of herself. That's what they kept telling her. But even so, she could not just sit here all afternoon.

What she needed to do—Hope had been thinking about this for days—was to check in on Maggie Kirk. The other woman had learned she was sick and not once come to check on Hope, which didn't seem like her in any other circumstance. Their last conversation had left Hope feeling rejected and guilty. She liked the other woman so much, respected her, and the idea that Maggie might feel disappointed or disdainful toward her was something Hope wanted to change.

Though the distance between the two camps was negligible, Hope had to steel herself. She reminded herself to be resolute in her walking into what could be a difficult conversation. Even from here, she could see that Maggie was bent over some garment in her lap, repairing a rip for one of her many active sons.

Hope cleared her throat when she got close enough to be heard.

Maggie looked up. "Mrs. Waters, how are you feeling? Why don't you sit?"

Though taken aback by the use of her last name, Hope was grateful to not have been turned away completely.

"Were you all able to get what you needed from the fort?" Hope asked, as she took the offered seat.

Maggie nodded as she turned her attention back to her sewing. "Some. Time will tell if it will be enough, though. Thank goodness these boys can hunt and fish, and contribute something to feeding themselves or I do not know how we would get by at all."

Hope made a small noise of agreement, wondering how to address her feelings with her friend. She cleared her throat. "I thought, maybe, you might like to hear that a couple of my children are speaking to me again. It took a while, and I'm sure there's still a lot of trust to build back up, but..." She spread her hands wide. "It's a beginning."

Maggie paused and considered before responding. "I'm glad, Hope. I know how much you love your family."

She nodded vigorously. "I do. And... Well, I told the boys this, but it's been made very clear to me what my keeping quiet meant for them. I wish I could go back. Everything might be different now." She cleared her throat, finding the courage to be vulnerable. "You were right, Maggie. I should not have kept this secret from them."

"I know..." Maggie said gently. "That's what I try to remember in every step of parenting. There are some things that cannot be undone. That's why I've always tried to be very careful in my interactions with my boys. I wouldn't want..."

She trailed off, but Hope could guess the end of the sentence. She wouldn't want what had happened in Hope's family to happen to her own. And now, being on the other side of that, Hope could acknowledge her wisdom.

"There will undoubtedly be things that I will regret," Maggie continued, "but my boys' trust in me and in their father is the foundation of everything we're building."

"I wish I had realized how important it was a year ago," Hope admitted. "I just took it for granted that I knew best—because I'm their mother—and I didn't think about what it would mean to them."

Maggie smiled sadly. "I'm sorry you had to learn it the hard way."

Hope let out a sad laugh. "Me too."

"Mama?"

Hope looked up in surprise. Her son Ernest was striding over from the Waters camp, and speaking to her.

"Ernest!" She stood, too quickly, and swayed a little on her feet. Her son was at her side in a moment, holding her steady.

"Come on, Mama. Davis caught some salmon and Nancy is making us quite the supper. It's nice to see you, Mrs. Kirk."

"You too, Ernest. Go enjoy your salmon. Joseph has promised he'll catch some for us as well."

"Thank you for talking to me," Hope said. "I really... You're right, in all of this, and I appreciate you taking the time. And being patient with me."

The smile Maggie offered her in return was far warmer than when Hope had first sat down. Maybe she was making amends after all.

Ernest walked Hope back to where her own family's campsite, next to the Kirks, was bustling.

All six of her children in one place. Her two bonus daughters taking care of supper. Her husband crossing the packed earth to greet her. In spite of the chill in her interactions with her children, Hope was not sure she could be happier. They had all been through so much, and even though there were still miles to go, and obstacles to overcome, the important thing was that they were together.

"Oh, Nancy, this is just..." She sniffed appreciatively. "What a wonderful supper, thank you so much."

But the younger woman did not even acknowledge she had heard her. Hope almost thought to repeat herself in a louder voice, but caught Colin's eye. He had heard her, and he was much farther away. No, Nancy was still refusing to speak to her mother-in-law.

"Colin," she continued, "you must be so proud of your wife."

That time, at least, the person she was speaking to looked at her, but he looked away again immediately without responding.

Hope nodded to herself, understanding. It hurt, but

she had gotten the other children to warm up to her. Colin and Nancy could still come around.

She needed to admit to herself that perhaps there was nothing else she could do. She had broken their trust, and the only way to win it back would be over time, with consistency.

Hope hated that reality—she had always ever made things happen through her sheer force of will. But at the same time, she knew now she had made a mistake.

She might just have to accept this new state of things.

Sadie brought her a plate, piled with rice, salmon and a fresh biscuit. It was far more food than Hope could eat, but she welcomed this small instance of excess after so many months of deprivation. One of her sons would finish her food, and in the meantime, she could sit back and listen with joy as her family interacted, laughing, all around her.

# CHAPTER FORTY-ONE

Colin and Nancy were still not speaking to her; Hope noticed them having whispered discussions away from the rest of the family. In spite of this, in spite of the increasingly cold weather, in spite of their dwindling food supply and concern for the other members of the wagon party, Hope was beginning to feel as though the worst of it was behind them.

They were almost to Oregon. After thousands of miles, they had to be close. They only had a couple weeks' worth of travel before they could settle into the territory for the winter. She had been through the worst of her children's anger, and it had not destroyed her. And though she had to admit her illness was progressing, it was not impossible that once they had stopped traveling every day and she could truly rest that it might improve.

Everything was still tense, but every day felt a little more promising.

After leaving Fort Boise, Captain Mills pushed the wagon company hard, and they traveled several days without stopping for a midday break at all. The next big obstacle would be the Blue Mountains, and with the cold weather coming, the wagon company needed as much time as they could eke out. Nancy and Sadie spent each night in camp hovered over the campfire, cooking long after dark. With so many mouths to feed and so little time in which to prepare food, the women were forced to give up the little rest time available to ensure they had enough cold biscuits and bacon to eat on their feet the following day.

Pushing the caravan that hard and that fast had its benefit, however, when in the middle of the third day of such a pace, the sky opened up and a torrential storm soaked any and all persons left outside. The wagons had to slow as they pushed through the mud. Hope had been riding inside the sleeping wagon, alone as usual, but without the strength or mental focus to be able to work on the sweater she had been knitting for so long. A crack of thunder, and a swift dimming of the available light made her look up, just as Faith, Sadie, and Nancy climbed into the dry of the wagon as fast as they could.

"Oh!" Hope gasped, as she got splashed with rainwater from Faith's bonnet. She scooted back against the canvas, allowing as much room as possible for the three people who suddenly appeared in there with her.

"The oilskins are in the other wagon," Nancy was saying to Sadie. "Does Angus know that?"

Sadie nodded as she untied her own sopping wet bonnet. "He did the last time it rained, but you know those men. He could have forgotten by now."

"Colin is the same way." Nancy glanced at her mother-in-law briefly before turning away again. She situated herself at the foot of the cot on the opposite side of the wagon, as far away from Hope as she could get in that cramped space. Keeping her gaze fixed outside the wagon, Nancy looked like nothing more than a caged bird just waiting for the exact moment when the door opened, and she could take flight.

After a long moment of awkward silence, Hope tried to make conversation. "Seems like this storm just swooped in on us out of nowhere, doesn't it?"

"I was going to go see what the Cole girls are up to today," Faith said, "but I didn't get more than a few steps before I got drenched and came back here."

"Of all the reasons I am looking forward to Oregon," Sadie said, "getting a roof over our head again just to stay dry is up near the top of the list."

Hope chuckled. "I told you this would be an adventure when we set out. I didn't think about bad weather being such a big part of it."

"Yes, well, it seems like there are quite a few things you didn't give thought to," Nancy said.

Hope blinked back her surprise at the fact that Nancy had spoken to her at all; the bite in her words was nothing compared to the cold silence she had endured for weeks.

"You're right," Hope said. "I'm sorry."

She did not take her eyes off Nancy, but the latter looked away, out through the canvas to the storm that raged around them. In her periphery, Hope sensed Sadie and Faith exchanging looks.

Though she did not know how this all would develop —or in fact how it would end—to Hope's surprise, the fact that Nancy cared enough at all to even be this angry seemed like a good sign. If she could just be a little more patient, a little more humble, she had hope that her son and daughter-in-law would come around.

"Looks like it's easing up," Nancy said, pointedly only looking at Sadie.

To Hope's ears, the torrential downpour seemed as heavy as ever, but she knew better than to disagree with Nancy at that moment.

"I'm going to go check that the boys found the oilskins," Nancy continued.

And with that, she had climbed out of the wagon and was gone. The rain was still so heavy outside that any sound of her footsteps disappeared immediately.

Sadie turned to her, a pained expression on her face. "I'm sorry, Mama. I think they'll forgive you in time. They both will."

Hope smiled sadly. "I hope so. But... I hope so."

"Patience."

"Stubbornness," Hope returned. "That I can do."

The storm dissipated later that afternoon, and the trail began its slow climb into the mountains. Each morning, Hope had to bundle herself up with as much warm clothing as she had on hand before she exited the wagon for breakfast. Most mornings, in fact, she sat holding her hot cup of coffee and allowed the heat to seep into her, putting off drinking it as long as possible. It was late in September, by now, and at this elevation summer was long over.

Each morning she looked up at the snow-topped mountains into which they were journeying. From the flats of the prairie, the Blue Mountains in the distance had seemed so tall, insurmountable. But now that every day they were climbing higher and higher, they seemed more like an unending grind. Hope knew, in theory, they were making progress up and over the range, but on a day-to-day basis it certainly did not seem that way.

But if she could just hang on, all the sacrifice and turmoil would be worth it. Just a little bit farther.

# CHAPTER FORTY-TWO

The Sullivan-Mills wagon company had been on the Oregon Trail for almost six months already. It had been weeks since they had begun the climb into the Blue Mountains, weeks since Fort Boise, weeks since they had been near any river deep enough for fish. Weeks of a precarious hold on survival.

Though Hope had reached such a point of exhaustion and illness that she stayed in the wagon most of the time, she still saw enough of the rest of the company to understand how dire the situation was. Mothers sent children foraging for pine needles and acorns so their children could have even a tiny bit of sustenance. Fathers went without meals entirely. Another two oxen had perished on the uphill trail, and though they had been butchered for the meat, there was scant flesh on the bones to feed more than the family it had belonged to.

This monotonous stretch of mountain trail was as

stark as some of the desert landscapes they had traveled across in months past. There was water but it was too icy to easily use for cleaning. There were pine trees for fuel, but the sap made it difficult to burn. There was no grass for the draft teams, and they were in too high elevation for there to be game to hunt. Having to feed the oxen from their own stores of oats and parched corn meant that the emigrants themselves had even less food to keep them going.

If it weren't for the belief that they must be close, they must be near to the end of this nightmare, many of the travelers would have given up entirely.

But there were other things that could be let go of. Hope still had not finished knitting her sweater, and she was beginning to wonder if she ever would. Maybe there would also be some unfinished piece of work, some open opportunity that never was resolved. It was all she could do to give her children the attention and energy they needed.

The incomplete sweater was now, perhaps, simply a reminder of when she had been well, when she could take on additional projects. A reminder of the life she had left behind in New York and the possibly naive optimism she had felt in proposing this journey.

But they were close. They were so close to Oregon. Hope just held on to that future day when all the work would come to fruition.

One day, a week into October, the wagon company had stopped for a midday break, even though most of the families lacked the food to actually build a meal when they stopped. The cold and the elevation were making Hope tired, but when the wagon train halted she wanted to at least stretch her legs. As soon as she had appeared at the back of the wagon, Davis leapt up to help her down.

At first, she just stood in one place. They would not be stopped long enough to build a fire, and Hope was shivering. But she rubbed her arms, huddled into her shawls and made herself walk the length of the wagons and back again.

Frank met her at the rear of the wagon when she made it back. "You all right? Should you be walking around?"

"It won't be for long. I just thought that I could take in some air while we had the chance. I thought I was cold in the wagon, but it's even worse out here."

"I know. It's too bad we didn't have more room for blankets and coats."

"Well, we thought we would be settled in Oregon long before this. What are we, in mid-October?"

Her husband nodded. "I've lost track of the exact day, but somewhere around there. We'll be settled soon."

"You mean we'll be in Oregon soon. There's still quite a bit to go before we can feel settled."

"We'll manage."

Something over Hope's shoulder caught his eye, and Frank's entire face lit up like a beacon.

Hope turned to see what had made him react so.

A pair of men, leading a horse, appeared at the top of the trail, coming around the bend in the mountain from somewhere in the Willamette Valley below. They were strangers to Hope. After months of traveling with the same forty families, any new face stood out. But beyond simply not being familiar to her, they also appeared to be strong, well-fed, rested, and able to think about something other than mere survival, unlike the members of the wagon company.

"Who is that?" Hope asked in a whisper.

"I didn't think anything would come of it, but here they are."

Hope looked back at the strange men, and noticed three more coming down the trail behind them. "Come of what?"

"They're from Dempsey, down in the territory. The captain sent his son on ahead to scout and bring back help. Too many of the families here are trying to push through with too little food, and for some the situation was becoming quite dire."

"Oh..."

"I'm going to see how I can help," Frank said, before leaving her alone by the wagon.

Hope felt a warm affection for these men—these strangers—that had risked coming up into the mountains on the eve of winter to help dozens of people they had never met. As she watched, two more men came down the trail toward the starving emigrants. The men from Dempsey dispersed throughout the camp, looking for the families with emaciated children, or that had lost members and needed additional assistance.

She noticed one short, blustery man spoke to Angus briefly before continuing on down the caravan. The Waters family had managed far better than others thus far, and Angus knew to direct the assistance elsewhere.

This was the kind of community that she wanted to live in.

This was the kind of world she could be leaving if her consumption did not get better.

She began coughing, lightly at first, but the tickle took hold of her and she could not get her breath.

"Mother Waters?"

Hope looked up, elated, excited, just at the mere mention of her name on Nancy's lips. It had been a difficult several weeks of feeling shut out of their lives, Hope had resigned herself to having to wait as long as it took for Colin and Nancy to open the door to her again. She still had not gotten her coughing under control, but Hope gave her daughter-in-law all of her attention.

Nancy held out a clean, folded white handkerchief to her. "You look like you could use a fresh one," she said.

Hope swallowed hard, determined to accept this small gift with grace and humility, and not do anything to make Nancy regret it. "Thank you. I do. Thank you."

Nancy nodded, but didn't say anything else. Whatever friendship or relationship they might have in the future would have to be built slowly.

Holding the fresh handkerchief to her mouth and saying a silent prayer that she would not find blood on it, Hope leaned against her family's rear wagon wheel, and watched the wave of charity and generosity pouring through the wagon company.

They were close. This was nearly the end.

Though the journey had certainly not been what she had dreamed, they had made it.

With the boon of the additional food and assistance

from the men of Dempsey, the wagon company had a new energy to close the final miles until they were on the other side of the mountain and down into the Willamette Valley. When the company broke camp the next morning, Frank stopped his wife from climbing into the wagon.

"Just for a little bit. Walk with me. I want to show you something."

She tucked her hand into the crook of his arm and followed. "I don't know that I can walk far."

"I know. We won't go far. Just trust me."

Frank put his big, rough hand over hers where it nestled in the crook of his elbow and led her a few yards down the trail to where it curved around the side of the mountain. From this height, now finally on the west side of the mountains, they could see at least a glimpse of the Oregon Territory, the rolling green hills, and their future home.

"Oh, Frank!" Hope exclaimed when the view opened up before them. Tears of gratitude sprang to her eyes. "I admit there was a part of me that thought I would never get this far. That maybe *we* would never get this far."

He wrapped his arms around her from behind, looking out at the view over her head and murmured in her ear. "It certainly was a much bigger commitment than we realized, wasn't it?"

"Not the least because I'm sick."

It was still difficult for her to say those words out loud, to admit to the weakness.

"Well, now we know for next time," he joked.

She laughed through her tears, and the pair stood gazing out into the valley in silence for a moment.

"Frank?" She finally turned away from the territory, from what would be her home, and forced herself to face the biggest concern. She looked up into her husband's face, pain and pleading in her expression. "I thought I overheard Colin telling Angus that he wasn't sure they would settle in the same place as the rest of the company. Do you think…" She swallowed back tears. "Is that true? Do you think they will be able to forgive me? This feels like a punishment."

"Oh, my heart…" Frank offered her a compassionate smile, before pulling her in for a hug. "I don't know if they are trying to punish you, specifically, but… You have to understand how much you hurt them. All of them. And each of the children are going to react to that hurt in different ways. Taking distance might just be Colin and Nancy's way of handling it."

Hope nodded, brushing away the tears. "I just… I wanted so badly for everything to be perfect. For this big change to be what we needed."

"I know you did. And I'm sorry it worked out this way."

"It's so much of what I wanted… It's not perfect, and I know that's my fault. But everything that has been good about this journey has been because of you and our little brood. I don't know what I would have done if you all had not been so supportive."

"I imagine you would have tried to cross all three thousand miles on your own anyway," he responded, with a teasing lilt.

"Oh, goodness, can you even imagine?" Hope laughed at the thought.

"But we're here now. You see that valley down there?"

Frank asked. "We're going to build you the coziest, most welcoming home. You'll spend every day surrounded by the people you love most in the world."

Hope nodded, beaming at him.

"I can't wait. This is all I've wanted. Thank you for helping me get to our new home."

Thank you so much for reading *Seeking Home*! This is one of my books that I am most proud of (I'm sorry if it's a bit dark).

I think we all know someone like Hope Waters—the kind of person who is just so enthusiastic and so adventurous that they conveniently ignore reality if it's going to infringe on their freedom.

I think we also know someone like Colin—the kind of person so rigid in their worldview that gleaning any grace or understanding from them is like pulling teeth.

They often know each other.

Hope's habit of ignoring reality when it is too painful was inspired in part by Scarlett O'Hara. If you've read *Gone With the Wind*, you know one of her regular refrains is "I won't think about that now. I'll think about it tomorrow, when I can stand it." And then, of course, that tomorrow never really comes.

This is all of course why I love writing women's fiction—seeing the characters grow and change and discover things about themselves. This is precisely why studies show that reading fiction promotes empathy.

Small Easter Egg: The story (that is really only alluded to) about Davis getting left behind and having to run after the wagon is actually a story from my father's childhood. He is the oldest of six boys, and the youngest one got left behind at the library when he was about five years old. They still laughingly describe his little child legs running down the street after the station wagon.

One of the fun (and difficult) things about writing this series is finding the very specific cultural research I need to do. I don't know enough details off the top of my head to know what hymns (for example) were written before 1850. It took me a while to find the song "The Blue Juniata". And just for one teeny tiny scene.

But I love it. I could write these books forever. Thank you so much for being part of this with me.

Read more about the Waters family in *Reluctant Spring*, book six of Oregon At Last.

I hope you love *Trouble and Grace*, the next book in the series, too!

— A.T. Butler

May 2025

# NEXT BOOK IN THE SERIES

**The next book in COURAGE ON THE OREGON TRAIL series is available now.**

**Grab TROUBLE AND GRACE here!**
**(on Kindle and Kindle Unlimited)**

Leah Atkins has long ago made peace with her spinsterhood. At thirty-five years old, she has been a schoolteacher for nearly two decades and is perfectly happy in her routine. Living with her cousins, the Robinson family, teaching a classroom of children, enjoying her flowers and books over the years have given Leah a beautiful life.

But when the Robinsons tell her they are emigrating to the Oregon Territory, Leah's perfectly crafted life is turned upside down. She has to make the choice between saying good-bye to the only family she has and leaving her students. Though the frontier life was never what Leah wanted, neither can she bear being alone, and so packs up to head west along with the family. Even once the choice is made, she is not sure it's the right one.

**Will Leah be able to find peace again in the west or will the struggle and deprivation of the Oregon Trail make her wish she had never left home?**

*All the books in the Courage on the Oregon Trail series take place within the same wagon company's trip west and run concurrently. They can be read in any order.*

# WHAT HAPPENS IN OREGON?

**She thought the hardest part was behind her.**

The Oregon Territory, October 1850: After nearly a year of living out of a covered wagon, day after day of grueling work and heart-breaking tragedy, Caroline Harper has finally reached the Oregon Territory where her new life will begin.

She thought she had given all she had to give; she thought she had become the strong woman the frontier requires. But every day brings a new challenge for the settlers.

When unexpected obstacles appear that keep her from getting married, from finally finding her security, Caroline learns that becoming the woman she needs to be will be far more difficult than she had realized.

Can Caroline find her new path or will this journey be the end of everything she thought she had achieved?

*For all the stories of how these brave pioneers got to Oregon, look for the book series Courage on the Oregon Trail by A.T. Butler.*

**Oregon At Last Series:**
***Journey's End*** (Caroline's story)
***Christmas in Oregon*** (Annie's story)
***Snowbound Promises*** (Nora's story)
***The Pastor's Baby*** (Olivia's story)
***Frontier Fortune*** (Rebecca's story)
***Reluctant Spring*** (Sadie's story)
***Summer of Promise*** (Margaret's story)
***Eden Valley Sunrise*** (Leah's story)

# FREE PRINTABLE OREGON TRAIL MAP



Sign-up to download a FREE custom printable map of the Sullivan-Mills wagon company's journey on the Oregon Trail.

You'll also get news of future releases, updates for promotions and discounts, as well as occasional other exclusive goodies, created just for my subscribers.

https://atbutler.com/ot-free

# ALSO BY A.T. BUTLER

**Courage On The Oregon Trail Series:**

*Westward Courage*

*Faithful Trail*

*Frontier Sisters*

*Unyielding Heart*

*Wild Promise*

*Fierce Dreams*

*Seeking Home*

*Trouble and Grace*

**Oregon At Last Series:**

*Journey's End*

*Christmas in Oregon*

*Snowbound Promises*

*The Pastor's Baby*

*Frontier Fortune*

*Reluctant Spring*

*Summer of Promise*

*Eden Valley Sunrise*

**Juniper Falls Series:**

*The Juniper Hotel*

*Building the Dream*

*Snowflakes and Sugar Cookies*

**Marrying a Sweet Sister Series:**

*The Sweetest Bond*

*The Sweetest Spark*

*The Sweetest Shelter*

*The Sweetest Gamble*

**Jacob Payne, Bounty Hunter Series:**

*Trouble By Any Name*

*Danger in the Canyon*

*Justice for Jasper*

*Blood on the Mountain*

*Outlaw Country*

*Death By Grit*

*Desert Rage*

*Arizona Legend*

*Fool's Demise*

*Silent Night*

**Bountiful Justice Series:**

*Loyalty's Price*

*Riding for Justice*

*Trail of Redemption*

**Other Western Novels by A.T. Butler:**

*Hawke's Revenge*

*Short Stories from Juniper Falls*

I grew up in the southwest—California Missions, snakes and constant threat of drought weaving the backdrop of my childhood.

But it wasn't until I moved to Texas a few years ago that the magic and mythology of the American West began to seep into my soul.

I'd love to write about western adventures, strong women and noble men for a long time.

If you enjoyed this book, a review on your favorite retailer would be greatly appreciated.

- A